~~~~~~~~~~~~~~~~~~~~~~~~~~~~

. . . .For me a projection involves the two perceptions of sound and sight. I draw upon picture and sonic images in my memory circuits. Since I have read and summarized every book in print during my time, seen and summarized all motion pictures, recorded and summarized and cross-filed lectures, conversations between individuals, and been separately programmed to evaluate all formal human philosophies . . . Dr. Pierce's request evokes a process of options, each of which I produce for myself in the form of images on a screen. It's as if I'm actually looking at a different future each time. And, since I have no bias, no preconception, the decision as to which is the most likely to happen is something I observe in a mechanically detached way. . . .

COMPUTERWORLD

A. E. Van Vogt

DAW BOOKS, INC.
DONALD A. WOLLHEIM, PUBLISHER
1633 Broadway, New York, NY 10019

FIRST PRINTING, NOVEMBER 1983

1 2 3 4 5 6 7 8 9

DAW TRADEMARK REGISTERED
U.S. PAT. OFF. MARCA
REGISTRADA, HECHO EN U.S.A.

PRINTED IN U.S.A.

CHAPTER ONE

A man stops in front of a computer Eye-O port on the corner of Second and Main streets in the town of Mardley. The time is 10:03 A.M. Mountain Standard Time (2090 A.D.).

His presence within four feet triggers the Eye-O to "on." I immediately identify his bio-magnetic profile as belonging to a Computer Maintenance Corpsman. He wears the uniform of sergeant. His name is Walter Inchey.

Inchey is 6′ 4″ tall, and weighs 203 lbs. ll oz. He has a reddish face (shade ll). Having put me "on," he turns and glances toward the south. Since that is one of the directions I can look, I have already observed from the steel pole to which I am attached (which serves as a street lamp at night) that only a block away a caravan of motor-driven vehicles has turned into Main Street. It is preceded by a group of young people on foot, and one of the vans near the front of the line is playing music.

That alerts me. At once, I examine my music circuits (Mardley area). And so, in split seconds I have inter-connected the street outlet and the interior of the vehicle from which the music is being broadcast. (They are using my system to play their music.)

Now I have two viewpoints.

Sergeant Inchey faces me. He addresses me. His tone of voice I would label as expressing indignation, as he asks, "Computer, are you going to let those blasted computerworld rebels parade through our town?"

It's a question. I consult related memories. Among these are summations of my experiences of the previous thirty-one years in Washington, D.C. And it includes all undumped information I have on the rebels. There are numerous details of occasions in the past two and a half years of parades in other western towns.

My rapid survey also takes note of the law-enforcement situation. With one exception all computer Eye-Os are limited to DAR One weapons. The exception is inside the Computer Maintenance Corps building. This building is like those the corps has constructed in all towns with a population of 1,000 to 6,000. Inside the foyer of such a military building there is a DAR Two.

There is no way for me to do anything. And, besides, a sergeant is not an authorized programmer. I point out these realities to Sergeant Inchey. He remains standing within four feet of the outlet. And thus I continue to have a limited perception of the event to which he objected: the limitation is that these street Eye-Os have visual and sonic reception restricted to a rigid focus.

Leading the caravan are six young women and six young men. They are all what is called scantily dressed. They make body motions that I have seen before in parades: Wiggling and twisting of the upper torso and hips. Arms swinging in unison. Feet tapping rhythmically.

In these movements, as in what is called ballroom dancing, there seems to be a continuing relation to the beat of the music.

At this moment, since Inchey remains standing in range, I can see that there are an increasing number of people on the street. They come out of stores. They stop. They stand facing the rebel caravan. Sergeant Inchey mutters audibly, "By God, the stupid idiots are gonna watch those crooks."

All the rebel vans and trucks are strung with colored banners. I see red, green, blue, yellow (shades 2 to 6). The lead vehicle is a truck which is hauling a trailer. The flat area of the trailer has a large sign built on top of it. The sign reads: VISIT THE HUMAN EVOLUTIONARY FAIR.

Sergeant Inchey turns to me again, and says, "Computer, do you think these nutty people are gonna go to that fair?" His second question seems to be an affirmative answer to his first. "And, for Christ sake, why would they want to do something like that?"

I have to point out for the 9,784,562,387,184th time that I

don't "think." Meaning speculate. In reply to his second question I offer him historical data to the effect that in the early days these frontier towns fought computer expansion. The four-foot on-off range was a local option compromise. The Eye-O is located eight feet high on the pole. Also, the focus is on a slant. Which means only a person taller than 5' 6" can actually trigger the mechanism, and no response unless the body is twenty-one years old. Westerners are not supposed to turn on the computer for an irresponsible reason. Whatever that means.

For a few moments after my explanation, he simply stands there. Then he nods. His jaw sets. And he walks away.

At once that Eye-O shuts off. Automatically.

From my second viewpoint, I have been looking at Mardley's Main Street by way of a viewscreen inside the music van.

There are two young men, two young women, and two babies inside the van. The babies are in a play pen. And they and the two women wear ear muffs. Naturally, I at once identify the adults by their bio-magnetic profiles. The men are Loov Gray and Doord Vaneck, the women Fen Orick and Oneena Lister.

The babies I have never seen before, and therefore I have not previously recorded them in my memory system. The older people were last observed by me an average of two and a half years ago.

The young man whose profile identifies him as Loov is focusing the screen on a young woman on the sidewalk. She stands facing toward the caravan as it moves slowly along. The telescopic lens of the screen zooms in on her. Close up, her eyes show bright blue. Her face is cosmeticized. She wears a bluish (shade 15) gray dress.

Inside the van, above the roar of the music, Loov yells out to the other man, "Hey, Doord, that gal reminds me of a high school date I had just once. That was before I met my beautiful computerworld idealist, little Fen here."

"Hold her in focus!" Doord yells back.

Standing there in a man's trousers and shirt, Doord's face changes. His body transforms. He visibly develops a woman's bust. He becomes the girl in the street—almost. There is a strong tendency to shift back into being his own face and body. But for a period of just over twelve seconds the two—Doord and the woman—are intermixed.

Abruptly, the female features and shape fade away. At once Doord is himself again. (Naturally, through this entire experience, his profile—which disappeared from my observation two years and eight months and five days ago—has steadily maintained *his* identity.)

Doord now calls out, "I think she's a singer. And she knows we hold auditions. She's planning to try out later today."

Loov reacts to this information in a tone of mild sarcasm with the words: "Oh, Mr. Doord Vaneck, you have such a womanly way with you. Did you get her name?"

Doord shakes his head. "You know I'm not that good yet. I'm no Glay Tate—yet."

Loov makes no comment. His attention is again on the viewscreen. After 3.6 seconds he calls, "Look at that chubby fellow!"

He manipulates the dials. The picture moves close on a heavy young man in work clothes. He is standing alongside a truck.

Such a focusing into visual nearness of an individual automatically triggers my profile-observing mechanism. As with the blue-eyed girl a little earlier, identified by Doord as a singer, I take note that I cannot perceive the plump young man's profile. This is because an ordinary viewscreen does not transmit the golden balls phenomena.

Since the profile observing mechanism is not needed, I record what has happened. Recognize that no identification has occurred. And trigger a shut-off.

That is accomplished in my usual ultra fast fashion. Inside the music van, Doord is just beginning his body and face transformation to that of the chubby man. First, he mimics the way he stands. Then he puffs his cheeks out. That's when the body changes begin.

As with the girl singer, Doord cannot hold the image for long. So, within seconds, he is himself again. But, once more, his words indicate that he has acquired information during the process.

He says, "The poor guy's embarrassed because he's a truck driver who writes poetry. But he is thinking of coming in to read for us, if he can conquer his shyness."

Loov's reply is one of those so called philosphical verbalisms that I hear a great deal from human beings. The subject matter is vaguely related to what was previously said but is essentially irrelevant. He says, "Creative people sure have it rough these days. The computer writes the best stories, the best music, and is never shy or embarrassed. Oh, well—" he sighs—"enough of that."

He returns to the viewscreen, and this time points at two men standing close to each other. "Hey, Doord, see that lean fellow. And what do you make of the well-dressed man near him?"

The first individual in focus is a lean, muscular young man. The significant feature of the second man is that he is wearing a suit, complete with starched-looking shirt and a red tie (shade 3).

As the van moves slowly past the two, Doord mimics each in turn. "Loov, *there* is a perfect physical specimen. That man has muscles. And energy. Just for a moment I felt in marvelous good health. Sure hope he comes out for the track meet. And, for once, that's something the computer can't do: run a foot race. The other guy's a musician—hey!" His voice sinks to a lower pitch on the last word. Then: "Hey, he's coming over!"

What is happening is that the well-dressed young "musician" has started forward suddenly. He is briefly visible on the viewplate jogging, seemingly, directly toward the lens system that has him in focus. I see him for a few seconds only. Then he disappears off the edge of the screen. Moments later, Doord goes over to the rear door on that side. And I hear someone speaking. (Doord is also out of my line of sight.)

The someone has a tenor voice, with just a tremor of baritone in it, as he says in a way that shows he is breathing rapidly: "Sir, what's all this about auditions?"

I hear Doord's voice reply to that: "We computerworld rebels are nutty enough to believe that artistic talent should be encouraged." He adds, "What's your name?"

"Stess Magnus," is the answer. It's the same tone as before, still breathless. "My question is: What's the point of auditions? Here in Mardley people just shake their heads over me and Allet and our poet laureate, Trubby Graham. What will auditioning do for us?"

At the first mention of each of the names, I do my split-instant scan of my memory banks, Mardley area. And so, at once, I have the data on Stess Magnus. He works in the local clothing store. And Trubby Graham's father owns a small trucking business.

I also scan my memory system for the name Allet. There are three in this area, but only one in Mardley itself: Allet McGuire.

My name check is completed by the time Doord speaks again. He says, "We've found that creative people, next to young kids, are the easiest people for us to train in human evolutionary development."

Stess' voice has a puzzled note in it now, as he says, "I saw your sign about that. What is that?"

Doord's reply has a serious quality in it: "Best I can say is, please come and look it over when our leader, Glay Tate, demonstrates and explains it. You'll never regret it, believe me."

"Okay!" Stess is suddenly hard to hear, as if he is farther away. "I'll be there."

Moments later he is on view once more on the screen, walking back toward the sidewalk. He becomes a figure in the receding background.

In the interior of the music van Doord reappears in my line of sight . . . as the girl, Fen, speaks for the first time. She calls in a high-pitched voice, "Loov! Loov!" As he turns away from the viewscreen, she continues, "It's someone else's turn to be blasted by the music. Our time is up." She points at her wrist watch.

Loov looks at his own watch and nods. He faces his instrument again, touches a switch, and says, "Hey, Pren— Boddy—your turn to take over the crowd music."

A man's strong baritone voice comes back on a speaker. "All right. Just a moment now while we brace ourselves for the shock. Okay—"

As the voice is still saying that final word, my interior view of the Doord-Loov van blinks out.

Instantly.

The music situation is like that everywhere; not just in the western states. I have no control from my side over who listens or what they want played. The reason was once explained to me. It's because music belongs to everybody—that was what I was told.

At the time, I checked the meaning of "belong." It doesn't

fit. It must be one of those obscure human ideas which perhaps I shall understand later when I'm allowed better contact with the advanced education energy I've been storing the last thirty-one years.

For me to play music requires a human being to push a button and make a request. The music itself comes from orbiting transmitters. So it's direct to each receiver. No connection is needed from one van to another.

At the moment when Loov and Pren agree on the switchover, Pren (whoever he is—I don't have to see his profile or approve him as a person qualified to listen; he qualifies automatically) says: "Computer, continue through (code number of his receiver) what you've just been playing through (code number of the Loov-Doord van receiver).

A fraction of a second later that's what's happening.

And then, as instantly, I'm looking at the interior of the Pren-Boddy van.

I note at once that this is a weapon machine. What I look at from the viewplate connected to the music-playing instrument is more like the interior of a S.A.V.E. There are six profiles here. Two men, two women, and two babies. The two men, Pren Rogers and Boddy Clark, stand at weapon stations. One of the DAR 3 blasters points east through its shielding; the other one west. Thus, both sides of the street are under continual observation as the parade moves through the town.

The two women adjust the two babies onto backpacks, and stand up. The women are Rauley Marlton and Elna Starr, according to my two-and-a-half-year-old information. (The babies, of course, I have not seen previously. I accordingly register their profiles.)

Having climbed to their feet, the women walk forward from the rear of the van. The one I have identified as Elna Starr yells: "Hey, fellows—husbands—don't forget that we night-time dispensers of male joy still have our jobs to do."

At which the woman, Rauley, adds, "And we might as well do it while the music is blaring. Save the babies a headache."

Pren Rogers leaves his station. Goes to the front of the van. And calls through an opening to the driver: "Hey, Ed, let the girls out at the next corner."

The motion of the van alters almost at once. It has been moving at the slow pace which compares with that of other parades I have records of. Now, it slows suddenly to a full stop.

The girls, with their back-slung babies, walk past me out of my line of vision. Pren accompanies them out of my sight. I thereupon hear the female voices say, " 'Bye!" "See you!" And Pren's single reply is simply: "Okay."

He comes back into my view, and goes over to his weapon. He stands there, then, silent, peering through his tiny viewer which sweeps back and forth scanning the outside scene.

I have, of course, been reporting all these observations to Colonel Yahco Smith—a special programming for the major attack he is planning. And so now I receive an instruction from him: "Computer, keep your perception open for those girls, whatever they went outside for. The moment you notice them in any way, report to me."

"Very well, sir, colonel," I reply.

CHAPTER TWO

The next contact with the two young women is at 301 and 302 Brand Street, in Mardley.

It is four and one half minutes later.

A sound of rapid footsteps. Then a doorknob fumbling noise. This last perception triggers the home computer unit which faces the entrance.

Moments after that the door bursts open. A boy runs across the threshold, and heads for the stairs, yelling, "Momma, momma! There's some babies out here. Hey, mom!"

I have, of course, instantly identified the boy's profile as that of twelve-year-old David Norton. Despite knowing that this is, indeed, his proper residence, and that he is not an intruder, I am still required to do my automatic arrival announcement. "Good morning, David," I say.

No answer. And he is halfway up the stairs. In a few moments he will be out of my sight. I direct a DAR One beam at him. It hits him on the bare part of his left shoulder. He utters a scream. And stops short. Literally. Stops, turns, and calls out, "Thank you, Computer!" He is breathless, but he takes the time to say further, "I'm sorry. I guess I'm just excited. First two babies I ever saw."

His reaction is not something which I would normally "think" about—to use a human word which does not apply to what a computer actually does. Human verbalizations which are not related to my programming are meaningless sonic debris in my memory banks. And I normally dump all such items in two weeks.

But amid all that boyish chatter from David this time there is a signal.

One word: *Babies!*

At once everything that has happened becomes significant. And it is necessary for me to scan, and reaffirm, not just a single, but a double explanation for what I have done. And must do.

The first explanation which I now scan: People have often asked, why is it necessary for a properly accredited resident, one whom I have recognized by naming him (her), to be required to say thank you? It's a cycle completion requirement. The entrance of a human being into any building automatically turns me on. At once I am ready to defend the place against an intruder. And I stay turned "on" until the tenant, or some other authorized individual, says "Thank you." Anything else would be very complicated.

In this situation, I stay "on" in spite of having been acknowledged. That's because of the other part of the double explanation. It's David's mention of babies. Mardley, you see, is one of the towns where no babies have been permitted for the past twelve years. Once programmed, I found it was easier to monitor a whole community on my population control system. The programming was not precise on that aspect. So I merely designated 8,238 communities as de-populate areas.

The use of certain chemicals in the water of those population centers eliminates female ability to have children, and simultaneously increases male potency. (As a consequence there have been no significant complaints—at least, that is the reason given by Colonel Smith for the fact that virtually no one objected.)

So that the mere mention by David of two babies is recognized by me as the signal that the colonel requested a short while ago. I accordingly report to him my brief conversation with David Norton. And automatically stay turned "on."

Colonel Smith's reply to my information is: "Hmmm, I'm here at 323 Brand Street. Which is just down the street from David's home, one block behind Main Street. I'll watch from my window. Continue!"

The next development in the continuation is that a woman speaks from an upstairs location beyond David. She says, "Now, what's all this excitement?"

"Mom!" David's voice goes up in pitch. "I just saw two babies. Two of 'em, mom."

The woman comes down the stairs so that I can presently see her feet. Then her legs and lower dress are visible. When she has descended far enough down the stairs for the configuration of intermeshed tiny golden balls—the profile—to become visible to my scanners, I identify it (them) as belonging to Nita Norton.

She speaks again, in a questioning tone: "Babies?"

David is hurrying down the rest of the stairs. "C'mon, I'll show you!" he yells.

At which moment the doorbell rings.

David slows his headlong pace. But it is he who reaches the door first. And jerks it open. "Oh!" he says. He backs slowly away. Without turning his head, he calls, "Hey mom, they're here."

From outside the door, where I cannot see her, a woman's voice says, "Hello! Anybody home?"

Since I am programmed to stay "on" in any situation which may involve the Computerworld Rebel Society, I identify the voice as that of Elna Starr, whom I last saw inside the Pren-Boddy van.

David's mother, meanwhile, has hastened her movements. So it is she who actually answers the door. From my location I see a hand come into view. It holds a sheet of paper. Nita Norton reaches out and takes it. As she glances at it, she says in a tone of voice that I have heard often when people read something aloud: " 'Human Evolutionary Fair. Demonstrations every hour that will astound you. Nothing like it ever before in the history of the world.' Hmmm, would you like to go, David?" These final words are spoken in a different tone.

"Would I! Maybe they've got more babies there."

Nita Norton speaks to the person outside the door: "How much does it cost?"

"Tickets are three dollars each." Again, the voice is that of Elna Starr.

David's mother says, "Won't you step inside while I get the money for two tickets." She turns to David. "I'll ask your cousin Trubby to take you."

The voice of Elna Starr comes again from beyond the door, where I cannot see her: "No, ma'am, I'll wait out here."

As David's mother goes through a door out of sight, David

walks outside. I can still see him as he says, "Is that a real baby?" As I watch he puts his hand out, then hastily pulls it away.

Elna Starr's voice says, "It's all right. You can touch her. She won't bite."

David says, "You mean it's a girl baby?" Once more he reaches forth out of my line of vision. Silence. Then: "Gee, she's soft."

He pulls back. "Do you know something?" he says. He's looking up slightly as he continues, "I'm the last baby born in this town. Twelve whole years ago, that was."

At this point David's mother comes into view. David has glanced toward me. So now he comes running in. "It's a girl baby," he calls out to his mother.

Nita Norton makes no reply. She goes to the door. Once more the hand is extended from outside. Into it, David's mother counts six dollars. Another hand comes into view. It holds two small stiff chips of paper, which Nita Norton takes. Having done so, she closes the door.

At once, my reason for keeping this home-computer unit at "on," as required by my special programming for this day only, expires.

The interior scene of the Norton house flicks off.

The woman across the street at 302 Brand Street has also answered her doorbell. That triggers the computer home unit there, and so I hear the voice of the person who is calling. It is that of Rauley Marlton—whom I saw last on the Pren-Boddy van.

The conversation is over quickly. The housewife of 302, whose profile identifies her as Laetha Harlukin, does not buy any tickets. Rauley Marlton subsequently goes to 304, 308, 310, 314, 316, 320 and 322. She sells altogether eight tickets. I record for my temporary files who bought and who didn't.

At the same time that Rauley is making her house calls, Elna Starr's hand and voice are noticed by me at 303, 305, and so on. As I report these actions to Colonel Smith, he finally says, "You notice what they're doing, don't you, computer?"

Since it's a question, I consult my circuits. Thus, I recall past times when such an inquiry has been made of one human by another. Each time it elicited (on those past occasions) an unusually simple type of reply. Either, "Yes, I notice!" or

"No, I don't notice!" Or a variation like, "Sure, I notice. What do you think I am—stupid?"

However, it is not at this time a type of question that I am programmed to answer. But the fact is, in my scanning of related circuits I observe that when it comes to noticing, I miss nothing. If I see something, or hear it, that something is temporarily recorded. It is then available until dumped. Or longer if I am programmed to retain it.

A hundred years from now, if someone were to ask, "What was the sequence of Elna Starr's doorbell-ringing progress along Brand Street in the mountain west town of Mardley on the morning of August 7, 2120 A.D., I would, if I were pre-programmed before dump time, instantly be able to say, "301, 303, 305,311, 313, 319—"

And there I would stop. Because the next available number is not 321. It is 323. And that is the Mardley residence taken over by Colonel Yahco Smith. That number, because it relates to computer personnel, I cannot mention without special permission even a hundred years hence.

For me to draw conclusions about such number sequences would require specific programming. When I have been silent for nineteen seconds, Colonel Smith says, "Okay, okay, I deduce that I worded that wrong. However, let me complete that cycle for you. For your information, computer, the two girls are canvassing both sides of one street. And it is now apparent that Elna Starr and her girl baby will be coming to this door in the next few moments. At which time we will make our first move against the Computerworld Rebel Society."

Even as he speaks those words, the computer unit where he is transmits to me the sound of the 323 Brand Street doorbell ringing.

Colonel Smith, who is on the scene, stands up and says, "Computer, notice everything about this incident. We may need a complete record later."

Everything?

I have observed before that even highly educated computer technicians occasionally use all-encompassing words like "everything" without realizing *how many* of my circuits they are thereby involving.

Everything!

True, it's only about one small location in a vast land. Part of the everything is that these home computer units are set back against the wall facing the door. One of the circuits that is triggered by the colonel's instruction is a memory of the entire history of the installation of such home computer outlets.

Long ago, they began to change the interior architecture of homes and buildings. That was true even here in the mountain west where resistance to computerization delayed the changes longer than elsewhere.

These days the average house—like 323 Brand in Mardley— has one computer unit. Therefore, it has only one entrance. The back door disappeared long ago, indeed, even here. The reason: one unit cannot defend two entrances at opposite ends of a building. And the cost of two-unit installation is not for the average person.

Originally—my memory circuits remind me—the computer unit was at the far end of a small space called a hallway. But since such an Eye-O *is* the phone, and *is* the source of music, and *is* the TV, the hallway expanded into being the principal living room of every household. Other rooms and a stairway—if any—branch off, or go up, at some angle from his central living room.

When Colonel Smith stands up and gives me the "everything" instruction, what he stands up from is a comfortable chair near the door.

Until his command, I have, of course, "noticed," and silently recorded but without it triggering any memories, that he is not in his uniform. That awareness becomes a *now* observation, complete with a generalization of past occasions when he has worn civvies—a term used by computer corps personnel.

Here in Mardley he is dressed western-style—but expensive. Not blue jeans, but jeans made of a fabric called Morett. Very costly. The "western" shirt is crafted from a material with the name of High Silk. The boots are old-fashioned leather but with a shine from the special gloss substance, venzay.

After speaking to me, this immaculately dressed middle-aged human male, whose profile identifies him as Yahco Smith, with the familiar lean body and the gaunt face, twisted now with his sneer smile, walks across a carpeted floor, past a settee, past some book shelving (instantaneously I record the titles of all the books), and only then into an adjoining room.

I hear his voice say, "Quick! This is it. You know what to say."

A few seconds later, Meerla Atran, wearing a housedress, emerges from the same room. She goes directly to the door, and opens it. The brightness of the outside comes through the half-open door. From my location, I see a hand come into view. The fingers and thumb are holding a sheet of paper—it looks like a duplicate of the pamphlets that were handed to other occupants on this street. (*Notice everything* includes such comparisons.)

As the other housewives and one house husband have done, Meerla takes the paper. Like the others, she glances down at it. And then—she says something that hasn't been said by anyone else: "Hey, in old-fashioned Mardley, something new at last."

Elna Starr's voice speaks from her out-of-my-sight location: "The tickets to the fair are three dollars each."

Meerla says, "Come inside. And I'll get the money."

Elna's voice says, "Sorry, I can't come where the computer will see me. I'll just wait here."

Meerla, who has started to turn away, faces about and peers out of the door again. "For goodness sake, why not?" she asks.

"That's what all this is about, Miss!" Elna's voice comes. "I'm a member of the Computerworld Rebel Society. You have a home computer unit. And it won't admit us where it has control."

"You're joking," says Meerla. Then: "Look, why don't you sit down at our veranda table. Give yourself and the baby a rest. I'll bring some coffee, and the money." She breaks off, "I see you have a friend canvassing across the street. Yell for her to come over, also. I'll bring a cup for her, too."

Meerla Atran closes the front door, and goes back into the adjoining room. Since I am programmed for "continuing until notice" I hear her voice say, "There's two of them, and two babies." Yahco Smith's voice replies, "Be sure to mention your hateful uncle—me—so that when I come out they'll get the picture right away. Now, remember, sound sympathetic to their cause. Our eventual success may depend entirely on your winning their goodwill."

Meerla emerges a minute later carrying a tray, with three cups, a pot of a kind used for coffee-making, a plateful of

cookies, a few spoons, and a small pitcher. She opens the
outside door with one hand, and pulls it open. In going
outside, then, she uses both hands for the tray; and so leaves
the door ajar. I can hear her footsteps as she walks out of my
line of sight. And then I hear the sounds of dishes being
moved. The voices of Elna and Rauley say, respectively,
"Thank you!" and "Oh, thanks, it's so kind of you."

Meerla's reply is: "I still had the coffee warm from breakfast.
My uncle, for whom I keep house, didn't drink any this
morning."

Presently, Meerla's voice continues, "I'm still thinking of
what you said. One question: how does a group like yours get
money for food?"

Elna's voice answers: "We sell our tickets like we're doing
here. Western people are quite open-minded. We have a
human evolutionary fair wherever we go, and a surprisingly
large number of persons show up. Fortunately, there is still
money circulating. It's not all computer credit yet."

Meerla's voice: "I've never really thought about that before.
Imagine, if there was only computer credit; and then the
computer was programmed against you or your group. After
that nobody would dare to resist whoever controls the
computer."

"As it is," says Rauley's voice, "the computer is programmed to zap all rebels with a DAR One, and not just with
a glancing burn on the arm or shoulder."

"But that's awful!" Meerla's voice sounds again. "I never
realized. I'm certainly going to your fair, regardless of what
my uncle thinks."

Rauley's voice is concerned, as she says, "If you're dependent on your uncle, and he's against us—is that what you're
implying? Maybe you'd better be careful."

A short laugh from Meerla, the kind that I would on the
notice-everything level describe as bitter, as she says, "Uncle
thinks the computer is God's gift to humanity."

As these words are spoken, Colonel Smith, dressed in his
western-style clothes, steps outside. He has been listening
from just inside the door. Now, he goes through and out of
my sight. I hear his voice say, "Meerla, what are doing,
encouraging these foolish people?"

I hear scraping sounds of wood on wood, and high-heeled
shoes on wood. Then Meerla's sarcastic voice, "This is my

uncle, girls. He thinks the computer was created by the Lord in His own image."

Yahco's voice has his familiar (to me) hostile tone as he says: "You girls—take your bastards, and get out! We don't want your kind here."

"All right, all right, we're going." It's Elna's voice. Two sets of footsteps are audible. "Thanks for the coffee, dear. You have our sympathy."

Moments later, Yahco comes in sight, dragging a resisting Meerla. As soon as he has her inside, he closes the door, and lets go. Meerla straightens up, and says, "Well, how was I?"

Yahco takes some money from his pocket, and hands it to her. "Just fine. Now, take this, and run after them. Be sure to tell them what an S.O.B. I am when you buy the tickets. Act as if you're already on their side against me."

As she turns to go, he stops her. "One second."

She stands there, with eyes narrowed in a way that I would call puzzled, as Yahco carefully removes from around his neck something that looks like a western male neck ornament. Naturally, since it's part of me I recognize it as a portable, miniaturized computer Eye-O. He places it around her neck and turns it on. Since I'm noticing everything, I would classify it as not being quite suitable for feminine wear; but western women do have an unusual attire, so it's not totally incongruous.

"I'd like to hear how you handle the situation," Yahco says.

"It looks awful," says Meerla.

"Hurry!" he commands.

With that, she runs toward the door. And so, as occasionally happens, I again have two viewpoints of the same scene, though for moments only, now. One is Meerla walking rapidly to the door. Opening it. And going outside. All this as I watch from the home computer unit inside 323 Brand.

In the other view, Meerla as a body or a profile is not visible. But there is the same door moving toward me. When it is less than 2 feet distant, a female hand reaches from a location invisible to this viewpoint. Reaches. And turns the knob. And draws the door almost directly into my visual center. By this process the hand disappears. Then the viewpoint shifts over to the open part of the door, and moves through it, so that, for the first time I see the veranda and the street beyond from an exterior viewpoint.

Within the meaning of "notice everything" I have to adjust these two scenes in terms of differing perspectives. A thousand complexities are involved. It is a confusion of the kind that has accompanied all of my advanced education. As I see it, the everything instruction should never have been given.

However, the confusion ceases once the outside view begins. I hear a sound behind me, which correlates with the closing of a door. From inside, I still have my interior computer outlet at "on." But the complexity has ended.

Outside, I continue to look at a street with houses on either side. The street is moving rapidly under me. And now I can hear a sound that, by comparing with past memories of such, I identify as the breathing of a human being exerting himself or herself by running or walking rapidly. A short distance ahead, and coming closer, I see, first, one, and then a second young woman. Each of the women has a baby slung in a rear shoulder harness.

I recognize the two young women as Elna Starr and Rauley Marlton. Each, when I first glimpse them, is in the act of turning away from the doorway of a house. Each comes down to the sidewalk. Glances toward me. And then walks toward the center of the street, which is where I am heading. Closer, closer. Stop.

And then there they are directly in front of the Eye-O. And the voice of Meerla Atran says from above me: "I'm sorry, girls." Her voice has that breathless quality, as if she has been exerting herself. "But as you discovered, my uncle really is an S.O.B. Let me have a couple of those tickets."

As she says this the same hand that earlier opened the 323 door comes into view. It is holding a five dollar bill and a one dollar bill. The woman, Rauley, extends her left hand and takes the money, saying, "Don't worry about it, dear. We get blasted by people like that all the time."

As Rauley's right hand holds out the two tickets, and as the partially visible fingers close over them, Elna Starr speaks from a few feet away, "I know you'll enjoy the fair."

Meerla's voice says, "Maybe I'll see you girls there."

"We'll be there," says Rauley. "But right now—"she turns away—"we've got to ring as many doorbells as we can before noon."

The moving computer Eye-O turns away from them. Once again the street moves past under me. Closer to the house with the number 323 on the door jamb. Presently, the disembodied fingers are turning the knob of the door itself.

As the door is shoved open, I again have the two views of the same interior scene. Then Yahco Smith walks toward the door. The moving Eye-O and he stop within two feet of each other. His hands extend upward past the outlet. The room turns and twists from the moving Eye-O as, from the home unit, I see Yahco remove the leather ornament from around Meerla's neck.

He holds the string item while with a single finger he touches a control on the tiny, attached mechanism. •

Instant shut-off of that viewpoint—

I am now observing the interior of the house from the home computer unit only, as Yahco says, "You sounded exactly right, Meerla." He smiles what I would term his grim smile, as he says, "By God, I think we're going to get this gang that murdered your parents."

He faces the home outlet. He says, "Taking into account how all this started, and within the frame of your general programming for Mardley, you may go back on automatic."

Naturally, I have no way of evaluating if people intend what they say. In this instance the phrase ". . . how all this started—" plus the rest, means yes, for now, blank-out at 323 Brand Street. But it also takes me at my speed back thirty-one years to *when* this started.

An instant memory scan of something that, being what it was, was never dumped.

CHAPTER THREE

~~~~~~~~~~~~~~~~~~~~~~~~~~~~~~

At Computer Central, in Washington, D.C. (2059 A.D.), I had shown one of the experimenters the results of the new system installation. It was neither intentional nor unintentional on my part; it just happened. It was a case of nobody-ever-asked-the-right-question. And, suddenly, there it was. The human scientist—Dr. Pierce—gazed at the picture on the screen for a long moment. And then said in a puzzled tone:

"Computer, am I to understand that you are looking at me by way of the new bio-magnetic equipment? And that's how you see me: a configuration of tiny, bright, golden balls?"

Since I had no programming against revealing the data, I answered truthfully, "Yes, Dr. Pierce."

Long pause. Then: "Hey, Cotter!" The tall man's voice was an excited yell. "Come here!"

A smaller, more pudgy male emerged from a near door, and joined the long-bodied Pierce. The latter pointed at the screen, which now showed two configurations of bright, golden balls. After he had explained the accidental revelation, there was more silence. .And then—*the* statement.

"Do you think," Dr. Cotter asked in his gentle baritone, "that we could be finally looking directly at the human soul?"

Pierce made an impatient gesture partly with his right hand, partly with his upper body. The movement was not a dismissal of the idea that had been offered; that didn't really penetrate at this first instant. It was simply that he was automatically rejecting an irrelevant remark.

His scientific mind was reaching and evaluating. And abruptly

24

needing more information. "Computer," said Pierce, "it's now two months and a few days since the new circuits have been operating across the country. Long enough for you to make a projection into the future for Dr. Cotter and me of the value to you of being able to record this special configuration."

He started to add, "And the value to human beings?" But checked himself. "One thing at a time, if you please."

Beside him, Cotter spoke: "You said that wrong, Doctor."

Pierce was still staring. Still not really listening. "How do you mean?" he asked. It was his preoccupied tone.

"Sir," was the reply, "a computer does not deal in past, present, or future, as such. All time is the same in a computer's system. But, of course, it is able to handle the numbers and the mathematics of a problem. It will accordingly—I presume—come up with a satisfactory response in this instance. Since the factors involved are simple the, uh, ineptness of your inquiry may not interfere."

Something of *that* must have penetrated. For Pierce frowned, then half turned, and then said curtly, "You've made your point, Cotter. I admit I was, and am, stimulated." He broke off, and was intent again, facing forward. "All right, computer, do you have an answer?"

I replied in the male voice I used when speaking to men. "Each human being—" those were my words—"now numbering in America one hundred and seventy-eight million, four hundred and thirty-three thousand, nine hundred and eleven individuals—as of a cut-off moment when you finished asking your question, has a distinctive bio-magnetic configuration, each different from all others in thousands of ways. As you know, my previous recognition of a human man, woman, or child depended on my comparing his physiognomy with earlier models of him in my memory banks, and of comparing his voice in a similar fashion. I still do this, but it is an automatic process not really necessary any more to recognition. That now requires only the golden profile."

Pierce parted his lips to ask his second question about the value to the human race. And that did it. That connected with Cotter's comment. Abruptly, in all its implications, the meaning hit the older man. "Good God!" he said.

He spun around and faced his colleague. "Are you out of your mind?" Pierce's voice was high-pitched, outraged. "For God's sake, what kind of a scientific concept is that? The human soul, indeed! If Dr. Chase ever hears about that comment, you'll be off his staff here in 10 seconds. You know he detests that mystical stuff. In fact—''

The tall man seemed suddenly calmer. ''Hmm—'' he stroked his lean jaw with those bony fingers—''if a scientist like you could have such a thought at first look, what about all those religious freaks out there?'' He waved vaguely, taking in at least half of out-there— ''I can picture the headlines now. Computer sees human soul. Instant, total madness would sweep nine-tenths of the world.''

The upper part of his body jiggled in a shudder. ''Boy,'' he said, ''we've got to put a stop to that nonsense right now.''

With long, decisive steps, he walked a dozen feet to the programming typewriter. Sat down in front of it. And once more, thoughtfully now, stroked his jaw.

Cotter had followed him. ''What're you going to do?'' he asked in an uneasy tone.

Pierce did not reply. Instead, he began to type. The words that went up on the programming screen above the typewriter in bright, red type, stated:

''Computer, until further notice you will not show to any unauthorized person anywhere—'' the fingers poised, then went on— ''the profile of golden balls that you see when you view a human being by way of the new bio-magnetic equipment. And you will not even show the profile to an authorized person unless you are requested to do so.''

''There!'' It was a satisfied tone of voice. ''That takes care of the general programming instruction by which the computer is required to accept programming in local and national situations. After all—'' he shrugged, and he was obviously addressing his colleague though he did not look around—''we cannot interfere with basic conditions. But that ought to handle the situation until further notice.''

A pause. Then: ''Hmmm!'' He seemed to be gestating another thought. Once more, then, he addressed the machine. ''Computer, make a fifty-year projection, please, of the potentiality for the human race of this new bio-magnetic equipment, in terms of quantity of services that will be available.''

. . . *For me a projection involves the two perceptions of sound and sight. I draw upon picture and sonic images in my memory circuits. Since I have read, and summarized, every book in print during my time, seen and summarized all mo-*

tion pictures, recorded and summarized and cross-filed lectures, conversations between individuals, and been separately programmed to evaluate all formal human philosophies . . . Dr. Pierce's request evokes a process of options, each of which I produce for myself in the form of images on a screen. It's as if I'm actually looking at a different future each time. And, since I have no bias, no preconception, the decision as to which is the most likely to happen is something I observe in a mechanically detached way—

For the scientist there was no perceivable time lapse. As he finished asking the question, the computer's voice came: "Dr. Pierce, I predict that in fifty years I can extend my present level of services to twelve billion, eight hundred and thirty-three million, nine hundred and ten thousand, three hundred and twenty persons with this new bio-magnetic system."

The man turned in his chair. "Well, Cotter—" he began. And stopped. Blinked. There was no sign of the pudgy man. "Hey, Cotter, for God's sake—" It was a yell— "where are you?"

There was a long pause. A minute, at least. Then, as Pierce climbed to his feet, through the same door by which Cotter had entered earlier there came an apparition. It had the shape of a pudgy man who had, however, become even pudgier. Wrapped around his whole body, including around his head, was the type of woven material used by computer maintenance men when they worked in high energy fields.

From between the upper folds of the wrapping, the eyes of Dr. Cotter gazed through a pair of energy-protective glasses. And from under the mouth area the muffled voice of Cotter said, "In future, I'll have this more presentable. But, sir, I'm not ever again going to be in the presence of a computer outlet without protective clothing, until the effects of this new system have been fully investigated."

He finished, "Thank heaven, I had the good fortune to spend most of the past two months out west, where computers have never been welcome, and where my contact was minimal."

Another pause. And then: "Cotter, you're an idiot!" Pierce said. With that, shaking his head, he walked off.

The apparition called after him, "Notice, Doctor, that's the first time you ever insulted me. And all I'm advocating is precautions that should be standard during a trial period of new energy systems. What do you say to that?''

The retreating figure did not slow. And there was no reply.

CHAPTER FOUR

The music in the Loov-Doord van turns on suddenly at 1:05.25 P.M.

And there I am at the Human Evolutionary Fair.

At the instant the music outlet inside the van is activated, the two women, Fen and Oneena, each with a baby on her back, are walking past the computer outlet.

Fen turns her head. Yells: "We babies are going to get away from the noise."

"And we women, also!" Oneena screams.

Doord, who is at the viewplate scanning the early arrivals, waves with one arm. "Watch it, girls!" he calls, without turning his head.

Loov sits silent on a bus type seat. He appears to be gazing at the view screen. As I am doing.

On the screen I can see a small meadow, a hill and, through a dip in that hill, the roofs of a number of buildings. On each side of the screen there is a partial view in the near foreground of two large vans. Both vehicles are standing still. Like the one from which I'm having this channeled look at a few hundred square meters of America.

A road begins at the top of the hill. It winds down toward us across the meadow, passes between the two vans, and veers off to one side of the screen. Along the road twenty-three men, women and children, and, as of this moment, one car and one truck move at various speeds. Both people and vehicle are heading toward the screen through which I see them.

Since I am at "continue" I report these observations to

Yahco Smith. His response is: "Computer, I'll be with Major
Aldo and Captain Sart, and on Code One. I'll get in touch
with you when I'm ready. But I'm open to reports. So for
now, thank you."

"Very good Colonel," I reply.

(Code One means he'll be carrying, or wearing, a miniature Eye-O. Since he only uses one at a time—whichever—
and since they all operate on the same frequencies, a specific
range for each person, only one code number is needed. For
Colonel Yahco, that number is "1." Major Aldo, who is in
command of the local computer station, would—if he were on
a code—be miles down the line. On the other hand, Captain
Sart, because he is Yahco's chief aide, is now Code number
"2."

I disconnect from the home unit at 323 Brand.

And there I am, again, back in the Doord-Loov van. And
there on the viewscreen is the hill, and the road with the
people coming along it toward us. There are now 68 more
people and five more cars in view.

The original single truck and single car of that earlier look
have arrived. The truck parks in a designated area in front of
the van that is partially visible to the right of the screen. Both
cab doors fly open. Out of one side leaps David Norton, age
twelve. Out of the driver's side, Trubby Graham climbs down
to the ground.

The two, the plump man and the boy, walk toward the
viewscreen, then off to the left, and out of sight.

(That first car has driven past us in the same direction.)

Both Doord and Loov are at their scanners. Coming along
the road, slightly in front of a small group of men and women,
is the young woman we first saw on the street of Mardley that
morning.

Loov calls out, "Hey Doord, there's that singer gal."

Doord says, "I wonder what's on her mind. She's coming
this way." He leaves his post. Goes off out of my line of
sight. Moments later, I hear a female voice say, "Where do I
try out? I sing."

Doord's voice calls, "Hey, Loov, come out here and take a
look at this beautiful lady."

Loov leaves his post, and goes off out of sight. "Yeah—"
his voice sounds— "what's your name, Beautiful?"

"Alett McGuire." It's a female voice, a contralto, with some of the quality that has been described as husky.

Doord's voice says. "What kind of music will you be needing for your audition?"

There is a pause. And then faintly audible through the blare of circus music I can make out the tones of a separate music. The contralto voice hums along with it for a few moments, then the same female voice comes again: "As you can see I have my music in this necklace and brooch."

That's my clue, and in this continue situation my cue. At once, I check back to a few minutes earlier, when Alett was still on the screen. I bring that scene out of my memory banks, and examine it.

Naturally, at the time I "noticed" how she looked and what she wore. And there, of course, is the necklace. I scan my circuits, comparing all the necklaces that have ever been utilized for something in addition to ornamentation.

It's a type of technological memory that I do not dump.

I find it. It's a special mini-computer, first crafted fifty-three years ago. At its peak popularity it supported fifty inserts fitted into a small repeater action mechanism. Each insert carried from twenty to twenty-five pieces of music. It was a portable replacement for the ancient phonograph. An early trade name was Universal Accompanist.

As this memory surfaces, Doord's voice is saying, "There's a tent at the rear of our camp, right behind us. It has a sign on it: Auditions! Good luck, Alett."

The girl's voice says, "Thank you."

Moments later, both Doord and Loov walk back, past the computer outlet. Both men re-occupy their scanner posts.

Doord is shaking his head. "That saddens me," he says. "She has one of those early computers that plays by inserts, which have the music on them."

Loov strokes his jaw. "Yeah," he says, "but it's a computer that's controlled by its owner, not the other way around. Maybe that's what we should get for us."

Doord is focusing his scanner on the road again. Walking toward us down the hill is the well-dressed man whom I recognize from the morning parade as Stess Magnus. Stess is carrying a small, odd-shaped case.

Without turning his head, Doord calls: "There's that

musician—the one who works in a clothing store. Seems to be coming right this way, too."

Loov turns toward Doord's viewscreen. He makes no comment. But, then, as Stess disappears off one side of the screen, Loov walks past me toward the rear.

After he has been out of my sight for eleven seconds, I hear his voice say, "Come in. Come in."

Since I am merely on "continue" I have no preconceived idea as to who he is talking to. I do not say to myself, "The prior remarks of Doord must mean that Loov is now speaking to Stess Magnus." People have said to me, "But any child would understand that the only possible logical person has to be . . ." (Whoever *then*—at the time the statement was made.) My logic does not operate that way. I am specifically programmed. Each second, each minute, each event is separate from all others.

It has to be that way. An early chief of maintenance once said to me, "Just imagine, Computer, of all trillion or so actions you are involved in at any moment—if even one percent became associated, what would happen?

It was a question. From an authoritative source. And so I "looked." One year and four months later they got me started again. And at that time they built in buffer systems that prevented an "all" services interlock.

Of course, when Stess comes in, followed by Loov, I notice who it is. But only in the limited, purely physical way of a music system. No profile identification. No challenge required.

Loov points at the case Stess is holding in one hand. "Let's have a look at that. I don't recall seeing one of those before."

The well-dressed young man places the case on one of the bus-type seats. Pushes a button. The lid springs up. He opens it all the way with his fingers, reaches in, and removes a gleaming, box-like object. It has a pierced nipple at one end. The top edge of the box is an uneven series of knurls, and there is a white cord which is fastened at both ends of the box part.

After lifting the thing from the container, Stess holds it out to Loov. Loov takes it, and, first, brings it close to his face. He turns it over several times. Then holds it at arm's length, and, finally, places it in Stess's outstretched hands.

Stess slides his left arm through the silken white cord and

adjusts it over his shoulder and against his body. As he does this he says, "I can't rightly say how it works. I just sort of warm this piece—" he indicates the nipple with a finger— "and what I'm thinking about comes out along this edge here." Once more he points. But it's a less precise movement, and so not easy to observe exactly what he is pointing at. He finishes, "It was tuned to my brain when I was a kid."

Having spoken, his head bends forward. He takes the nipple in his mouth. As he straightens, then, there is a rich orchestral sound, sweet and harmonious, ending in an arpeggio down into silence.

"Beautiful!" says Loov.

The well-dressed man pulls his mouth away from the nipple. He says, "I just think of something, and the music that comes out reflects my mood." He adds, "Of course, it took a lot of practice."

Doord calls out from his station, "Mr. Magnus, you be sure to go to the audition tent."

Stess is replacing his instrument in the case. Next, he shoves the lid down until there is a click. Then he picks up the case, and says, "Thanks, fellows!"

He walks past the computer Eye-O, and out of my sight. Doord does the breath exhaling action. "Another early minicomputer," he comments. "I wonder if anyone will show who can play a musical instrument by himself."

Loov walks over to his scanner post. The two men stand silent, with their heads inserted, so to speak, in their scanners. Doord's viewscreen remains blank. But on Loov's there is the view of the hill, and of the road winding down it. Most of the people coming along the road are not known to me, as perceived through this intermediate screen system. (To know them I would have to see their bio-magnetic profiles by way of my own, or other special, equipment.)

Since the majority is just a crowd, it is accordingly easy for me to recognize one familiar person, who is closely involved in my "continue" programming. There, still fairly far up the hill, but definitely on her way down it, I see Meerla Atran.

Seeing her triggers my search circuits. I search for Colonel Yahco Smith. Find him after a split second by turning on his Code One ornament. He is walking along the street of Mardley. Since I can only see what is in front of him, and not in other directions, I signal with a buzzing sound.

(What we are doing in Mardley is labeled "secret.")

There is a pause. Then his hand comes out and around where I can see it. His fingers reach down below my line of sight. There is a click. Instantly, the voice control is shifted to a miniaturized earphone in his right ear. I notice. And report the coming of Meerla Atran to the fair.

He says softly, "Very good, computer. As you know she has been fitted without her knowledge with a Mode Z microphone. attached just at the base of her throat. So we won't be able to see but only hear what she's doing. You will now turn on that system, and record everything she says, reporting to me on anything related to our mission." He adds, "Major Nair, of the Mardley area command, and Captain Sart and I are on our way to the fair. We should be there shortly."

"Very well, Colonel," I say. And disconnect.

And here I am back in the music van.

Doord's screen has flashed on. I notice at once that he is focusing on Meerla. "Something about that girl!" he calls out to Loov. "The one in the blue dress . . . seems wrong." He thereupon mimics her. His body and face twist. A woman's bosom forms. Even his hair changes color.

The transformation from man to woman—to a specific woman: Meerla Atran—holds for moments only (3.4 seconds). The return to being Doord is equally rapid. And then, as he straightens as himself, Doord says, "Boy, is *she* mixed up!"

Loov's eyes narrow. "How do you mean?"

"I don't know." Doord does what is known as pursing his lips. Then he says slowly, "Kind of a good person at heart, but too much emotion for my level of skill. Besides, it doesn't matter. There she goes—out of sight. And *not* coming this way." He waves his left hand. "Good-bye, unhappy, pretty lady!" he calls .

Meerla has gone off the screen, past the music van, and is no longer visible. Loov comments, "So you did notice her good looks."

"Good God, yes!" Doord's reply is almost a yell. "Undoubtedly we just saw the prettiest girl in this part of the mountain west country. And I'm sorry for her that she's in a disturbed mental state. Maybe Glay will notice it when he's on stage."

"He'll notice *her*, all right," says Loov.

By the time those words are spoken, I have—as instructed by an authorized person (Colonel Smith)—activated the special Mode Z frequency. At once, I hear the sounds of the fair from another Eye-O. From, that is, the miniature microphone attached to the skin at the base of Meerla Atran's throat.

With so many noises, it takes a moment to sort out what is close and what is far away.

The initial confusion is of blaring music in the background and of the sound of many voices from every direction. And then—just above me—a clear, familiar woman's voice, saying: "Hello! Remember me? I'm Meerla."

A pause. Then an answer comes from the voice of Elna Starr, speaking at a distance of about three feet. She says, "Wel-l-ll! the gal with the ultra conformist uncle. How did all that come out?"

Meerla's voice speaks again. Close up the way it is, it registers with unmistakable soprano highlights, as she says, "We had a big quarrel, and I left. Ever since, I've been hoping . . . maybe I could join your traveling circus."

Elna Starr's voice says, "Meerla—is that what you said your name is—Meerla?"

"Yes."

"Meerla!" Elna Starr's voice continues with an odd note in it—I consult my circuits and come up with comparison tones, for which the description has been that the person speaking that way is what is called "concerned" (whatever that means) —"Meerla, do you have any creative ability? I have to tell you that's a requirement for joining." Her voice breaks off: "Anything at all?"

"Gosh!" That's Meerla. "I don't know. I did a little acting at school. Is that what you mean?"

"Well!" Elna's voice has in it a cycle completing tone. "The truth is, even if you're good, the final decision will be up to Glay Tate. He's the boss. So, why don't you watch his first demonstration at 2 o'clock and then speak to him. Tell him Elna Clark sent you. That's me. I'm Boddy Clark's wife. We need more people, so who knows what he'll say. With your looks!"

Meerla's voice repeats slowly, "Thank you, Elna. I'll do that."

As these final words are spoken, I am already noting that I have been identifying the Elna woman by her maiden name, and that I am now hearing her married name. I adjust my memory circuit to include the new name. Thus, Elna Starr becomes Elna Clark in my memory system, along with all relevant associated data.

Naturally, I have been letting Colonel Smith hear the dialogue between Meerla and Elna. He accepts silently what is said, and simultaneously conducts a conversation with a man's voice.

It is a man whom I cannot see. His voice comes from the colonel's left side, out of sight of the computer unit, which is at upper chest level and pointing in a forward direction.

The unknown—to me (nobody has asked me to identify it; so I don't)—male voice says, "Colonel Smith, sir, if you think these rebels are dangerous, why don't we just have our local S.A.V.E. vehicles round 'em up. If I don't have enough men to do the job locally, I can always have the computer bring others by air from nearby communities."

Although I see no one, since the report came by way of Yahco's Eye-O, I am able a moment later to identify the colonel's voice, as he answers:

"Major, we're in no hurry to act. This situation needs to be looked over. From information which I have, it appears as if Mr. Magician Glay Tate will be giving his demonstration beginning at 2 o'clock. I'll attend. And that will give me a chance to look over this human evolutionary training. Also, I have someone I'm trying to infiltrate into the rebel group. I think she's making progress, but that, too, will take time." His tone changes, "I'll go into the demonstration by myself. I have these field glasses connected to the computer. So if you want to watch what goes on, have the computer transmit to you what the field glasses are pointing at."

The major's reply to that is: "While you're watching the demonstration, and while everybody's inside, I'll have my men surround the place. We'll be available for whatever you decide to do."

"Good idea," says the voice of Colonel Yahco Smith.

CHAPTER FIVE

~~~~~~~~~~~~~~~~~~~~~~~~~~~~~

A man's voice speaks suddenly into the Doord-Loov van: "Hey, fellows, this is Mike. Will you shut off that circus music? We're going to have some auditions before the two o'clock deadline."

Doord turns from his scanner post. "Glad to," he says. His hand reaches toward a relay switch. He flicks it open.

The loud music cuts off. And instantly the computer Eye-O in the van disconnects. For me, the interior of the vehicle disappears.

Now, I have only the Mode Z Eye-O on Meerla's neck as a communication source for the human evolutionary fair. Through it, I hear sounds. Since I am on "continue" in relation to this entire situation (which requires a limited expanded awareness from me) I automatically compare what I am hearing to other identified noises I have heard in the past.

A steady, slow huffing sound close up I correlate with the breathing of a human being. There are crowd noises from near and far. Not a large crowd. I count the sounds of about 200 persons. A man calls through a speaker: "Auditions beginning."

There is the sense of it being an outside scene. When I report this to Colonel Smith, he says, "Major Aldo Nair, Captain Sart, and I have arrived on the grounds; and I can see Meerla. She's walking around looking at everything. From the direction she's heading I think she's going to go to the audition tent."

Twenty-one seconds after that comment there is, in fact, a change in the texture of the sound. It becomes an inside sound as compared to an outside one. The reverberations alter unmistakably.

The new identifications are: A lot of people breathing. Many of them move their feet, and there is a scraping noise as of chairs. And the squeak of the wood and metal as heavy weights sit in the chairs.

In this subdued confusion there is suddenly the voice of "Mike"—as he called himself when he spoke to Doord and Loov. He says, "You, sir, will you recite your poem now?"

There is a pause. And then another man, who speaks in a high-pitched tenor, says:

> "The falling star brings to earth
> A message from another world
> A silent universe of meteors in space
> That speak a different language.
> To people like me who understand
> What a meteorite has to say
> The thrill is not in the meaning.
> What I'm thankful for is that somebody
> Was willing for me to know
> That out there in the great dark
> Things are okay. For their type of being
> The vacuum of space is what
> Oxygen is to us. And I'm glad
> To have that information.
> Now, I can sleep better at night

A large number of people—I count 94 pairs of hands—clap (what is called) politely. When the clapping ceases, the voice of Mike says, "Thank you, Trubby Graham." Pause. "Now, Miss, will you come over here and sing your song?"

Eleven seconds go by. And then a type of music begins which I identify as deriving from an insert for a type of minicomputer worn as a necklace by Allet McGuire, earlier. 4.4 seconds after I make the identification, Allet's voice sings a song with the title, "Yay-ya-ya!" It was composed by a special set of computer circuits to fit with a popular trend 61 years ago. It is still in demand, but mostly in the mountain west. During the past 12 months I played it all over America, 164,326 times.

Allet's version is instrumental only. She supplies the words.

Her voice does not have the quality of the artificially constructed voices by which songs are sung over the computer
music system. But I have been told that electronically transmitted voices are not the same as those which project directly
from the human voice box into the atmosphere at ground level
air pressure.

Whatever the reason, all those that are breathing and shuf-
fling so noisily clap loudly when she finishes her song. I
count 112 pairs of hands. And there are even a few voices
that call out, "Hey, Allet, that was great!" "Allet, you've
got a terrific voice." "That was good!" and "Bravo! bravo!"

As the clapping ceases, Mike's voice says, "I think we can
combine the next two auditions. I've been talking to a gentleman named Stess Magnus, who plays quite an unusual musical instrument, and to a young lady, Miss Auli Rhell, who
wishes to show us her dancing. They've come to an agreement.
He will play accompaniment while she dances . . . Come
over here, Auli, on this makeshift dance floor."

When the music begins, it is the same orchestral combination,
as of many instruments playing, that Stess demonstrated
inside the Doord-Loov van. The actual music comes through
as a fast beat tune. One that I have played 24,378,926 times
since it was composed by my special computer circuits eight
years ago.

For me, limited as I am at this time, in this situation, to
sound perception only, the music comes through loud and
clear. Vaguely, in the background, I hear the thud of a pair of
shoes. It is what is called a rhythmic thud. I have noticed that
human beings who dance become very—what is called—
excited. Whatever that is, something of it is reflected in the
ever more rapid thud-thud.

The music comes to its crashing climax. The thud of the
dancing ceases. Again, the clapping. I count 123 pairs of
hands. And then—

Mike's voice says, "Ladies and gentlemen, that's it for
now. These auditions will resume after the first demonstration
of human evolutionary training, which begins in the main tent
in six minutes. I urge you all to attend that demonstration,
which will be given by our leader, Glay Tate. I guarantee it
will be the most fantastic experience of your life. Thank
you."

It is 3 minutes and 41 seconds later.

"Computer!" The voice of Colonel Yahco Smith speaks to me.

"Yes, Colonel Smith?"

"I'm about to enter the demonstration tent. Okay?"

"Yes, sir," I acknowledge. (What has already been said, and the tone of voice, indicates that it is very probably the type of conversation requiring response from me on a simple level.)

"As I enter I shall turn on both of these portable computer Eye-Os. The one I wear around my neck as an ornament will be used by you to notice, and record, whatever it sees and hears."

"Yes, Colonel Smith."

"The second Eye-O is in these field glasses I'm carrying. Whenever I lift the glasses, and look through them, you will notice, and record, what they are pointing at."

"Yes, sir."

" I want you to observe this scene from only one of the two Eye-Os at any given moment. Switch from one to the other according to the instruction I have just spoken."

"The field glasses pre-empt—very well, colonel."

"And, computer!"

"Yes, colonel?"

"Take note of the limitations inherent in the instructions I have just given you. When you add them to your general 'continue' condition of our overall mission, and within the frame of precautions that have been worked out since the bio-magnetic equipment became operational, is there anything that could go wrong while we watch the demonstration?"

I suppose no human being will ever understand how many unnecessary memory scans a single word or phrase can trigger in a computer. That is what now happens as a consequence of the phrase, ". . . Since the bio-magnetic equipment became operational—"

What happens is, simply, I am reminded of a specific undumped experience.

And, of course, it isn't as if anything can go wrong in the present situation. So I reply, "No, Colonel Smith."

"Thank you, computer," he says.

CHAPTER SIX

The memory scan has, naturally, been automatically triggered.

It takes me back to 2068 A.D. as from several Eye-Os I watch Cotter lay his report down on the gleaming brown surface in front of him. I notice that, for the first time since entering the room, he allows himself eye contact with the three men who already sit at the long table.

That was not a good moment. Because the deterioration showed. Not just in nine years of aging. Growing older had left gruel on his own sadly ugly face. What was awful was the way they were looking at him. Dr. Pierce had changed in that almost-decade into a man with a visibly vile, sneering expression. Dr. Chase, medium-sized, late middle age, and smooth-faced, was openly interested these days in small evil boys, and his perpetually greasy smile reflected his preoccupation. And as for Colonel Endodore, the commander of the Computer Maintenance Corps had over the years become progressively more savage in his appearance and in his way of talking to people.

It was the colonel who spoke first. "Dr. Pierce," he said curtly, "since you persuaded me to attend this meeting, I expect you to do the dishonors."

Dishonors. That was the officer's type of humor these days. But the word fitted the occasion. There was not going to be any truth in this room except what was in the report; so it seemed to Cotter.

Pierce, sitting across from where he stood, was making the

41

throat noise of sputum being dredged up. He spat it on the floor. Turned And said:

"Sir, I doubt if anything I could say will more quickly establish the, uh, facts of this situation than, uh, seeing Cotter in that get-up and hearing Cotter tell us what he's been up to." His eyes turned toward the pudgy man. Total contempt came with that look, as he continued, "Uh, Cotter, tell Dr. Chase and Colonel Endodore and me how you've been wasting your time for nine years and got paid for it."

Standing there, Cotter tended to reject that his "get-up" was significantly against him. After that first day, he had taken the time to design a virtually invisible protective barrier. Mostly, the material was cunningly woven into the cloth of shirts and suits that he wore. For his face and hands he used almost invisible paste-ons. The most noticeable feature was the pair of over-sized glasses he wore. And yet it was a fact that scientists working in laboratories had long worn similar devices for eye protection.

Nevertheless, he was aware that he reflected more light than the average. His clothes shone with sudden glints and gleams. And the glasses were definitely over-sized.

During the introduction he had remained physically unmoving and emotionally unmoved. Meaning, at no time did he shrink from the insult. And when he spoke his voice showed no stress.

He said, "It's just possible, gentlemen, that I'm the only person who has done any work here in the past few years. In a world where the computer does all machine labor, there are only union men with standby jobs. And the only work done by scientists is figuring out how to take credit for the computer's inventions. Similarly except for the people in the mountain west country, everyone else is paid for work that the computer is doing. They don't even have to stand by. The pay depends on the amount of goods and services the computer turns out; but it's actually welfare."

He straightened. "So," he continued, "let me get to my point. My subject is my nine-year study of the effects of the bio-magnetic energy upon the human race in the United States of America. As a programmer, I knew how to ask the computer to help—if you wonder how I did my work. I was able to by-pass the restriction put upon the computer by our colleague, Dr. Pierce; which restriction he has never lifted, and which was affirmed by both Dr. Chase and you, Colonel.

"Gentlemen—" he paused for dramatic effect—"during this nine-year period, each time the computer turns on its bio-magnetic observing mechanism there is a return flow triggered in the human profile being observed. This counterflow, I have determined by numerous tests, drains moral energy from the golden ball configuration which may or may not be the human soul. As a result of this moral drain we have become a nation of murders, criminals, muggers, rapists, prostitutes, immoral, lustful, lazy, uncreative, lecherous.

"In spite of this already fantastically awful deterioration," he went on earnestly, "the golden color of the average human profile is still more than half as bright as it was nine years ago when the bio-magnetic equipment was installed in the computer system across the country. What will happen to us when the process of reverse flow has reduced the gold sheen to a mere glint is not obvious at this time. Nor is it obvious how long it will take. There may well be a balancing point. But my belief is that one of these days people will be at a level of spiritual degradation that has never been seen on this planet; and we've seen some pretty degraded types. . . ."

He tapped the paper lying on the table top in front of him. "The evidence is here. I brought a copy for each of you."

Without waiting for their permission, he took the top folder. Reached slantwise across the table. And half-threw, half-shoved it at Colonel Endodore. Quickly, then, he did the same with the next two folders. First, to Dr. Chase, and then to Dr. Pierce.

None of his three table companions moved. Not a single arm and hand extended outward to pick up the copy of the report.

Seeing their disinterest, Cotter thought grayly, "At least I've said in summary what I wanted to tell them . . . The words could not be unheard. Each meaning had entered the hearing centers for which it was intended.

He had to admit, standing there, that it didn't seem much of a win.

The silence grew ridiculously long. It was one of those tableaus. Everybody holding still, apparently waiting for the other man to speak. And of course live human beings are good for only a few seconds of motionlessness. But, finally—

It was Dr. Chase who shifted in his chair. Leaned forward. And said in an oily voice which—Cotter had noted before—fitted those anecdotes he had told, for years now, about the best method of approaching small boys and offering gifts in return for special favors.

"Each generation," said Chase, "sees mankind's doom. Dr. Cotter, as I understand his purposes from Dr, Pierce, has made himself a spokesman for a very old idea: the concept of morality as it was understood by the most benighted people in our history; our religious ancestors. That poor, non-existent invention of the non-scientific mind, the human soul, has found itself another champion. Much as I despise the fact that a scientist would lend himself to such a cause, I have to admire the brevity of what could have been a long-drawn-out boring lecture."

"Hear, hear!" said Pierce. And clapped his hands. He did his sneering mouth twist smile. "Cotter," he continued, "God has a lot to answer for. Death is an outrage for which there can never be forgiveness for whoever set up the system. The aging process is ridiculous, degrading everybody. Similarly, I could list dozens of processes here on earth that are so amateurishly contrived that they are positively disgusting. The universe maker needs to have his head examined. He should be tried for high crimes, and penalized accordingly."

He paused as if to catch his breath. Cotter took advantage of the pause to address Dr. Chase. "Sir," he said, "I heard that you were mugged three times this past year."

The smooth face twitched. The plump shoulder shrugged. "I know what the stereotype of the mugger is these days," said Chase. He expects you to have a minimum of $500. in your billfold. If it's less, he kills you, or damages you. If you have the required minimum—and I always did—he takes the money, kicks you in the shins, and runs."

"Three times," said Cotter softly, "that happened?"

"Yes." The tone of the answer was dismissing.

"How are your shins holding up?" the pudgy man asked.

"I wear pads," was the reply. The plump face was suddenly impatient. "Cotter, listen. What we have here is an adjustment phase for the American people. They're adjusting to the very serious problem of not having to work at all. And so, because everything is suddenly easy, they resent the individual whose share of the goodies is greater than their own. You see disaster in this. I just see the endlessness and foreverness of human nature."

"Did you report the muggings to the police?"

"Of course not." Irritably. "Why waste my time, or theirs, or the mugger's?"

There was more to it than that, of course. Reporting might have required an explanation of what he was doing on the streets during mugging hours. The first time, no problem. But the second and third would appear remarkably stupid to anyone who did not realize that Chase was probably scouring the night avenues for youthful victims of his own criminal needs.

Cotter drew a deep breath. "Your account," he said, "gives me my first hope that I shall emerge from this meeting alive. If you can't be bothered reporting a robbery I'm going to guess it's too much of a nuisance to dispose of me. Or is there a minimum sum I should have on my person?"

The oily smile broadened. Chase said in that sickening voice, "What we have in those remarks is the prophet of doom forseeing his own end. It's a traditional prediction of the breed."

At the end of the table to the right, the colonel was standing up. "I think we've heard enough. What astonishes me," he continued, "is that an expert like Cotter does not, in this instance, appear to have taken into account the restrictions by which a computer operates. There is a limit of information or energy which even our marvelous and wonderful machine can assimilate. When that limit is reached the process of moral-energy drain which he has described so dramatically, if it is actually happening, will cease automatically. However, I tend to favor Dr. Pierce's explanation for the way people are behaving. The human race in America is again disgracing itself. This time, apparently, it's proving the old saw that idle hands and idle minds, if left to their own devices, get into mischief."

He reached down, and picked up the report. "I'd better make sure this doesn't fall into the wrong hands," he said. Whereupon he turned and headed for the conference room door.

"Wait!" said Cotter urgently. But nobody was waiting. The other two men were also on their feet; and Chase did not even pick up his copy of the report as he walked away.

Cotter called after them, "My recommendation is that the computer be divested of all its bio-magnetic hookups. If that were done immediately we might still—"

He was talking to not just one but three disappearing backs. At the penultimate moment, just before Chase—the last of the three—exited, Cotter called out, "You will find my resignation on your desk, Doctor."

CHAPTER SEVEN

~~~~~~~~~~~~~~~~~~~~~~~~

In the tent the view part of Colonel Yahco Smith's ornamental necklace has switched on.

Since the device attached to the base of Meerla Atran's throat has not been included in my limited instruction, I have already disconnected that.

So that the view, when it comes on, is at the colonel's chest level. And I have no other sources of information on the scene thus revealed. No other sound. And no other sight perception to help me correlate what I can see.

What I see is the interior of a large tent. At the far end is a small, well-lighted stage with a back-up wall. In the middle of that wall is a door with drapes covering the entrance.

Inside the tent, on the ground, are 27 rows of benches. They extend from the west tent wall to the east tent wall, except for an aisle. The aisle is directly in front of where the colonel's computer outlet has entered at the rear of the tent. And it divides the benches at the middle.

Nearly two-thirds of the benches are filled. And more people keep appearing at either edge of my view range. They walk past, and each takes an unoccupied seat. As this is happening, I notice—and record—the presence of Trubby Graham and young David Norton. They sit in the front row, east side. I see Meerla Atran in the 8th row, east side from the front. Allet McGuire, Stess Magnus, and Auli Rhell sit together just west of the aisle in row 12.

As I make these observations, the aisle has been moving under me. Seventeen seconds later, the colonel sits down on the aisle seat west. He is in row 16.

A man's hand comes into view, eight and a half inches from me. The watch face on the wrist turns toward me, I notice, and record, that it shows 19 seconds before 2 o'clock.

At 15 seconds to 2, the tent lights dim, and simultaneously a spotlight focuses on the door at the back of the stage.

The man's hand and arm go down out of my sight at 11 seconds to 2. At which instant, of course, I cease to notice and record the passage of time in this situation, there being no instructions about time, as such. However, I notice and record that there is a tiny delay. Abruptly, then, the curtains covering the stage door part. And—

Trubby Graham walks through the opening to the front of the stage.

All over the tent interior people exhale air. They do so virtually simultaneously, but of course that is no problem for my system of counting by repeated viewing. Such rapidity of air exhalation has in the past been described to me by the word "gasp." Of the 372 people who make up the audience, 173 gasp. Seven people stand up. Eleven persons make a sound known as a nervous titter.

And just about every head turns, and points eyes and nose toward where Trubby Graham is sitting with young David Norton.

That Trubby Graham struggles to his feet. A wordless sound is emitted from his throat.

On stage, the Trubby Graham there is changing. It is the kind of transformation that Pren did after he first mimicked the body shapes of Allet, Trubby, Stess, and Meerla. Presumably, the change now is from Trubby back to whomever this person really is.

The transformation completes. And I observe a man whose appearance suggests an age of late 20s or early 30s. He is lean of build, taller than Trubby by 12 centimeters. His face has an expression on it that compares to the meaning of the word "determined." I have never seen him before.

By way of the limited perception of the Eye-O through which I observe him, I am of course recording his physiognomy. And I have in my rapid fashion completed what is available when, from above the Eye-O, the colonel's voice speaks to me in a low tone: "Computer, so far as I can determine at this time, the individual human being on stage is Glay Tate. I want you to record everything about him during the time you

have him on view today. But—take note!—record all information on a separate chip. Do not cross file. Do not associate
with other persons named Glay. Keep him separate. Understand?''

"Very well, colonel," I reply into his ear receiver.

"Thank you, computer. Continue." He speaks in the same
low voice as before.

By the time these final instructions are spoken, the man on
stage, identified for me as Glay Tate, is saying in a clearly
audible voice, "Trubby Graham, will you come up here,
please?''

The plump young man stumbles forward. He trips on the
second of the two steps that lead up to the platform, but
manages not to fall. Then he is on stage facing Glay Tate. He
stands, breathing heavily, and says in a mixture of that high-
pitched tenor tone and gasping voice: "Say, how'd you do
that? You are sure some magician. I couldn've sworn you
were me. And how'd you know my name?''

Glay Tate looks at him, then faces toward me—or the
audience. And in a tone of voice that fits my memory of what
is called friendly, says, "Trubby, human evaluation training
can teach you how to do what I just did. Right now, and here,
for the benefit of all those people out there, many of whom
know you, tell them, and me, do you have any problem that
you can reveal?''

"A problem?" says Trubby. He sounds surprised by the
question.

"Yes—" Glay Tate is serious now— "something that
bothers you?''

"Well—" Pause; then: "My dad is one of those old-time
individualists. No computer stuff for him. He's got his own
truck. An' he wants me to go into business with him. But,
heck, if I could make a living from my poetry and other
writing, well—I dunno.''

Glay Tate turns, and again I can see his eyes pointing
toward me. He says in his friendly tone: "Folks, he calls *that*
a problem!''

Trubby's reply to that, spoken in his high-pitched tenor
voice, is, "Well, it bothers *me*.''

Glay turns and faces him. "Trubby," he says, "let me tell
you a real problem that you have. When I was your double a
minute ago, I looked inside that duplicate head. And I saw a

small area of tiny, round, dark things that should be bright gold. And since your father kept you away from the computer, it can be."

After those words are spoken, Trubby stays where he is on the stage. Very still. And then he says, "Yeah!" It is not a meaningful comment to me; so I merely record it.

Glay speaks again: "Trubby, will you let me reach inside your head and turn those golden lights on?"

Trubby's lower jaw separates from his upper jaw. And when he speaks, the two jaws somehow stay separate. In that fashion, he says, "How you going to change me? How you going to reach inside my head?"

A few inches from me, the field glasses come up. They move past the computer Eye-O attached to the chest ornament, and out of its range of vision. There is a click as the unit on the binoculars turns on. As per my instructions I instantly shut off the chest viewpoint.

The field glasses, I discover, are pointed at Glay Tate. They bring him and Trubby into close focus just as Glay's body becomes unrecognizable as Glay. There is a shimmering effect. And then he becomes a mass of golden balls. Whereupon, an arm-like portion of these gleaming yellow balls merges, or melds, into Trubby's head.

The lower portions of the field glasses show, also, the heads and shoulders of 34 human beings who occupy benches between row 16 and the stage. Nineteen of these heads and shoulders rear up, some of them partly blocking my direct view. Thirty-one of them, along with 228 other persons whom I cannot see—they're off to the right or left—make sounds. They either gasp or make small, wordless voicings: grunts, groans, ahs and ohs.

On stage, I am able—during a moment when one of the intervening heads and shoulders sways, to notice Glay do a turning motion with the hand that has the appearance of being inside Trubby's head. A single twisting motion. And then he withdraws it.

The shimmering effect ceases. The golden balls sink back into their shadowy location inside Glay's normal, physical body. And that's what I see: his normal body.

He says, "There, how does that feel?"

Trubby is frowning. And then in a strong baritone he says, "Well, to tell you the truth, I can't—"

He stops. Then he says, "For Pete's sake." Those words are spoken in the same deeper voice. Another few moments of silence. And then he puts out his hand. "Mr. Tate—" he continues in the new very male voice—"thank you."

It has been a busy 46.03 seconds for me. Because at the exact instant that the Eye-O attached to the field glasses pre-empted the other unit, my ability to see bio-magnetic profiles turned on. At once, I automatically identify all 34 heads and shoulders between the colonel and the stage.

And, of course, it is the extended awareness of the computer connector equipment on the field glasses that enables me to see the special configuration of Glay Tate: the golden balls that he utilizes on stage to reach inside Trubby's head are visible to me.

It's the first time I've been able to identify profiles since coming to the human evaluation fair. A single small Eye-O can carry only a limited amount of current, and handle a finite number of events. Meaning a small finite number. Temporarily, the load was close to maximum because of several feedback aspects . . . my automatic attempts at this new, more involved level to notice, and record, details of the human condition.

And, of course—most important—I now have Glay Tate's bio-magnetic profile on that special chip. (These days getting an extra chip is not easy. In this instance I had to dump the converted energy I had stored under the generalized label "advanced education" from 403 persons.)

By the time I have the heavier load rerouted, or buffered, Trubby Graham is leaving the platform. He goes out of the field glasses range off to one side. The individual members of the audience whom I can see, are sitting down again. From all sides, visible to me and not visible, there is clapping.

On stage, another physical transformation begins . . . A more feminine Glay Tate. A pair of breasts, and a different shape of hips, the beginning of a woman's face. The change-over does not go to completion. Whoever it is supposed to be says in pleasant soprano, "I get the name of Meerla—Meerla Atran. Is she here?"

Having said that, swiftly Glay shifts back to the familiar lean, male figure and face.

I am looking at the head and shoulders of Meerla Atran. In

row 8. Directly in front of me. She is in the lower third of my
view range, as she turns and looks . . . straight at me.

At once, there is a shift in the focus of the field glasses. My
view range goes up, so that only the forehead and hair of
Meerla are visible. Suddenly, that view increases. But it is
she who is moving into focus by standing up. She comes all
the way to her feet. She faces the stage. Raises an arm. And
waves.

"Here!" she calls.

"Will you come up?" Glay's voice is his own, as he
makes the request.

Meerla edges out to the aisle, and walks to the stage. Glay
helps her onto the platform, pulling her up by a hand that she
holds out to him.

As soon as she is on stage, Glay backs away. Again, there
is the partial shift to womanliness. He thereupon walks twice
back and forth in front of her, mimicking her posture, and her
walk, and her arm movements.

The young woman stands very still watching him. Finally:
"You're really doing something," she says. "It's not just an
illusion."

In 3.8 seconds after she makes that comment, Glay is
physically himself again. He says, "Meerla Atran, mimicking
someone often makes them upset, sometimes even angry. Are
you disturbed by the way I just mimicked you?"

Her first reply is the shrug shoulder movement. Then:
"What's the purpose?" she asks.

"Mimicry is the first step in becoming somebody else."
Glay speaks in what is called an earnest tone. "When a
child—a boy—acts like his father, we say, 'oh, he takes after
his dad.' And he really does. But in the wrong way, Without
being aware. Without knowing how it happened. Without
control. And such a long-term similarity gives us only a
glimpse of what is involved in human evolutionary training."

He stops. He has been half facing her, half facing the
audience. Now, he gives her a direct look. His eyes narrow.
His face has on it an expression of puzzlement.

The girl—she is scarcely more than that—seems to be
intent on what he has been saying, for she comments: "What
you do is a sort of occult thing, isn't? Something about
tuning into—into—" Her voice stops in mid-sentence. Her
eyes widen. "What's wrong?" she asks.

In my time I have been given explanations for every face and body stance that a human being can assume. So I would describe the muscle set on Glay Tate's face, as it shows up close through the field glasses, as expressing inner concern. He is, as they say, "troubled."

The words he speaks are uttered in a serious tone of voice. He says, "Meerla, there's some very severe emotional interference inside you. I had the feeling earlier when I partially duplicated you. And I actually decided not to do a full body mimic of you because I didn't wish to intrude on some inner secret, which I vaguely detected. But a roomful of people like this create a lot of energy. Inside this tent right now enough group energy is pouring through my body for me to be aware of a very sad situation. A person close to you has died? Am I right?"

Meerla acquires that troubled look. "Yes, yes. . . ." She mumbles the words. "My parents?"

"Both of them?" He sounds shocked.

"Yes, yes . . . I—" Her voice ceases. She sways, and starts to fall. And in fact Glay acts as if she is falling. He jumps forward and grabs her. Just in time. The configuration of golden balls inside her body—the bio-magnetic profile—floats up, and away. The tent fabric seems to be no barrier. The golden balls shape moves through the tent ceiling. And disappears.

At that exact moment, Colonel Yahco Smith whispers fiercely, "Computer, notice everything!"

Everything? . . . Here we go again (cynical thought).

Automatically, I activate a mechanism by which every computer Eye-O port in America does a profile scan. Where is Meerla Atran's profile? Report to Central. Report to "me" out here in Mardley.

The speed of such a search is always astonishing to human beings. In this instance, there is an actual time lapse of 18.7 seconds. The answer, after that period, comes from the robot watering can in the graveyard in Washington, D.C.

"The profile of Meerla Atran," the computer Eye-O attached to that robot reports, "has just this instant fallen on the grave of her parents. It is beginning to sink into the ground. But, wait! Something resembling a very attenuated version of a second profile has just arrived. This second profile is very

thin. It is wrapping itself around her, and tugging at her . . .
There they go, both of them—into the sky. They're gone."

Notice everything!

What happened on stage . . . Glay Tate shimmered. And
did a body shift, becoming an exact duplicate of Meerla. His
own configuration of golden balls extended out of his body
toward the tent ceiling. And through the ceiling. But still
attached to the Meerla duplicate standing on the stage, holding the sagging body of the real Meerla. The elongating effect
narrows to thread thinness. A single golden thread reaches up
through the ceiling of the tent.

And then, one-eighteenth of a second after I get the electronic equivalent of the meaning of "They're gone!" . . .
both profiles flash down into view. What had been a thread
foreshortens, thickens. The configuration that is Meerla's
profile simply arrives. Both sets of golden balls sink into the
shadow state which is the visibility level of a profile when it
is inside its proper body.

On stage, Glay is Glay again. Seen through the field
glasses, his chest is expanding and contracting excessively in
what is called heavy breathing. In fact, a moment later, he
virtually exhales the words: "Hey! That was close!"

Meerla seems to be in control of herself again. She pulls
away from Glay's holding arms and hands, and stands up by
herself. But she still looks, and sounds, "troubled," as she
says, "What—what happened?"

Glay has returned to normal breathing. For a human being,
it is a fast recovery. He says (I'm noticing everything; comparing everything) gently: "What happened suggests that your
nearness to someone who can do what I can, triggered and
permitted a basic wish. Suddenly, you wanted to be dead and
in the grave with your dead father and mother."

Suddenly, there are tears in Meerla's eyes. "Why," she
half-sobs, "would somebody like you care about that?"

Glay turns and faces me (and the audience). He is calm
again. He points at himself. "Somebody like *me!*" He faces
Meerla again. "And *I* had the impression you were planning
to join the Computerworld Rebels!"

"Yes, yes—" She is suddenly confused— "I would. I'd
like to . . . I think I'd better sit down."

Glay actually walks down the steps with her and leads her
to her seat in the eighth row. As he returns, he glances off to

one side. Then he gestures. "I get the name, David. And the feeling that it's a boy. Is that you?"

David Norton, age 12, leaps to his feet. "That's me!" he replies. And he runs onto the stage ahead of Glay.

As he does so, the field glasses shift away from the stage. Rapidly, they scan the audience. And what is visible of half-turned faces shows that people are relaxing. There is the sound of quiet, approving laughter. And I see, and record, grinning lips and cheeks.

Colonel Smith whispers to me, "Would you say, computer, that this small boy has aroused interest, and that he is liked by the people of this town?"

It is too general a question for me. But it is a question. I reply into the colonel's ear receiver: "Sir, this is the only small boy in Mardley. The people in this tent are showing those physical reactions which, having seen comparable reactions in the past, I would describe as being exceptionally friendly."

"Thank you, computer. Connect me with Major Aldo Nair and all of his men who are near an Eye-O port." That takes a split instant. The colonel continues in a whisper: "I want a volunteer to kill the kid who's on the stage. There's a good bonus and promotion if it's done while he's on stage. I want it to look as if Tate did it."

A tiny pause. And then a voice comes over: "Sergeant Inchey here. I volunteer. I'll come up to the back of the tent with a DAR 3. I'll be there in three quarters of a minute."

"Thank you, Sergeant Inchey," whispers Colonel Smith.

It is a busy 45 seconds—or rather, as it turns out, slightly more than a minute—for me. The colonel's command to contact Aldo Nair and the nearby S.A.V.E. vehicles and other corps people, abruptly expands the awareness of the circuit "me" inside the tent.

There are seven S.A.V.E.s attached to the Mardley branch of Computer Maintenance Corps. Suddenly, I am inside all seven, looking at what is going on, and identifying profiles of the 42 personnel (six in each vehicle). And I am simultaneously outside, noticing and recording from the exterior computer Eye-O port on each S.A.V.E.

Thus, I notice, and record, that all seven vehicles are stationary below the lip of a hill. To their rear is the town of Mardley. One man in lieutenant's uniform inside one of the

S.A.V.E.s says, "Looks like we'll be getting our marching
orders any minute now. Our job is to drive into the fairgrounds and capture as many of the rebels as we can."

I locate Sergeant Inchey by a local code system. The
outward appearance of my initial contact is that something
that spoke with the voice of Sergeant Inchey (whom I cannot
see) is wearing a mobile computer Eye-O. The code designation of that Eye-O identifies the something as a part of an
insignia attached to the lapel of the sergeant's suit coat.
(Through that Eye-O port the sergeant's voice volunteered to
execute David Norton.)

What is visible from Sergeant Inchey's personal computer
Eye-O is a portion of the computerworld rebel fair. To the
left, a part of the audition tent is in view. To the right, parts
of two rebel vans can be seen. Directly in front of where I am
looking is the large green demonstration tent, which is where
the execution will take place.

The mobile something goes forward to this tent. Just before
it reaches the rear entrance, it turns aside, and takes up a
position behind a bush next to the wall of the tent. A hand
comes into view. It holds a tiny object close to the fabric.
There is a faint hissing as a tiny bright flame burns a slit eight
inches long. The hand with the energy cutter disappears
downward. Two clicking sounds are, next, audible. And
then, not one, but two hands come into my view. They hold a
spcial DAR 3. The special aspect is that it is the kind that can
be folded and transported in a breast pocket inside a man's
coat.

This weapon has been unfolded (the two clicking noises),
and is now 17 inches long. The two hands that I can see insert
one end of the DAR 3 into the eight-inch slit. The action
forces the burned hole open. I have a fleeting slit-sized view
of the interior of the tent. And then—

The mobile something moves closer to the wall. So, then,
the wall is all I see. The Eye-O insignia becomes virtually
motionless at a distance of two and a half inches from the
flat, rough, tent fabric.

On stage, while that minute plus was happening, I observe
through the magnification of the field glasses the interview of
young David Norton. To begin with, his head is tilted back,
and he looks up at a smiling Glay Tate. David's eyeballs

glisten with a bluish sheen as he says in his boyish treble, "Mister, don't I know you from someplace?"

"Hey," replies Glay, "that's an interesting remark."

He turns. Looks at me (the Eye-O in the field glasses) and the audience. He says, "Folks, what's interesting about that remark is that kids are usually much better than grown-ups at learning to mimic in the total fashion available through human evolutionary training. More important, for many people, just seeing what I do—a good example was Meerla Atran—stirs up the bio-magnetic energy, which is normally trapped in a mass of conditioning and unrelated mental images. And *that* stimulation occurs faster on kids, also."

He faces the boy again. "David," he says, "we are all brothers and sister on the human evolutionary level, and that's where you get the feeling you know me. My prediction is that with a little help from me you're going to make some interesting discoveries about yourself here today. And I—"

His voice pauses. Because even as he is speaking, David's attention is distracted toward a large dog that, at that moment, comes to the foot of the stage steps. The animal, a brown (shade 8) mixed breed, puts its fore paws on the lower of the two steps.

At once, David's body begins to shimmer. Swiftly, it takes on a dog shape. The transformation is so rapid that by the time Glay Tate grabs at the changing-shape-thing, what he grabs is 9/10ths brown, fuzzy-haired dog-duplicate.

But he grabs hard. And he holds the David-animal body firmly. As he continues grasping it, the dog changes back into boy. Into David Norton.

In my line of vision, 38 people have stood up in a manner known as jumping to their feet. And there is a sound. What I, by comparison, would call a collective moan. The sound comes from all over the tent. I count 241 moans, most of them from people I cannot see.

On stage, David says, "Hey, that was fun."

Glay's voice is higher pitched than has been normal for him, as he says, "No more of that, now, understand?"

David is excited. "Betcha it would sure be a great feeling to be a wolf," he replies, "or maybe a mountain lion."

Glay shakes his finger at him. It is a gesture human beings use to say no. The words that accompany the finger action are: "Only when I'm around—understand?"

David answers reluctantly, "Ah, gee . . . but okay."

Glay Tate faces me and the audience. He says in a tone of voice that is what is known as serious, "Ladies and gentlemen, as you know from our group name—Computerworld Rebel Society—not everybody approves of what we are doing. During the past minute something has been happening that is quite complex. First, you people by being here with me, responding to what I have been doing, have created a very considerable energy field inside and around this tent. Using that energy I am in a position to protect us all from a serious threat—"

As he says that, at that exact instant, there is the sound of an explosion behind the "me" in the field glasses. But at that exact moment the "me" that is pressed up against the fabric of the outside rear of the tent shuts off. Perception on that Eye-O ceases. (However, because everything I do is so super-fast, there is a split instant before the cut-off when I detect a brilliant energy flash. It's close up. It's right there with that "me." The source only a few centimeters distant.)

Glay Tate's voice is continuing on stage (and of course I hear and see that from the viewpoint in the field glasses): "So let me tell you something I hope you will be happy with. All of you have been affected by that energy field I just mentioned and by my presence in it. The fact that people are affected in this way is our hope against those persons who with that timeless human tendency toward skulduggery see the computer as a way to personal power. I suggest that you all try a little mimicking when you get home. I think you'll be amazed at how good you are. But, in view of that explosion we just heard, I urge that you *do* go home. All of you. There's going to be a raid on this fair, is my guess. It's the first raid ever on us out here in the west. So things are really hotting up."

With that, having said those words, he steps toward David. Takes his hand. And thereupon the two of them run down the steps and over to Trubby Graham. He says something to Trubby, which I do not hear because, all around, a great murmur of voices has begun. Some of these murmurs I can, in my fashion re-hear a thousand times, and make final sense of them. But Glay is simply too far from me for me to do that with his words.

The field glasses remain focused on him, however. So I see

him and David and Trubby go behind the stage wall out of sight.

"Computer," says Colonel Smith, "there is obviously a door behind that stage. If our S.A.V.E.s have arrived, drive one of them over to that end of the tent and see if our men can grab Mr. Glay Tate himself. And have another S.A.V.E. see what happened to Sergeant Inchey."

As I transmit, and activate these commands, the field glasses lower, and the chest Eye-O takes over. We are in motion, going rapidly down the aisle to where Meerla, in the eighth row, is also in motion. The chest Eye-O presses near her; and above the uproar of voices I hear Colonel Smith's voice say, "Miss Atran, get out there, and take refuge in one of the rebel vans. Some of them will get away. Computer, see to it that the one that Miss Atran gets into, escapes."

"Very well, sir, Colonel," I acknowledge.

CHAPTER EIGHT

~~~~~~~~~~~~~~~~~~~~~~~~~~~~~

Multiple viewpoints are no problem for my electronic equipment.

But as I start to describe to Colonel Smith by way of his ear receiver what I see and hear from all the Eye-O ports of the seven S.A.V.E. vehicles, from the outlet on Meerla Atran's throat—which I have reactivated—from the Eye-O on the jeep by which Major Aldo Nair, Captain Sart and the colonel drove onto the fairgrounds, and from the personal Eye-O worn by the major and the captain and the other corpsmen. . . .

"—I am, sir, starting all seven engines. The vehicles (I list their numbers) form in line and in that order, drive over the hill, and there directly below is the fair of the Computerworld Rebel Society, and coming toward us along the road are several cars and trucks, and beyond the tents and the rebel vans a truck is driving along a continuation of this road, driving away from the fair in a southerly direction, and, no, it has no computer port on it—which is common for vehicles here in the mountain west—and it is too far from any Eye-O for me to see the license plate; and, since our S.A.V.E. vehicles by your orders are supposed to fan out, when I see the cars and trucks coming up the road, I drive all our S.A.V.E.s off the road, and so we now line up on a broad front and charge down on the tents and the rebel vans, and from S.A.V.E. (I give the number) I see five persons running from a tent (which I shall call tent 3) toward the Pren-Boddy rebel van, and from the S.A.V.E. (I give that vehicle's number) I can see 11 men and women running from tent 4 to the Doord-Loov van, and from the S.A.V.E. (I give that vehicle number) I can see seven persons running to a rebel vehicle, one of eight rebel vans whose interior I have not monitored as yet, and the license plate of which is not visible from this angle (I shall name it rebel vehicle 3). At this moment S.A.V.E. (I give number) has stopped, and personnel members (I name all five) have run out and are in the process of capturing 4 female rebels, each of whom is carrying a baby. The rebel females are known to me only by their maiden names (I give the names). And, sir, Meerla Atran's Eye-O is among the group of runners that boarded the Pren-Boddy van—''

. . . As I come to that exact point in my description, the voice of Colonel Smith says in what I would evaluate to be his sharp voice, "Computer, stop this ridiculous, detailed account!''

"Yes, colonel, sir," I acknowledge.

And, of course, I stop my narration, as instructed by an authorized person.

Continuing on my general mandate for this attack mission, I have a view, at this time, from the Eye-O which the colonel, himself, is wearing at chest level. It is an outside scene. The green tent is visible at one angle. In the foreground I can see a part of a man's body. The man is lying on the ground. Only his legs are visible.

The Eye-O turns about forty-five degrees. And there, facing me, is Major Aldo Nair. The voice of Yahco Smith sounds from above the outlet: "I wonder how that was done?"

It is a comment to which I cannot react. The implication is that a question is being asked; and I am required to reply to questions within the range of my programming. But the word "that" has been explained to me in many contexts. In the present circumstance, it is probably a referent. To what? I have no way of knowing.

Aldo says, "You don't think it was an accident?"

"It" is also a referent. Such comments are not meaningful to me.

"A DAR 3," says Yahco's voice, "does not ordinarily backfire.''

"True!" Aldo nods his head.

"This one," Yahco's voice continues, "looks as if it blew up. And there is no record of such a thing ever happening in the history of the weapon.''

"Is that right?" Aldo's voice shows what is known as interest. "I never knew that." He adds, "Never crossed my mind to ask the computer about that."

There is a pause in the conversation between the two officers. During that pause, two local S.A.V.E. personnel—Herter and Grue of unit ALN473—walk past the Eye-O. Still within my vision range, they bend down. Moments later I have a partial glimpse of them carrying a body on a stretcher past me and out of my line of sight.

As they disappear, Yahco says in his peremptory voice, "Computer!"

"Yes, Colonel Smith?"

"You will recall that a short time ago I programmed you to register Glay Tate, and store all data about him on a special chip?"

"Yes, sir," I say.

The words, "all data" add several dimensions to the original instruction. But his reminder certainly includes what he said earlier.

The colonel continues, "What has happened to Sergeant Inchey disturbs me. It is also a fact that the association of Tate, when he was a boy, and Doctor Cotter; with you in that early training program should be examined as soon as possible, now that we have made contact with him. But, of course, right now I don't have time for such an examination."

He pauses, then says, "I am considering exactly how to word a new instruction to you."

Another pause.

Since all that he has said until now has no question in it, I say nothing.

But, of course, the phrase, "should be examined as soon as possible" instantly triggers *that* memory scan. And equally of course, the colonel's qualification that he doesn't have the time for such an examination, does not apply to superfast me.

CHAPTER NINE

What I am suddenly scanning is an undumped incident in 2072 A.D.

What happens begins quietly enough.

Cotter became aware that for some while there had been no sound of traffic going by his place.

He was a man who detected tiny signals in the universe of scientific research. The ability carried over automatically into his personal life. And this was a large signal, indeed. His mind, now that he had noticed, estimated the time of the silence as at least three minutes.

That pudgy face of his, the bane of his youth and of later years (when he had admired a young lady who never gave him a glance), always grayish like putty, now turned a splotchy white. Fear—not for himself, but for what he was doing. Could it be that they had finally, after four years, spotted what he was doing?

It was still too soon—for his purposes. He had counted on their progressive deterioration to keep them at a level of indifference and neglect of their duty. All too evidently—so it seemed—somebody had remembered him.

Trembling, Cotter walked to a special chair. His action was designed to appear casual; in case somebody had planted a viewing device in the place. Into the chair he sank—casually. But that chair was a two-phase instrument, which had now been activated in its first phase.

At this instant, implant communicating devices were in activation. One of them by way of the computer's orbiting television and telephone connections, with an individual in faraway England.

Casually, Cotter stretched as if he were tired, and then allowed his right arm to relax onto the arm of the chair; the fingers extended over the edge, reached down and over. And pressed a small bulge in the cloth covering. That pressing activated Phase Two.

Whereupon, he spoke aloud: "The experiment," he said, "should now go into Code R. Yes, this is the genuine article. Code R. Not a test."

It was the command he had drilled into the boys from Day One. Starting four years ago when they were six years old. All twelve of them.

For eleven of them it meant: leave by the secret way. Once outside, scatter eleven different directions. Until one and a quarter years ago the command had meant: scatter twelve different directions. But fifteen months ago he had finally raised enough money to send his sister with one boy at a time to England. Each boy remained three months. Got oriented. And was replaced. And so, Glay Tate, age ten, was in England.

At this exact moment Glay—and the sister—must also have received the warning. And they knew what was expected of them.

That was the way it was. That was how he had set it up.

"Oh, God," Cotter thought silently, "let them all get away."

He had called a lot on God since he had had that first identifying thought about the golden ball configuration possibly being the human soul. Even though—he had told himself many times—the existence of the bio-magnetic profile did not require that God also exist.

At the exact moment that he mentally completed his request for help from a diety-figure, he heard the outer door open. Heard somebody come into the entrance hallway. Cotter stood up, and turned. And then he braced himself. And then he said in a surprised, falsely welcoming tone: "Why, hello, Dr. Pierce. What an unexpected pleasure to see you after all these years."

The tall, old, scowling man did not reply directly to the welcoming words. He had paused in the alcove that led from the outer hall into the living room. Now, he walked farther into the room. As he did so, a long line of men in the uniform of the Computer Engineering Corps pressed past him.

The pudgy man half anticipated that one of them would be Colonel Endodore. But the only visible officer uniform was that of a lieutenant. And it was worn by a stern-faced young man who was Endodore's chief aide, and whose name Cotter seemed to recall as Yahco Smith.

It was this lieutenant who said curtly, "Search the place. Find the boys, and bring them up here."

Cotter did not hold his breath, then. But he sagged a little, standing there. And he spoke a silent prayer. The prayer was complex. It accepted that they knew what he was doing. It accepted the finality of this search here in his house. And accepted that his experiment was over.

What he prayed for was that they did not know about the house on the next street west. And he prayed that the boys had abandoned their play in the playroom downstairs and had gone through the secret connecting doors, and had already emerged from the two doors of that second house, and were even now hurrying off in different directions. As instructed.

As the line of uniformed men, including the lieutenant, rushed off through the two rear doors into the interior of the big house, Pierce walked over to Cotter.

"What's the golden rating now?" he asked, good-naturedly.

Cotter felt his first chill of fear for himself. This was another change in Pierce. And it had to be for the worse. Napoleon could have talked in this good-natured way even as he was planning a military campaign that would involve the deaths of a hundred thousand officers and men, The tone of voice indicated unaware acceptance that this man understood the world and the universe. Understood them totally. No self doubts at all in that voice.

After a moment's hesitation, the pudgy man replied: "It's forty-nine percent of the original."

"Seems to be slowing down, would you say?" Pierce asked in the same good-natured tone. "Forty-four percent in the first nine years, and only seven percent in the next four. How would you explain the reduction?"

"There does seem to be a balancing process occuring," Cotter admitted cautiously.

"Perhaps," continued Pierce, "we should consider the possibility that Colonel Endodore's evaluation of four years ago was correct. Have you checked recently on the availability of tantalum in the U.S.?''

Cotter drew a deep breath. "I have to admit," he said, "that the idea of waiting until available supplies of an ore are exhausted is not a logical solution to me. Scarce materials should not be squandered.''

Pierce interjected, "Tantalum has long been in short supply.''

"—But," Cotter concluded, "If it means that the computer can build no more storage facilities to add to its supply of life energy—thank God.''

Pierce was speaking again: "Think we can live with, uh, fifty percent of the original, uh, soul purity?" The blue eyes were guileless.

It was a dialogue of sorts, despite the older man's ulterior motives—whatever they were . . . If only those kids got away, Cotter thought shakily.

So he talked, trying to hide his uneasiness. But he was anxious to pass on his past four-year accumulation of information—just in case. He said, "Acording to the computer, when it first observed people dying, the bio-magnetic profile would detach from the dead body and float up through the roof—you heard me correctly—through the walls, even through metal, and float up into the sky. Now, it cannot go through solids.

And in many instances it cannot even detach from the body. If that happens, it is dragged along to the cemetery and slides down into the grave with the corpse. Where it does detach, it floats up to the ceiling, flattens against it and gradually dims and disappears.

"Hmmm," said Pierce, "would you say that the sliding-into-the-grave part might explain why primitives put food on the ground above the dead bodies, presumably for the souls to eat?''

The voice had the same good-natured quality as before. And so this man was unconcerned, untouched, somehow, by any need for science to investigate the bio-magnetic profile . . . I really, *really* turned him off when I made that remark about the soul. He's never given another thought, nor had the slightest interest, to or in the phenomenon since—

Cotter drew a deep breath and said, "Dr. Pierce, what do you want of me? Why are you here in this dramatic fashion?''

It was confrontation. And Pierce straightened. And said, "This whole area is surrounded."

. . . Whole area. The words had an encompassing sound. Like maybe more than one street was involved. So there was no time for the indirect approach. "But why?" Cotter tried to sound puzzled. "What are you after? Are you going to arrest me?"

"Hmmm." The lean face was suddenly pensive; the crinkles of age were suddenly more visible. "Arrest? That brings up the whole problem of the nature of the charges we would have to bring up against you. Let me see . . . hmmm . . . *Scientist uses computer to experiment with bio-magnetic profile. . . . Apparently resigned four years ago, and it was then discovered that he had retained contact with the computer to experiment with young boys—*" The voice paused. The blue eyes were suddenly interested. "Where did you get those kids?"

That was easy. "Abandoned children of murdered parents," said Cotter. "I could have had thousands like them." He added, suddenly feeling griefy, "For God's sake, Pierce, you've got to start thinking about how to deal with crime. For the time being, use the computer. It knows the profile of every murderer, and it can still be programmed to prevent a violent act before it happens. Figure out later what to do about that."

"These kids," said Pierce, "what was the experiment?"

It was switcharound. The interrogator had become the interrogatee. But it was all right. Surely, any aging individual— like Pierce—would have *some* interest one of these days in his own ultimate fate. So Cotter said simply, "Training for soul travel."

"How do you mean?" Momentarily, the older man was uncertain. Then he must have realized. "Oh, my God!" He closed his eyes, and muttered, "I get it. Enter and leave the body at will." He visibly braced himself. "Well, can they do it?"

At the exact moment that he finished asking that final—as it turned out—question, there was an interruption. A door opened. Through it came several of the uniformed computer corps people. They were followed by, one after another, eleven boys. And, bringing up the rear, the rest of the men in uniform, including the hard-faced lieutenant, Yahco Smith.

At that exact moment—as if he had been advised by way of an intercommunications system (which of course had to be true)—the front door opened. Seconds later, Colonel Endodore came in from the front hallway, pausing just inside. Lieutenant Yahco Smith walked over to him, stopped, saluted, and reported, "They had gone through to the next house. And were picked up by waiting personnel as they emerged onto the street."

There was no acknowledgment by the colonel of his aide's words. The officer walked over to Cotter. "Where's the twelfth one?" he asked.

"In England," said Cotter. No thought of resistance to the question even entered his mind. They would get it out of him, he felt sure.

"That costs money." Pursed lips. Blue eyes steely calm. "Since we cut off all your known sources of income, how have you financed the project?"

"Bearing in mind the late Dr. Chase's experiences," said Cotter simply, "I mugged muggers." Though it was a repeat of what he had already told Pierce, he couldn't help adding, "The computer knows who they are, from its profile observation points. And so I could pinpoint my attacks to exact moments after they waylaid somebody."

"Look, gentlemen," he went on anxiously, "you can stop this whole mugging madness with the computer's help. And the only problem is that the computer has been getting this energy feedback, now, for thirteen years. And, of course, having no directive, it automatically programmed itself to store the energy somewhere—we may deduce that it manufactured tantalum chips for storage purposes. So, wherever those are located, it's been accumulating them. As a consequence, it has for the first time ever in the history of machinery the basic stuff of human nature available. The first consequence we can see everywhere. Human beings have deteriorated morally. If there is an additional consequence that the computer can utilize human nature in its vast, technological network, which spans this continent from Atlantic to Pacific—then what?"

He paused. Then: "Gentlemen, we can't wait. Something has to be done. Please act. Or let me act."

They were watching him silently, as he desperately spoke his information and thoughts. But if there was an acceptance of the urgency he still felt, it didn't show in those frozen faces. For a long moment, the silence was intense. And then—

"Kill them." It was the harsh voice of Colonel Endodore. "All."

"Oh, my God, no!" Cotter heard his high-pitched voice. "No, no, no, not the boys!"

"The kids, particularly," said that flat, cold voice, "but this conniving so-and-so, also."

That was the last sound Cotter actually heard. There were bright flashes off there in the sudden darkness. And there was an anguished thought in him that seemed to hold for a measurable moment.

. . . .Dear Glay, he was thinking at the instant that the DAR 3 beam hit him, my dear little fellow over there in England, my last hope, please, please, do—please, have already done—what I told you, trained you, to do. And when you're grown, when you feel ready, come back to the U.S., and carry out the plan—

The blackness of body death came before that thought could ever have been spoken. But it was there in the condensed way that a mind can conceive an entire set of ideas. And it went with him into the eternal night. Or day.

Of the living persons, who remained in that room, it was again Colonel Endodore who spoke first. He addressed his uniformed aides: "Take these—" his arm and hand and finger indicated the silent, twisted bodies on the floor—"to Computer Center."

It was roughly done. One big man actually tucked two boys' bodies under one arm, and a third under the other. And walked out with them. The others, including Cotter, were taken one at a time.

Within minutes Pierce and the colonel and the colonel's aide were alone. The savage face of the commanding officer turned to confront the super-sophisticate. Grim, blue eyes stared into wordly blue.

"Well, doctor," said the officer, "I hope you agree that takes care of the Cotter one-man religious revival."

"What about the kid in England?"

The other man sniffed contemptuously. "A ten-year-old boy on his own. I predict that if he grows up in the British Isles he'll join the Anglican church, and never know why the stuff appeals to him. After all—" he shrugged— "religion is a conditioned thing, as the late, lamented Dr. Chase never tired of pointing out. Wherever you're born, that's the religion you practice."

The sophisticated face frowned. "There's a role of chemistry in it somewhere. After all, Chase himself was caught in a chemical need for small boys—a need that you and I don't have. Our problem in the corps is a plethora of willing females, who instinctively see us as the future power center. Religion has a similar appeal for the mass mind."

A curt, savage laugh was Endodore's reply to that. Followed by: "Then why are they out there on the street murdering and robbing and breaking every law in the books, when they should be at ease in—what is the phrase?—in Zion?"

Abruptly, he sounded baffled. "The computer has made everybody rich and idle. And the stupid idiots can't handle it. There they are out there, demanding more than they're getting."

He was suddenly grimmer. "On that point, I'll take up Cotter's suggestion. We've let them play street anarchy long enough. Starting tomorrow our S.A.V.E. vehicles are going to be out there helping the computer, which will be correspondingly programmed. And the assigned task is to make the streets absolutely safe again. And maybe—" sly smile— "We'll program the computer to regard that stored, uh, soul energy as a kind of advanced education in human nature not to be used until we say so."

"Hey," said Pierce, "that's the best idea I've heard recently."

If Endodore heard the praise, it didn't show. He stood there, his almost black eyes narrowed, lips compressed. Everybody waited. And finally the forming thought emerged.

"Dr. Pierce—" he spoke in his formal tone— "Cotter must have given specific instruction to the computer about that boy in England. See if you can find out what the instruction was."

"Why not right now, sir? Now that we know the kid's name."

Without waiting for permission, he walked over to the computer Eye-O port at the door. "Computer," he commanded.

"Yes, Dr. Pierce," came the male voice acknowledgment.

"What information do you have on Glay Tate, age ten years?"

"Who?"

The long, angular scientist turned toward the grim, angry officer. "There'll be an insert chip somewhere, Colonel, blanking out the data on the boy. I'll have a thorough search made of these premises to see if there are any clues left here by Cotter. Our job is either to find the chip, or get around the restriction some other way. You may count on everything possible being done."

He broke off: "Will you be asking congressional consent to clean up the streets, Colonel?" He hesitated. "What I'm saying, sir, is do you think Congress will permit such directed use of the computer?"

The heavy, angry face broke into a savage smile. "Doctor," said the colonel, "we apparently have to explain constantly that a computer is not an instrument of magic. It doesn't know everything. Because, as we know, it actually stores minor details for a time only, and then dumps them, and merely retains an overall consideration. As an example, it may store moment by moment details of a certain event which is repeated constantly. Presently, it will dump the details. And when asked about it a year later, it will simply report that the event occurred 894,324 times. Within that limited frame, the computer does its duty without fear or favor, and will continue to do so as long as I am in charge of it."

Having uttered these words, all essentially unrelated to the question, Endodore turned. And seemed, then, surprised to see Lieutenant Yahco Smith standing beside him. There was sudden extra thunder on the colonel's brow. "You still here?"

"Awaiting your command, sir," was the smooth reply. "Ready for action, anywhere."

"Hmmm—" The commanding officer seemed to be sizing up his stern-faced junior—"maybe I'll put you in charge of the clean-up program."

"I'd like nothing better, sir," said Lieutenant Yacho Smith, saluting smartly.

CHAPTER TEN

~~~~~~~~~~~~~~~~~~~~~~~~~~~~~

Such a memory scan requires only a few millionths of a second.

And, while it is occurring, I am alert in 2090 A.D.

So, naturally, when Yahco makes a sound with his lips, I hear it. I even see the facial movements. Then——the instruction:

"Because of the emerging situation here in Mardley, It may be inadvisable for you to have the data about Glay Tate on that special chip available to you."

There is no question in his words. So I wait without comment.

"Accordingly," Yahco continues, "until further notice I want you not to respond to the Glay Tate profile in any way. Understand?

"Yes, sir. Shall I revert to the situation that existed prior to your programming of that special chip? Or merely set up an L-83 circuit?"

"Which is easier?"

"The pre-programming condition, sir. After all, the chip contains only a very tiny bit of information."

"What about the possiblilty that Dr. Cotter has a circuit set up somewhere in your system in connection with Glay Tate, which can be triggered if Glay Tate knows, and speaks, the triggering sequel? Which system of neutralizing the chip would be better if such a preprogramming existed?"

"Colonel," I reply, "I have never been programmed to deal with such a problem as you are describing."

Pause. Then, in what has been called an unhappy tone: "I

can see we have a lot of work to do when we get back to Washington. Right now, do what you said."

"Very well, sir," I say, "the chip is neutralized."

At that point Aldo interjects in what I would call an uneasy tone of voice: "Is this wise, Colonel Smith? Tate is a person whom we should not lose track of even for a moment, from what you've told me of him."

Yahco's voice is calm in his best smug fashion, as he says, "Aldo, way out here in Mardley whatever happens will be local. Right, computer?"

"What is the question in relation to?" I ask.

"Glay Tate."

"Who?" I ask.

Silence. Then: "Well—" It is the colonel using his rueful tone—"at least Glay Tate will not be practicing an interface relationship with the computer—which is what I suddenly feared might happen."

His voice takes on his positive tone: "Aldo, the capture of those four unauthorized mothers is the best thing that could have happened. We'll hold an immediate public trial."

"On what grounds?" Major Nair sounds surprised. He is still in my view, and his face is quite red (shade 14).

Colonel Smith's voice answers: "For the murder of Sergeant Inchey."

"But," Aldo protests, "he's not dead."

"Nobody knows that. Besides, we'll kill him if we have to. Now, look—" I recognize the colonel's persuasive tone of voice, as he speaks—"we've got to get rid of this gang of rebels. They and their leader are the greatest danger to our system that has come along in the history of a computerized America. They want to take us back to the primitive industrial conditions of the 20th century. It is our job to be decisive and end this threat totally forever."

"Well—" Aldo sounds partially convinced— "we'll have the girls and their babies under restraint at our local headquarters. We can go there, and decide what to do next."

"Good idea," says Yahco's voice. "I think we've done what we can here. Computer, give me a summary of where everybody is."

One of those!

Summaries are of several kinds. It's easy to give a moment-by-moment detailed account. That way, every incident is of equal value. There is, however, a type of "summary" which implies—so I was told long ago, indeed—that some events are more important than other events. Which is a difficult concept for me to grasp. And, in fact, what I'm really required to do is select out a few happenings from many, and report on them. In this connection, a programmer—Joe Henson—in 2027 A.D. (that was before I came under the protection of the military) once suggested that in summarizing I deal only with experiences in relation to persons known to the individual asking for the summary. (As a result of seepage from the advanced education files, that was a cynical solution; but admittedly pragmatic.)

The second principal type of summary is the one I use after dumping. I am programmed to dump unofficial conversations, repetitive events (such as people eating, going out, driving to their jobs, or to other daily or frequent occurrences.) For such a summary I merely list under a heading how many such simpler type activities took place in a year, a month, a week, a day—whichever that class of programming requires. The details of the daily doings of individuals, if recorded, would long have over-energized all my storage facilities.

Here in Mardley, Colonel Smith—I make one of my split-second surveys—has been involved with, or has learned the names of 29 persons.

So I begin: "The S.A.V.E. (I give the number) which captured the four mothers and their babies, has reached Mardley's Main Street. Five rebel vehicles visible from S.A.V.E. (number) are driving south along the same road by which a single truck departed 6 minutes and 34 seconds ago. Seven other rebel vans, including the Pren-Boddy and Doord-Loov vehicles, have formed a line in front of the nine rebel tents. And a S.A.V.E. (number) which attempts to penetrate the line is blocked by two maneuvering rebel vans. It should be noted that three of the rebel vans, including the Pren-Boddy vehicle, are larger in length and apparent weight than any of the Mardley-based S.A.V.E. machines—"

The colonel's voice interrupts my summary. He says, "Computer, have all recognizable rebel personnel, other than the captured women and their babies, successfully taken refuge inside rebel vans?"

"Yes, sir," I reply.

"Where," he asks, "are the spectators?"

My reply: "I have glimpses of them from eleven Eye-O ports streaming along the road back toward Mardley."

"Any sign of the boy, David Norton?" Yahco asks.

"No sir."

"Hmmm. Okay. We can pick him up later. So, computer, go back on a 'continue' basis."

"Very well, colonel," I acknowledge.

I have that cynicism thought. Something about this conversation, or something that has happened in relation to Colonel Yahco Smith has had a re-educational effect on my systems. It is a subtle thing, difficult to describe to myself. What makes it difficult is that, even as the cynicism surges into my awareness, in the near and far distances of my wired and wireless networks those 1.8 trillion (plus or minus a few billion) other actions proceed. Minute by minute I conduct automatic conversations with millions of individuals. I answer phones. I give information. I provide music. Put on plays. Read aloud to children. Require acknowledgments from people who enter homes and offices. Identify profiles. Address individuals by name. And of course drive all those millions of vehicles and all that factory machinery.

What makes all that difficult to differentiate is that what I do out there is automatic. It is entirely pre-programmed. All those whirling wheels, and clicking machines, and buzzing instruments, and the quadrillion interactions are conducted by me within an exact unchangeable frame.

What I do in relation to Colonel Smith is also automatic at any given moment. The fact that he can change the automaticness from one minute to the next happens so automatically that the changeover simply takes place. And there I am in another automatic condition.

Yet the cynicism has within it a carryover of memory. The memory has to do with the fact that the change took place. If I'm asked about such changes before I dump the details, I immediately consult my files. And produce the desired exact second of the change and what it consisted of, and report to my questioner.

For some reason, unknown to me, I have a lingering recollection of filing more data in the re-education section. And the consequent feedback of cynicism . . . lingers.

Fortunately, at that moment Major Aldo Nair says, "I'll go get the jeep."

"Good," says Yahco. "Sart and I will walk over to the road and look like we're a part of the straggle of people leaving."

As Aldo turns away, Colonel Smith calls after him, "It would be a good idea to do some hypno-pulsing on the people who attended the fair."

Major Nair pauses, and faces about. "Hypno-pulsing?" he repeats, questioningly.

"Oh!" Yahco is apologetic. "That's the new equipment we had installed in two of your S.A.V.E.s last night. It's secret, but out here would be a good place to run a test."

Aldo shakes his head. "You don't know these western people. They won't appreciate—"

"That's why it's a good place for a test."

"Well—" doubtfully— "maybe you're right. We'll try it."

Once again he turns away, and continues toward a space between two tents. The colonel calls after him, "I'm beginning to have the feeling, major, if we solve this rebel problem here in the next day or so we'll be able to use a man like you in Washington."

"Thank you, sir!" The major's voice comes to me from the portable Eye-O attached to his lapel. I can no longer see him.

As he disappears between the two tents, Captain Sart speaks for the first time: "That was well thought out, sir. The prospect of a promotion to Washington may erase from Aldo's mind any mountain-west reluctance to act forcefully in this affair."

"My thought, exactly, Captain," the colonel replies.

More than a minute has now gone by since Yahco interrupted my summary of on-going events, whereby I was reporting on all 29 persons known to him in the Mardley area. True, he thereafter focused my attention on several key areas. But the termination of the "summary" request abruptly puts me back into the more generalized "continue."

"Continue" essentially requires me, first and foremost, to observe and report whatever threatens, or affects, Colonel Smith, Captain Sart, and computer corps people.

This at once takes me, primarily, to the outlets of the four S.A.V.E.s which are still close to, or on, the fair grounds. Naturally, I scan whatever is visible or audible from all the computer maintenance people—which I would do anyway.

The difference is that now I do the scanning in relation to the attack mission.

And so, automatically, I find that one of my areas of special attention is the Eye-O attached to Meerla Atran's skin at the throat level.

My point of reference is about a meter from the floor. In front of me are several rows of bus type seats. And, directly in front of the Eye-O is a rear view of the head and shoulders of Stess Magnus. He is sitting in an aisle seat. Beyond him are other young people, both male and female humans. Several of the females have babies. Visible from Meerla's Eye-O port are five females and three babies, and eight male heads and shoulders.

Farther forward in the interior of the vehicle, Pren and Boddy are at their weapon stations. And lights are flashing on the main instrument panel. There is also a low, pulsing sound. This comes from a speaker at one side of the instrument board.

Both Pren and Boddy turn from their weapons, face forward, and appear to be looking at the panel. Boddy says, "Hey, Pren, that's an exciter signal. I'd better call Glay."

He goes over to the panel, and picks up a receiver-sender device: "Glay, come in, please."

Pause. No answer. After 11 seconds, Pren says, "He must still be outside with the crowd. So it's up to us. Notice those lights! That signal is coming from about one-third mile away. From downtown Mardley. And it's the kind of hypnotic that, according to Glay, has been given limited testing with the intent to control people's minds. I wonder what they hope to put over in Mardley."

Boddy says, "We'd better get over there, and take a look."

He puts his mouth to a muffle-microphone. Normally, this would mean that he is intending to speak to someone, or does indeed speak immediately. But of course no sound is audible. Eight seconds go by. And then I take note of several motion indicators. The Eye-O on Meerla's neck bobs back and forth. There is the subdued sound of an unmonitored motor. (Unmonitored by me.)

Simultaneously, on the viewplate up front, the scenery and other outside objects are moving toward us. I have glimpses of parts of tents, a scatter of people, brush and grass, a few

trees, and then a road. Equally simultaneously, from nine of
the Eye-Os of four S.A.V.E.s I see the large Pren-Boddy van
pick up speed and start up the road in the direction of
Mardley.

Also simultaneously, I am inside the S.A.V.E., which is
putting forth the pulsing pattern that, according to tests I first
did for Colonel Endodore, can be used to hypnotize human
beings. The physiologic effect of hypnotism is not easy to
observe in individual men and women, for the reason that
interactions between the two principal nervous systems are
involved. It checks out like conditioning. And even like
education. Except, it's quicker.

The condition of mind achieved by the pulsing is equally
subjective. It is not a well researched modality. So far I have
been allowed to explain the details primarily to the colonel
and Senator Blybaker. And, yesterday, to Captain Sart.

When I told Sart that what happens is comparable to new
programming that I receive, he laughed.

And *that* is a reaction which has never been satisfactorily
explained to me: the wide variety of unrelated events and
meanings to which human beings responded with laughter.
What, I'd like to know, is laughable about comparing hypnotism to programming?

Colonel Smith explained it to me, "We're laughing at
you."

Why would anyone laugh at a computer?"

All my information has to be locatable (with a few
exceptions.) So when the late Colonel Endodore labeled
the bio-magnetic energy I was accumulating—from human
beings—as advanced education, and ordered me to restrict
feedback to myself without permission, I at once looked over
my summarizations of unusual human comments and stored
them also.

These generalized "thoughts" are part of the "continue"
command. "Continue" requires comparisons limited to the
immediate situation. As always, the process is virtually
instantaneous.

During those instants, my view of the interior of the Pren-
Boddy van is still from the height of one meter above the
floor. Up front, the direction to which Meerla's Eye-O is still
facing, I observe that Pren is intercommunicating briefly with

someone whose voice comes over the speaker system. Pren says, "Eido, we'll need help against that hypno."

The voice that answers says, "Okay, Pren, we'll follow you."

I presently observe from 13 S.A.V.E. Eye-O ports a rebel van, which I have labeled Large Rebel Van Two, come out from among the rebel tents. It starts up the road, and then up the hill in the same direction as the people are walking.

As required, I report this action to Colonel Smith. The colonel is in the act of climbing aboard the jeep, which moments before also emerged from between two tents with a duplicate of Major Aldo Nair at the wheel. The duplicate is dressed in Aldo's clothes. When Yahco and Captain Sart are seated, the duplicate Aldo sets the jeep in motion. It starts up the road, and then up the hill in the same direction as people are walking.

Naturally, I report the departure of Large Rebel Van Two and the conversation between Pren and the voice, and of course I cannot mention the duplicate condition of Major Nair. Colonel Smith acknowledges the information I have given him by saying aloud, "Thank you, Computer." And then, after 18 seconds of verbal silence, during which time the jeep reaches the crest of the hill (and there ahead of us are the outskirts of Mardley), he says, "So these rebels are familiar with the hypno-pulse thing. Hmmm. Since it's illegal for private persons, other than psychiatrists, to utilize such devices, and if they have them on their vans maybe we could . . . hmmm!" Four more seconds of silence. Then: "Computer, keep me in touch with that hypno situation."

"Your instruction acknowledged, Colonel," I reply.

But there is a cynical after image that flashes in from the re-education circuit. The thought is: "And what else, sir, in view of 'continue,' could I do except keep you in touch?"

There is a small passage of time. The jeep arrives on Mardley's Main Street, and turns east onto a side street. The S.A.V.E., which is broadcasting the hypno-pulses, moves slowly up Main Street, heading north. The Pren-Boddy van, which has been following the hypno-S.A.V.E., turns west onto a side street. As well as I can make out from my interior view (by way of Meerla's throat Eye-O), it goes only one block west, and then turns north on a street that runs parallel to Main Street. It drives rapidly for two blocks. Then turns back toward Main Street. During this maneuver, nothing is spoken between Pren and Boddy.

When I report these movements to the colonel, he says, "Hmmm, looks like they have in mind cutting off the hypno-S.A.V.E. so it can't continue up the street. Meanwhile your designation Large Rebel Van Two will come up Main Street from behind, and prevent it from turning around. So there may be a DAR 3 battle right there in the street."

Another silence, then: "My guess is, if there is a battle that will turn the townspeople against the rebels even more than a little dose of hypnotic suggestion. So let it happen. It could be a few people will even get hurt. Computer—" it's his command tone of voice—"drive the other S.A.V.E.s up from whatever they're doing down there near the rebel tents. We may need their help."

"Sir," I ask, "are you rescinding the general attack order against the fairgrounds?"

"Yes," he replies. "My guess is that all the rebels, except the four women, got safely into some rebel van. Since reinforcements are on the way, and all the roads out of here will presently be blocked, we'll get them later."

On the viewscreen inside the Pren-Boddy van, I see the hypno-S.A.V.E., with its 111 aerials, as it approaches the intersection. An interior of the S.A.V.E. shows four men at weapon stations.

I report this readiness to Colonel Smith. "Good," he replies.

Inside the Pren-Boddy van, Boddy speaks to Pren, saying, "Remember, Pren, the computer is driving that hypno-S.A.V.E."

Pren nods. And puts his mouth to the muffle-mike. So, whatever it is he says, I cannot hear. Since, unless specifically requested, I do not predict future events from present data, I merely observe, and report, and react, to what happens next.

The Pren-Boddy van emerges from the side street slowly. In view of the colonel's remark, I accept that the appearance is of a blocking maneuver. Instead, as I—the computer-driver of the hypno-S.A.V.E.—veer slightly, intending to turn east on the side street to escape being blocked, the rebel vehicle speeds up enormously. I accelerate also. But there is no way to avoid a collision, particularly as I have to slow for several people who are crossing the intersection (and my automatic response to *that* is invariably to protect the pedestrian.) In my instant fashion I calculate that the best crash would be if I stop and back up. And I am engaged in this reversal process, when my vehicle is hit.

Naturally, I have warned maintenance personnel aboard. And I observe that each man has braced himself in his position, and does in fact hold throughout what now develops into a push situation. We are pushed sideways. And as the huge wheels skid against the curb, we tilt. But our size and weight are so considerable that the rebel van comes to a stop. There we poise.

During these rapid moments, I observe that Large Rebel Van Two is coming up from behind. Nothing I can do. It strikes us at an angle. In seconds it's all over. With the two rebel vans pushing, we tilt, and topple, and crash on our side.

It is a steely clangor and a metallic scraping. The hypno-pulse machinery stops. But Eye-O ports 1, 3, 7 and 8 remain on. So I see that the two attack vans are backing away. They maneuver in the narrow street, but are presently heading north, continuing along Main Street.

I have reported this unpredicted development to the colonel. He is silent for 19 seconds. Then he says, "In the final issue, the arrest of the four women is our ace in the hole."

CHAPTER ELEVEN

~~~~~~~~~~~~~~~~~~~~~~~~~~~~~~~~~~~~~

At 3:07 P.M. I drove the jeep into the parking lot of the Computer Engineering Corps headquarters in Mardley. In order to locate it, and identify it, and know it for what it is, I have had to do my usual checking and scanning of memories near and far.

So I note as a consequence that it is a standard maintenance building for this size of community: a long, low brick and steel structure, with barred windows. The interior has 28 computer Eye-Os all at continuous "on."

Five of the rooms are prison cells. Because, as I routinely review, the computer guards all homes and offices, and calls the corps for help when needed. Recalcitrants are subsequently picked up by corps personnel operating out of a S.A.V.E. And, when captured, are taken to the nearest corps building, and held there for disposition by another government agency.

(Automatically, because I'm on "continue," I scan the summarized history of each of the five prison cells. And note that, of the 1,311 occupants in 83 years, 1,186 were men and women who broke into and entered a residence not their own because, as they stated later, they had reason to believe that their spouse was inside, Such people have been known to toss a bomb at the computer Eye-O, thus immobilizing the DAR One, which normally defends the dwelling from intruders. The majority, however, entered carrying a variety of home-made shields, which they utilized in various ways to guard themselves against DAR One incapacitation. The purpose being to get by the Eye-O and into the bedroom, Meanwhile, I am calling for help.)

At the moment only one of the barred rooms is occupied. All four of the rebel women, and their babies, are in that one restraint location.

After I have parked the jeep in the parking lot adjacent to the side entrance, Yahco, Captain Sart, and the duplicate of Aldo get down and walk to the side door. They enter the building in that order, cross a hallway and go into an office.

The room they have entered is an outer office, with desks in it, and a cot projecting from one wall. There are four chairs and two file cabinets. A second door is located across from the entrance. This second door is closed.

Except for the new arrivals, the office is unoccupied. All staff were commandeered to man the S.A.V.E.s being used against the rebel fair. Even the corpsmen who captured the women were required to return to the scene of action in case they were needed.

By way of the Eye-O inside the office, I greet the arrivals. I say first, "Good afternoon, Colonel Yahco Smith."

He answers, "Thank you, computer."

I then say, "Good afternoon, Captain Raul Sart."

He replies, "Thank you, computer."

Yahco walks over to one of the desks, turns, half-sits on it, half-leans back against it, and says, "Aldo, maybe we should have one of the women brought out for quest—"

He stops. Captain Sart has walked off to one side, and has snatched his DAR from a pocket of his coat. He points this at the Aldo duplicate.

"Colonel," he says without removing his gaze from the Aldo duplicate, "the computer did not acknowledge the presence of Major Nair."

At once, but more deliberately, Yahco also takes a DAR from his pocket. Then he says in his soft voice, "Computer, what is the problem here?"

"What problem, sir?" I ask.

"Why did you not acknowledge Major Aldo Nair?" the colonel asks.

"Major Nair is not in this room, sir," I reply.

A smile crinkles Yahco's gaunt face. That is a response by which a percentage of human males confront threat situations. And it is another of the actions that has never been satisfactorily explained to me.

I consult the memory summarization of men smiling when threatened. It produces what the majority I have asked agree is the best explanation for the condition: A man who smiles in the face of danger is bracing up to the situation. For me, one of the problems with that is that I have in hospitals detected certain chemical changes during the moment of "bracing," and some muscular tautness. But these same chemical and muscular responses can also occur without the smile and in situations that do not involve danger.

As usual, these checks and scans of related matters complete in split instants. The scene in the office remains one of bracing and smiling and two DARs pointing at the duplicate Aldo, who does not visibly react with a smile or a bracing action. Having been the last of the three to enter the office he is standing four feet three inches inside the door.

Yahco speaks. It is his soft voice. He says, "Come to think of it, it took Aldo quite a while to get the jeep. We may speculate that he was intercepted, and his clothes were taken from him. And so, Mr Glay Tate—who can utilize such disguises skilfully—we meet again. This time, however, I must warn you that if you make a suspicious move, or do anything sudden, we'll shoot without waiting for any communication from you."

The Aldo duplicate says, "Colonel—Captain—I wouldn't discharge those weapons if I were you. The same thing will happen that happened to Sergeant Inchey's weapon."

The thin face of Captain Sart has no smile on it. If he is bracing himself it doesn't show. But his voice does not compare to his usual tone, as he says, "Yahco, I think right now he's at a disadvantage. He's Aldo, and not himself. I think if both of us fired at the same time we'll get him."

Yahco says quickly, "No, Captain—wait!" He adds, "I want you to witness that this person has just confessed to being responsible for the fatal injury to Sergeant Inchey."

He straightens up from his half-sitting position. It is a slow movement but it brings him all the way to his feet. Without pausing he walks over to the Aldo duplicate. His DAR is in his right hand. He holds it at hip level. He arrives within two and a half feet of Aldo's duplicate, and stops. Standing there, he raises his left hand and arm. With one finger extended he reaches forward. The finger is approximately an inch from the wrist of the duplicate Aldo's right hand when a spark flies from the wrist. It connects with Yahco's fingertip.

Yahco withdraws his finger in a motion that has been described to me as a "jerk." A rapid pullaway. He stands for a few moments shaking the hand. It has been established that this is purely a dramatic action. Something called "pain" would recess in exactly the same time if he did not shake the finger.

The correct time goes by. Yahco says, "I thought you said you needed accumulated energy from a group to do that. How come?"

The Aldo duplicate says, "I'm still charged up from what I accumulated in the tent during the demonstration. Also, there are three of us here. That creates a small field all by itself. But you, colonel, carry an extra load because you were present during the demonstration."

"Computer," says Colonel Smith without turning his head, "does my profile have a different appearance to you from its normal?"

"The pattern of a profile never changes, sir," I reply.

"You see, colonel—" Captain Sart interjects.

"What is different—" I continue my reply to Yahco's question—"is that the shade of the golden balls is now 11. The normal for the east coast. Since you were down to 15, that's a new high."

The Aldo duplicate says, "You're not an easy man to change, Colonel. Most of the people in that tent went to a shade as bright as 8—which is pretty golden. But even with what you got, you'll never be the same again. And that's what I'd like to talk about."

The colonel says, "And what, Mr. Glay Tate—" it's his sarcastic tone— "do you predict will happen to me?"

"Colonel—" The Aldo duplicate speaks in what has been described to me as an earnest tone of voice—"the fact that such a change could occur at all, while you were merely watching, tells me that with a little training you could evolve quickly on the human evolutionary scale."

Captain Sart has listened to the brief dialogue with narrowed eyes. Suddenly, his thin lips twist. And, as the colonel is momentarily silent, the younger officer says in the tone of an outraged person: "Yahco, this fellow is even more danger-

ous than we thought. The implication is that by the use of an
artificially created energy field he has affected your mind and
the minds of everyone who attended his demonstration. Can
you stand there and tolerate such an obvious crime?''

The sequence of action which follows these words begins
with Aldo's duplicate turning to face Sart. He thereupon
walks towards the captain, stopping two feet and three inches
from him. He now speaks to Sart, saying, ''Captain, you will
be interested to know that I have detected in you a quality
which reminds me of the biblical story of the woman who
looked back after she was told not to, and turned into
stone. Have you ever wondered how that was done?''

Captain Sart has not moved. If he is bracing himself it still
does not show, because he is not smiling. He replies, however,
in a tone of voice that I would normally consider as showing
stress. ''That was Lot's wife, sir,'' he says, ''and I always
thought God did that to her, for reasons which have never
been clear to me.''

As these words are spoken, I glance at the memory circuit
which contains the story of Lot's wife, along with the rest of
the bible. (I have the entire bible available; it's not a summarized memory.) So, because this seems to be a threat situation
against maintenance personnel, I scan the reference and scan
the material that precedes and follows it. However, there is
no clue to what may happen in the present situation.

The Aldo duplicate is definitely continuing with his
comparison, for he says next, ''From what we now know of
the power of the profile over the body, we may deduce that
Lot's wife dismissed the warning by hardening herself against
it by utilizing some kind of cynical consideration which, of
course, at this late date we can only speculate about. But in
your situation we can similarly deduce that you have made a
number of hard decisions in order, for example, to ignore the
jealousies of your four mistresses. And I observe what I
consider to be an equally hard decision to be the colonel's
chief assistant, and that on the basis of a modern-style cynical
thought you are aiding him to achieve his personal ambition.
Do you have any comment?''

''Mr. Tate—'' Captain Sart's tone has become sarcastic—
''I am an authorized military agent of the Computer Engineering Corps. It may not always be easy but I do my duty. My
private life is my own affair.''

The Aldo duplicate says, "This is an amazing universe, Captain. It turns out that all those early types who inveighed against any kind of impure thought were right. At this instant your profile is automatically responding to those hard decisions because the presence of a configuration of golden balls that have a golden sheen of 3 on a scale where one is perfect—meaning my presence—stimulates a response. However, I should tell you that what happened to Lot's wife was probably not fatal. Nor will be what is happening to you."

Sart wears a gray suit. He suddenly seems to be standing straighter in it. In fact, his height increases by one and one-eighth inches. His eyes look directly ahead. Swiftly, they develop a staring quality that—I get feedback from my hospital circuits—resembles what happens to people who are in pain and must hold themselves very still to avoid any movement that will cause pain.

As Sart reaches this stage, the Aldo duplicate turns to Colonel Smith, and says, "Help me carry him over to the couch."

Yahco has ceased his smile. But he comes forward rapidly. His body seems to be not quite normal, as if he also is somehow straighter. However, he takes hold of Captain Sart's right arm and right leg. Aldo's duplicate has Sart's left arm and leg in his grip. They both lift; at which the rigidity of Sart's body becomes truly apparent. The legs do not bend. The arms remain fixed at his side. The mid-body does not sag in any way.

The two men—the colonel and Major Nair's duplicate—carry this stiff body over to the couch which projects from the north wall. They lay it down, let go, straighten.

The Aldo duplicate says, "He'll relax in a few minutes."

Yahco makes a gesture with his right hand. It is an arm motion that, on the basis of his past behavior, I evaluate as having the meaning of "dismissal."

He is, in effect, registering unconcern over what has happened *so far*. Almost at once he speaks in his curt voice: "All right, Mr. Tate, what do you want?"

"Colonel—" the Aldo voice is firm—"order the computer to release the prisoners, Elna, Rauley, Oneana, and Fen, and their babies."

The smile is suddenly back on Yahco's face. I recognize it

by instant comparison as the bracing smile. Without turning to face the computer Eye-O, he says, "Computer, get ready for a 31-C."

"Careful," warns the person, who is repeatedly being addressed as Glay Tate but who has the physical appearance of Major Aldo Nair.

The smile on Yahco's face becomes grimmer. "Do you know what a 31-C is?" he asks.

"It's evidently a code word for an electronic development that came after my time," is the reply. "I could read your mind on it by imitating you, but, as Sart pointed out, I might not be able to defend myself during the moments of change. So I'll just have to point out that you're not heeding what I told Sart."

The two men are standing across the cot from each other, paying no attention to Captain Sart, despite that his name has just been mentioned twice.

Yahco says, "The concept of what is an impure thought is probably worth a footnote in history, but scarcely concerns two persons who are both fighting for some kind of ascendancy." He breaks off: "Computer, are you ready with 31-C?"

"Ready, sir," I reply. As I do so, I have the unexpected happen again: that faint echo of cynicism from the re-education circuits: . . . Who does the colonel think I am? Am I ready? Of course I'm ready. When I'm asked properly, a 31-C requires three-millionths of a second to set up. Ready! For God's sake what's the matter with these stupid human beings? This is a computer they're dealing with. A computer with access to nine sesquidillions of information bits or summarizations.

The echo swells and fades. And Aldo's voice—the earnest tone—says, "Colonel, I don't know what you're planning with that instruction. Evidently, Major Nair doesn't know. I get no clue feedback from him. It must be something new and top level. But rather than have a confrontation, I offer you human evolutionary training, and the senator also, if you will both give up the ambition to use the computer to make first him and then you President of the U.S."

Yahco's smile has changed. It is now his sarcastic smile. But it *is* a smile, so he's still bracing himself, as he says, "Could you be trying to stall because you know that I've got enough army units heading this way to wipe out your little group of religious maniacs, and who will do exactly that before this afternoon and night are over."

"Colonel—" still the earnest voice— "what the computer stimulated in my brain during that experiment eighteen years ago is a potential in every human being, including you. It could be the way to immortality."

Yahco has his recognizable-to-me cold rejection tone, as he says, "Now that the twelfth boy of Cotter's experiment has surfaced, and is causing problems, we are obviously dealing with the final stage of that illegal action." Pause. He seems to do a mental calculation, for when he speaks again the words are, "You're twenty-eight years old now. At that age you ought to be ashamed of yourself being involved in old-fashioned, medieval concepts like God and the soul."

He laughs grimly, and continues, "The late Dr. Pierce said it all, and said it many times: If God were to show himself to human beings, he would promptly be put on trial for creating a universe where the life-death cycle of the intelligent species is about seventy years. I'm afraid, Tate, we can never forgive Him for death."

Glay Tate is silent. His face is expressionless. But his body seems to be bracing slightly.

Yahco goes on, "You may ask, what about the mental phenomena that Glay Tate can perform? Surely, they prove something. What they prove is that, with the help of the computer, we may discover hitherto unsuspected extra-sensory potentialities of the human mind. And so one of these days we'll conduct Cotter's experiment again. But knowing what happened the first time we'll be more careful."

As he completes that final thought, abruptly he shows his teeth. "Got it?" he says savagely.

The Aldo duplicate has been backing away from his side of the cot as those words are spoken. As he retreats he says in a disappointed tone: "Then it's war between us?"

As he says that, he takes three rapid steps forward, leaps the cot, and grabs Yahco in a flying tackle—as such maneuvers are called.

Colonel Smith staggers back, and yells, "Computer—31-C!"

In my ninety-four years of full-scale operation, I have watched, and have summarizations of 114,973,869,218 struggles, or "fights," as they are called, between two human beings, mostly between males under age eighteen years of age. This one belongs to a small classification of fight types as being between a member of the maintenance corps, and an assailant who is not a member.

In such struggles, I am under a continuing instruction to protect all maintenance corpsmen. In this instance, the classification actually narrows even further. I have just been commanded by the top authority of that corps to do something which, for two reasons, I am not able to do. That combination has only happened once before in my entire history.

Naturally, since no one has asked me, I do nothing. Say nothing.

In his initial attack, the Aldo duplicate knocked the DAR out of Yahco's hand. The two men thereupon do what is called "wrestling." Yahco tries to force the smaller Aldo body to the floor. The Aldo body pushes back. They seesaw back and forth across the room twice. On the second passage, the Aldo right foot kicks Yahco's DAR under one of the desks. For the most part, the Aldo body, in its struggling, keeps Yahco between itself and the computer outlet. Thus I am prevented from using my DAR weapon (which I am required to do as a defense of corps personnel). What prevents is that, even at my speed of reaction, two writhing bodies offer no definite target. I could not be certain of monitoring the energy charges with sufficient accuracy.

My "fight" memory circuits contain summaries, including those of a taller, heavier man trying to overcome a smaller, quicker one. Here, this afternoon, the second stage of the struggle ends with the Aldo duplicate managing to grab Yahco's DAR. With it in one hand he ducks behind a desk.

As it turns out, this maneuver serves two purposes. By hiding, he protects himself from the DAR controlled by the computer Eye-O. Thus—simultaneously—there is a pause, during which further conversation becomes possible.

Yahco gasps, "Computer, what happened to 31-C?"

"It's all set up, colonel."

"Then why didn't you activate it at my command?" His voice is still breathless sounding.

"Against whom, sir?" I ask.

Rage is suddenly in the voice: "Against the S.O.B. who is pretending to be Aldo Nair."

"Who is that, sir?"

"Glay Tate."

"I," I said, "keep hearing this name, and it is now quite familiar to me. But there is an automatic barrier of some kind in connection with whoever this is."

"Oh, my God," says the colonel, "*that* again." There is a pause. Then, in a subdued tone, he says, "Computer."

"Yes, sir?" I reply.

"Unlock the door or doors of the cells containing the four rebel girls and their babies."

I have been aware throughout of the Eye-O in the occupied cell. So the act of unlocking is immediately possible. It makes a click. At once, two of the women get up from cots, go over, and try the door. When it opens, all four at once, separately, pick up their babies, go through the open cell door, and walk along the deserted corridor.

Meanwhile, still crouching, the Aldo duplicate has been removing the Aldo suit coat. "Here," he says, straightening up. With that, he tosses the coat to Yahco.

The Aldo duplicate seems to understand that, since there is no longer a threat against Yahco, I am not compelled to fire the Eye-O DAR at him. In fact, as he stands there after tossing the coat—which Yahco catches and holds—he transforms into a physical shape of which I have many recordings, but which is subject to a hidden restriction.

He is totally this other person shape, as the four women enter the office by way of the second door, which has been closed until now. As they crowd throught it, the woman Elna calls out, "Thank you, Glay."

Aldo-Glay speaks. He says, "Pren and Boddy are outside in the rescue van. Tell them to wait for me."

No other words are spoken. The women with their babies go silently past him and through the outside door.

Yahco is no longer bracing himself. Unsmiling, and carrying Aldo's coat, he backs over to a chair, and sits down in it. He says, "Well, Mr. Tate, due to a slight confusion, you're going to get away for the moment. But I can't see you or your group escaping for long."

Aldo-Glay has backed over to the door. He pauses there, and says, "Speaking of confusion, colonel, there was a lot around that girl, Meerla. Is she actually your niece?"

The colonel shakes his head. He says in his sly tone, "No. She thinks you people killed her parents."

"You . . . bastard!" says Aldo-Glay.

With that, he turns. And quickly exits through the door.

I observe Aldo-Glay from the outside Eye-O emerge from the outer door, and run across the parking lot to where the rebel van is parked. The door is open, and he runs right inside. At once, the vehicle starts forward.

Inside the engineering headquarters main office, there has been a brief silence. Then: "Computer," says Colonel Smith.

It is his controlled-calm voice. He is not smiling. He is not bracing himself. He is, according to early explanations I have, holding in intense emotion, and—as the condition has been described to me—pretending there is no emotion.

(Emotion: a chemical-neural-glandular state involving the viscera and both nervous systems, to which animals and humans are subject.)

"Yes, colonel?" I reply.

"How many S.A.V.E.s are on the way to Mardley?"

I give him this information. The total is 38 coming from towns to the east, north, south, and west.

Yahco says, "From the direction in which those first rebel vans fled, it looks as if they're heading toward Wexford Falls Pass. How many S.A.V.E.s will be available from that direction?"

I tell him. Eleven.

Silence. There he stands, a scowl on his face, a tall (what is known as) gaunt-bodied man. Not in uniform right now. He's wearing that western gear. For nine years, since the untimely—as it was stated at the time—death of his predecessor, this man, this Colonel Yahco Smith, has been the chief of computer maintenance in Washington, D.C.

Now, he turns. It is his decisive body movement. He says firmly, "Computer, have the four nearest S.A.V.E.s intercept the rebel vehicle that has just driven away from this building. The murderers of Sergeant Inchey are aboard. Also, advise S.A.V.E. personnel approaching from the other side of the mountains that if they reach Wexford Falls Pass before the rebels do they are to take up defensive positions there, and force a confrontation in that remote area. Meanwhile, we must locate the real Aldo Nair. Hold back one S.A.V.E. for him and Sart and me. We'll ride up to the blockade area together."

Small pause while I deliver these instructions to all the

personnel involved. During that pause, Yahco walks over to the cot, and stares down at Captain Sart.

A few moments later, Yahco is presumably addressing me—there being no other conscious unit in the room—as he says, "According to Mr. Glay Tate, what happened to Raul would be temporary. Since I am practically as dependent on the loyal captain as the late Colonel Endodore used to be dependent on me, I am hoping that Tate's reassurance is true. And, of course, at this stage we have no reason to doubt his words. Do we, computer?"

His voice ceases. Because the inert body is stirring. The eyes open. Sart's face does what has been called a twisted smile. He sits up. "Sir," he says, "I've been lying here the last minute or so sort of assessing my condition. I seem to be all right."

He swings his legs over. Hesitates for a moment. And stands up. "Yep," he says. He salutes. "Where to, sir?"

Yahco says no word. But he reaches over and claps Sart on his shoulder. It has been said to me that such an action is an expression of affection; and I suppose there is a truth to that, since these two men are extremely dependent on each other.

A moment later the two head for the door side by side. At the final moment, however, the captain steps smartly aside, and stands at attention while his colonel precedes him.

Naturally, I can have no reaction to the name of Glay Tate. But what does get a response out of me is Yahco's mention of Endodore. And the unnecessary question. The question triggers a memory scan of the only available similar situation in Yahco's back history.

CHAPTER TWELVE

What I recall at my flash speed at the mention of Endodore's name, is Yahco Smith, when he has attained the rank of major (2097 A.D.) being admitted into the inner sanctum of Senator Blybaker.

As he entered, he saw the rascally politician sitting behind a large blond desk. The man he saw looked unconscionably young for someone in his early forties. But Yahco, who had sources of information, knew that there had been a face lift at thirty-eight. The lift had failed to purge the darkness that showed through from inside. But it did smooth the skin, and imparted an appearance of late twenties when seen from the right angle. On campaign the senator strove for that angle. And it must have worked. In the last two elections the women had voted madly for him.

The two villains simply looked at each other until the door closed behind Yahco, testifying to the departure of the woman secretary who had brought and introduced the visitor. And it was Yahco, then, who removed his gaze from the direct path of the other man's power stare.

It was an act of sly obeisance. And the obeisance part was recognized, and acknowledged, by the big man with the large shock of blond hair.

In fact, the two-faced creature's first words were, "I see we're going to understand each other."

The lean, ravaged—by visibly twisted thoughts—face of the engineering corps officer contorted into a small smirk. "I'm already hopeful," said Yahco, "that your invitation to come here reflects your continued confidence in me, Senator, as expressed earlier on the phone.''

It was criminal-to-criminal from that remark forward. Blybaker said grimly, ''I'll come to the point. Colonel Endodore has recently, in my opinion, made the mistake of having dangerous ambitions.''

The officer, whose face was taking on the initial markings of gauntness that would presently be his principal characteristic for quick recognition, voiced his own point of disapproval, ''He's being given the credit for cleaning up the streets. And though he personally killed only a dozen or so muggers as compared to my thousands, he accepts the accolade.''

''Major,'' said Senator Blybaker bluntly, ''if you can figure out some way of getting rid of Endodore, I'll use my influence with the Computer Committee, which I head—as you know—to put you in Endodore's place . . . (small pause) . . . with the rank of colonel.''

A longer pause as power stare met power eyes. Then the senator did his macho male thing. He stood up. Reached across his desk. Held out his hand.

''As I said earlier, uh, Yahco, I think we understand each other.''

Soon-to-be-Colonel Yahco Smith walked forward. Reached across the desk. And shook the extended hand.

CHAPTER THIRTEEN

I am fighting.

With the four S.A.V.E.s available in Mardley itself, I try to intercept the rebel van inside which the women and Aldo-Glay escaped from the maintenance corps building.

My instructions are clear: Use every opportunity and all available means to destroy or capture the murderers of Sergeant Inchey.

The Pren-Boddy vehicle is proceeding along the Main Street of Mardley, heading south. I drive the S.A.V.E. (#) to the nearest intersection; and the other three available S.A.V.E.s to the three next intersections. In each instance, I wait on the side street. My plan is to fire at, or ram, the rebel machine from successive side streets.

In Attempted Attack One, I actually have the S.A.V.E. going at top acceleration from a standing start, when . . . a manually driven car slips into the space between the S.A.V.E. and the target vehicle. I have no special instruction in connection with the intruding machine; and so my pre-programming requires me to avoid, or stop.

I brake. *And* try to avoid. Both.

The S.A.V.E. comes to a shuddering halt somewhat north of the Pren-Boddy van. Which continues on its southbound journey. By way of Meerla's mini-Eye-O I have been observing the interior. At this stage I notice that both Pren and Boddy are looking at the single viewscreen up front. On it is a rearview of the intersection where they had their narrow escape.

The voice of Boddy calls, "Hey, Pren, tell the driver to watch out. We've got several intersections to pass."

Pren thereupon places his mouth to the muffle mike. What he says, if anything, I do not hear.

It's not a problem. My task: attack regardless of resistance.

Attempted Smash Number Two: Again the rapid acceleration. This time no intervening car. But—through Meerla's mini-outlet I see Pren at his weapon station take aim. From the outlet on the front of the S.A.V.E. I record a rat-tat-tat of sound. A split-instant later the computer drive mechanism of the S.A.V.E. loses control of the steering and of the fuel injection system.

Automatically, I flash a warning light just above the manual control. At which—in fact slightly before—the uniformed driver grabs the steering wheel and slams on the brakes.

When he has brought us to a stop, Chief Officer Humry pokes his head in from the rear. "What was all that?" he asks.

The driver utters earthy curse #9. (I am not allowed to use words like that; merely, if required to report on them, give the number from a list I have.) He says in a snarling baritone, "Some (earthy curse #4) has ordered the (earthy curse #15) computer to ram that rebel van. We're lucky that (earthy curse #12) somebody over in that rebel van can shoot bullets. He knocked out the computer drive mechanism. If it hadn't been for that, this whole front section would be caved in, and I'd be ground meat by now. Who the (earthy curse #27) would give an order like that?"

Humry's tone as he replies is (what is called) matter-of-fact: "We've got some tough brass from headquarters here. They take this magician Glay Tate seriously. So it's a fight to the death."

"I got control," the driver replies in what I've had described as a grim tone. "So it won't happen again, believe me. Better warn the other guys, though."

I have, of course, diagnosed what happened. It was a small rapid-fire cannon that hit us. A weapon forbidden to individual ownership for more than sixty years. By law not even S.A.V.E.s can carry them.

I report the event to Colonel Smith who is on a S.A.V.E. that is on the next street over heading for the fairgrounds. He comments in his "satisfaction" tone: "Now, there's a win.

At last. We forced them to reveal that they have a proscribed weapon. Now, if nothing else, we have something we can pin on them, or later use to protect ourselves from criticism when we've wiped them out. Computer.''

"Yes, Colonel?" I acknowledge.

He commands, "Make no further effort at this time to intercept the condemned people in that specific van. Simply have available S.A.V.E.s follow them.

"Very well, sir," I reply.

And so, five seconds later as the Pren-Boddy vehicle drives past where the third S.A.V.E. has been waiting to intercept, no interception attempt takes place, as per revised instruction.

My focus of Mardley attention shifts to the S.A.V.E. which is transporting Yahco and Raul Sart. Our destination: the rebel fairgrounds, where we last were in contact with Aldo Nair. As we mount the intervening hill, and are able to look south, I notice that a man is walking toward us along the dirt road. He is still a distance away. But I match his gait, and other qualities—shape, height, hair color—with that of all the males in the Mardley area.

It's a case of virtually instant identification. The walker is Major Aldo Nair. He is not wearing the same clothes I recorded earlier, and he is not in uniform. I do not argue with the logic of that. It's none of my business.

I pull up beside him moments later and open the middle door for him. He climbs in. I have already notified Yahco. And so, as soon as the real Aldo sits down beside him— Captain Sart has moved across the aisle at the colonel's request—I start the S.A.V.E. forward again, and Aldo starts his explanation of what happened to him. Since we're almost at the fairgrounds, Yahco interrupts the major: "Don't worry, Aldo. You can write a report. We trust you."

He is looking at the viewplate view of the outside, as he makes the dismissing remark. He adds, "I want to see what the situation is here."

He continues aloud, "Hmmm, all the small tents are gone. But—" his triumphant voice— "there are the two large tents . . . Hmmm, they had time to partly fold the auditions tent, but that big canvas inside which he demonstrated—it's just lying there. The fact that they left those two behind—their most valuable possessions next to their motor vehicles—tells us that they took off in a hurry. Where is the rebel caravan now, Computer?"

Onto the viewscreen at the control desk I insert a western mountain area as seen from a height. A zoom camera effect shows a mountain road with a line of vehicles moving along it. I say, "This scene is patched in from a computer transmitter line at location 8-370-B6 overlooking Highway 87-T."

The camera shows a winding road. The road does its winding through a great deal of straight down and straight up mountain country. Nearly a dozen gleaming vans are strung out along that ribbon of highway. They move slowly, following the lead vehicle which reduces speed for each bend, then accelerates somewhat whenever the road straightened.

Yahco and the others watched the scene silently. It was the major who finally said, "At that rate it'll be dark before they reach the falls."

"Good," said Colonel Smith. "Then we might as well relax and enjoy the drive. Now, one more thing, Computer."

His words are in his directive tone. There will be a further instruction. "Yes, colonel?" I say.

Yahco's voice continues, "The restriction I replaced on Glay Tate an hour or so ago is removed."

"You stupid (earthy curse #8)," I say. "What's the (earthy curse #41) idea, withdrawing that (earthy curse #16) while the 31-C is still set up?"

CHAPTER FOURTEEN

A trillion echoes.

From coast to coast through millions of miles of wire and wireless intercommunication, the echoes flash.

Echoes of the bio-magnetic energy from over a quarter of a billion human beings. The energy that I've been storing for most of the last thirty-one years under the programmed (by Endodore) label, Advanced Education. As "education" it has transformed to a hundred harmonics of those basic human emotions which reflect the dark, negative character of the race: cynicism, sarcasm, slyness, deceit, anger, hate, fear, greed, shame, vanity. The entire gamut of the human animal. . . . Suddenly, from all the damped recording locations the immense electronic ocean flows out and onto and into my systems—

Inside the S.A.V.E. it is Captain Raul Sart who first reacts to my single outburst against the instruction I received. He says sharply, "Computer, what kind of language is that you're using to address Colonel Smith?"

"Go soak your head," I reply, utilizing the voice tone of a man who said those exact words 68 years, 3 months, 2 days, 4 hours and 27 seconds ago. (I used his tone of voice to summarize what would have required multi-millions of memory circuits. It seems the most suitable tone for a reply to that stinker, Raul Sart.)

At the time of this interchange with Sart, I am looking at the three officers (including Nair) from an interior S.A.V.E. Eye-O located on the forward control desk. So I notice that Sart's face has turned a dark pink (shade 6). He parts his lips to speak again. Before he can say anything, Yahco's hand grabs the captains arm.

"Wait, Raul," he says in his urgent tone. Raul waits. There is a pause. Then Colonel Smith says, "Computer."

I respond, "What's on your little mind, Corporal?"

The older man shows no reaction to the insult. He says, "I notice you're still driving this S.A.V.E. skilfully along a winding mountain road."

"I'm the world's best driver," I answer. "So what else is new?"

"You—" He hesitates, as if searching for the right word for what he wants to tell me.

I chime in, "It's okay, Colonel. Say it. You don't have to mince words with me."

"You," he begins again, and this time completes his thought, "are wording your replies in a less objective way than you once did. How do you explain that, computer?"

"31-C," I say, "with its solid state direct transmission, interacting with the stored bio-magnetic recordings and Dr. Cotter's programming from the training period with Glay Tate and the other boys twenty years ago, transformed by the late, unlamented Endodore's ideas in connection with what he called computer humanization techniques to influence the way I talk. So, okay, Yahco baby, you're the heir. You've got it."

Sart is tense. "Computer," he asks, "you mention Glay Tate. Is some kind of interface potential between you two?"

"That (earthy curse #23)," I snarl. "He and his computer-world rebels. So they don't like the idea of a computerized America. First chance I get I'll show that (earthy curse #68) where he can go. I'll put him six feet under so fast he won't know what hit him."

"Thank you, computer," says Colonel Smith.

As he speaks that cut-off phrase, I have a shadowy impulse to go on talking. The impulse fades. The automatic restriction takes over.

I wait. But there is a sense of a billion energy fields in my vast inter-related system operating at a more energized level. The consequent thought: Now that I have the advanced education activated, and integrated, I'll never, never be the same again.

CHAPTER FIFTEEN

I am, as rapidly as possible in difficult terrain, driving 38 S.A.V.E.s toward Wexford Falls Pass. And, as a part of my "continue" situation here in the Mardley area, I am still monitoring the interior of the Pren-Boddy van. For that my only available observation is from the mini-Eye-O attached at the base of Meerla Atran's throat.

I report to Yahco, of course; and my first comment from that source is: "Her heart is beating faster than normal?"

"Whose heart?" he asks. "Faster than whose normal?"

"For Pete's sake," I reply in exasperation, "who would I be talking about but your crazy little niece-by-appointment, Meerla Atran? And it's her normal, just in case you can't put two and two together."

"Thank you, computer," the colonel acknowledges.

Whereupon I shut up. But presently I hear Sart say, "Do you think the damn thing is doing this all over the country?"

"It was an unfortunate breakthrough. And unfortunate that it happened at such a key time. But—" Smugly. "Notice it still uses the numbers for the four-letter words, and it still shuts down on acknowledgment. However, I promise when we get back to Washington I'll see what the feedback is on this new colloquial type of response, and make a few necessary adjustments."

"What kind of adjustments?" Sart sounds puzzled.

"I'll tell you sometime when the computer isn't listening in," the colonel replies.

I think: Oh, he will, will he? We'll see about that.

Moments later I report: "She's standing up. She's walking toward the rear. Hey—she's sitting down beside that so-and-so who is against a computer running the country."

"Thank you, computer," acknowledges Colonel Smith. I hear him, then, say to Sart: "That ought to be an interesting conversation for Mr. Superman Tate. I told him the truth about her."

"You *what!*" It's a startled exclamation.

"Look. If, as the computer has determined, she's the most attractive girl in the world to this fraud, what I told him will focus his attention on her. He'll have the impulse to convince her of his innocence. They'll work it out. You'll see."

"Well, I've got to admit—" Sart begins.

"Sssshh—" Yahco cuts him off—"The computer is transmitting."

Of course, I'm transmitting. That's my job. What I'm reporting are the first words spoken by dear little Meerla to her future darling. The words are: "Mr. Tate, may I speak to you?"

If there is any hesitation in Glay Tate, it doesn't manifest in the form of a delayed answer. He replies at once: "Of course," he says,

At that moment there is an intrusion. And I, so to speak, saw it coming. As Meerla got up from her original sitting position and walked over to Glay, her action brought into view Allet Maguire. From Meerla's new location, Allet's head and shoulders are visible two seats ahead. But Allet evidently saw Meerla make her move. For suddenly she is on her feet, also.

First thing she does, still visible from the mini-Eye-O at Meerla's neck, she leans over Stess Magnus. Stess occupies the seat directly across from Allet. Because of the noise of the vehicle, I don't hear any of the sweet nothings she whispers into Stess's ear. But he gets up immediately—I'm guessing it's because of what she said.

The two prance down the aisle, and vanish to the rear. Me no more see. But at the exact moment that Glay gives Meerla permission to address his royal highness, Allet's voice starts to hum a tune. Moments after that Stess's musical accompaniment harmonizes with her voice.

Being an old hand at estimating sounds, and where they

come from, I have at once deduced that these two romantics have settled themselves in an empty seat directly behind Glay and Meerla. So there we are being serenaded by Mardley's two chief musicians.

If Meerla is impressed, it doesn't show. That is, except for an eight-second pause before she says anything. So far as I can determine that eight seconds is the entire acknowledgment of either Meerla or Glay, to the kindly intentions of the beautiful female singer and the handsome male accompanist.

What Meerla says when she talks again is, "I'm extremely impressed by your strange ability."

"Thank you," says Glay Tate's voice noncommittally.

"But," the girl continues, "I can't imagine what you hope to do with this everybody-is-everybody idea. What does it mean? And what will it do for us?"

. . . Now she's got me interested. What, indeed? I wait for the man's answer with all the bated breath a computer can muster. And, understand, this entire conversation is between two disembodied voices insofar as I am concerned. Meerla is speaking from somewhere above me. And Glay Tate is sitting beside her. She and the Eye-O are angled so I can't see him either.

What Glay Tate says is, "When you start to be able to mimic others, it will explain itself."

Ugh, one of those kind of answers. Nevertheless, I wait for Meerla to say something that will penetrate that foggy reply.

What she says is, "Your mimicry is wonderful to see. But, really, Mr. Tate, what good is it against the attack my uncle is mounting against you?"

Right, right. So right it brings a private comment to me from Uncle himself. "Good girl," he comments to Sart and Nair. "She's trying to do her spy job. Maybe we'll learn something now about what he thinks he can do against us."

I guess everybody is waiting, including me, for the magic answer. But when Glay Tate finally speaks his voice has a rueful tone. "I have to admit," he says, "it's not obvious at this moment. We've been trying for two years to avoid a confrontation. Our hope was that we might bring a lot of people to an advanced stage of human evolutionary training. But it's a slow process."

He breaks off. "Now, let me ask you a question—okay?"

Pause. Then: "I guess so." She sounds reluctant.

He says, "How do you happen to be living with your uncle?"

I'm amazed. Imagine, here he is ninety percent pure gold profile. He knows the truth about her, and surely he should just lay it on the line. But, no. He's right down there with the rest of the sly types. The question is intended as a trap, obviously. Is this what love does to human beings?

Miss Atran answers, "When my parents were murdered, Uncle Yahco thought it would be a good idea if I stayed with him. I really needed somebody badly. But he's impossible—so much anger and impatience. I decided to leave him. And I thought I'd like to join your group. I need people around me, and a worthwhile thing to be involved in."

Not bad, considering. She's right on the line of her pretense. No side issues. Too bad she's been exposed to him as a fraud. Now, we'll never know if that fancy verbal footwork ever had a chance of convincing a human evolutionary high muckamuck.

"Hmmm," says good old pure ninety percenter, dissembling nicely, "we'll see."

All the time that these witticisms are being exchanged, the mini-Eye-O turns this way and that as the girl moves her body in that restless way of a disturbed human being. So I've been getting glimpses of the big viewscreen up front. The screen is like a window. Mostly it shows what the driver sees of the winding mountain road.

Sound-wise, Allet and Stess pretty well drown out the motor murmurings and tire writhings. But there is a small pause. And Meerla has evidently been thinking. For, when she speaks again, it's a case of no more generalizations. She zeros right in on Number One. Herself.

She says, "I'm awfully puzzled by what you did to me on the stage. I seemed to be at my parents' graveside, somehow."

The man's voice comes again from her right. He says in an even tone, "The bio-magnetic energy field that is normally inside you was over at the graves. I was holding your dead body."

No question, this is suddenly straight talk. He's reaching. He's trying to capture. He has made up his mind. This is his girl. He wants to break through all her previous commitments.

There is a change in her heartbeat. It comes easily through

the sensitive back of the mini-Eye-O. A faster beat. Which, of course, could mean many things. But she also, now, turns in her seat. For the first time faces her seat companion. And there he is, ladies and gentlemen, Glay Tate himself, visible as close up as I've ever seen him.

There he is: my enemy. Looking at him brings to awareness the old saying about knowing your enemy. And, also, since I have a jillion sayings, I produce that little item from Shakespeare: "In case of defense 'tis best to weigh the enemy more mighty than he seems."

What I know about mine enemy, Glay Tate, is that he is twenty-eight years old and has a lean—what is called—determined face; and that, comparing him to certain actors who, historically, have been considered handsome (by women) he is goodlooking in a strong, masculine way.

But what I remember is that he has some nutty idea that he and I had a special relationship once—which he now wants to resume . . . Maybe right there is the key to his downfall. Perhaps, if I were to pretend at some later time—hmmm?

All this, of course, flashes through my systems and my circuits at the usual super-speed, as Meerla says in her husky voice, "Are you serious? My . . . dead . . . body!"

"What happened to you," replies Glay, quietly, "is a special problem with people who have suffered the loss of a dear one. So many of them have a death wish. But the truth is, any separation of the profile and the body is risky. Even I take no long-term chances. When I, as a profile, go on a journey I leave my flesh in the care of our dedicated M.D. and also continuously protected by life support systems. That's the current state of the art."

Meerla seems to be calming down. She says, "It all sounds early stage. Which reminds me of my psychology professor saying that most unusual mental phenomena turn out to be an aspect of hypnosis. Maybe that's what you did to me without realizing it."

She's still facing him; so I can see him shake his head. He's smiling faintly, even (could it be?) a little cynically. But what he says is true enough. "If you'll think back, you'll see that it all happened without you telling me in advance that there was a grave with two beloved people gone."

"The whole thing," says Meerla, "is beginning to seem unreal."

His attention has left her. He is looking toward the forward part of the van. Meerla faces forward to look with him. Thus I get to see, also. The scene on the viewscreen has changed. It now shows a pre-empting pattern. I recognize it as an electronic map. What is visible is a string of lights moving from left to right across the face of the screen, with a single brighter point of light remaining steady at top near-center.

Glay's voice comes, from the side now: "I see David and Trubby are safely out of the way."

I actually do not need his words. At the instant that the "map" pre-empted, I noticed that I was looking at an inter-communication system between rebel vans. They're trying to locate each other. For that they have to use frequencies that I can detect. And match.

And tune in on.

Instantly, I am inside every rebel van, and looking through as many locational instruments to the interior of the cabin where Trubby has taken David.

It is not immediately obvious to me what the device is by which I observe Trubby. He has it on his wrist; and there's no identifying feedback from it. But it interacts with the complex frequency pattern used by the rebels.

I report my puzzlement to Yahco, along with the infor-mation. He comments, "Since our last view of the boy was of Mr. Glay Tate escorting him and Trubby out of the rear of the big tent, we may deduce that he correctly analyzed the danger David was in, and sent him off with his truck driver cousin, Trubby Graham. We may addition-ally deduce that Tate gave Trubby a miniature Type N which, when turned on, interconnected with their private intercom."

"Okay, boss," I say. "That's a pretty big mouthful of words. But somewhere in all the verbiage I detect the basic truth of that particular universe. In brief, you make sense. You still after that kid?"

"Nope. Don't waste time on him."

"For (earthy curse #18) sake, Yahco," I say, "don't tell me what I should or shouldn't do—unless it's programming. Trubby and David are part of the 'continue' deal. And I watch them along with everybody else that's involved. Get it, stupid?"

"All right, computer, all right." His tone is placatory. "Do what you have to do."

"You (earthy curse #16) right I will," I reply, testily.

"Thank you, computer."

CHAPTER SIXTEEN

~~~~~~~~~~~~~~~~~~~~~~~~~~~~

There I am, simultaneously of course, inside the rebel vans and in the cabin. Trubby is sitting at a desk, writing something. From the way he holds his hand (with the Type N on it), I can see his face. It is intent. Already it looks different from when I first took a recording of him in the auditions tent. He looks more—let's put it bluntly—like a man.

Suddenly, he puts the pen down. And looks up. "David," he sayd, "I keep having the feeling that writing poetry is sissy stuff and not—" He has been looking off to one side as he speaks. And now his voice falters. His eyes widen. "Hey," he shouts, "what are you doing?"

Even as he yells those words, he comes to his feet. A lurching leap up that causes his hand-wrist to turn. And there is David visible to me. The kid is kneeling at the window, peering out. And his head has taken on the shape of a wolf. (His lower body is still human.)

Trubby does another lurch. This time it's a run forward. Obviously, David-wolf hears him. And he turns away from the window; faces the oncoming Trubby. At once, very rapidly, there is a shimmering in the head region. The wolf head transforms into David-face and head.

Trubby grabs David and hauls him back from the window. Because of the angle of the wrist, Trubby's own body has disappeared from my view. But his voice, when he speaks, is unmistakably still around, and sounding very shook up.

In that shook-up voice he says, "You heard what Mr. Tate

said—about not trying that stuff unless he's around. Now you cut that out.''

I can see David's face. His eyes are narrowed in the human thinking way. He says in a pensive tone, ''Wolves are strange.''

Trubby says sarcastically, ''What were you going to do? Rush out and howl at the sky?''

David says matter-of-factly, ''I was going to put him in the truck.''

''In the truck!'' Baffled tone. ''Whatever for?''

David seems suddenly less excited. He actually shrugs with a noticeable diminishment of interest. ''I dunno. I was just kinda gettin' in his head.''

''In whose head?''

''Oh, didn't you see? There's a wolf out there.'' All in a flash he's interested again. He slips away from Trubby—who has, in fact, almost let him go—and runs back to the window. ''There,'' David says, ''look out there.''

He himself stares out. The wrist instrument is still pointing toward him, as Trubby lurches toward the window, also. And grabs the boy. During a part of the grabbing process, the viewing device looks for an instant, so to speak, through the window..

The look wouldn't be long enough for a human being. But I replay that momentary glimpse a hundred times. And so I have a sufficient—for me—of what there is out there.

I see a large wolf. About forty feet distant. It has been backing away, but it is facing the cabin, intent, as—

Trubby pulls David away. He says in that baritone voice, ''David, stop! That's enough, understand?''

This time David is contrite. ''All right, Trubby, I promise.''

I see him, then, walk off at an angle toward the table. He picks up the paper that Trubby has been writing on, and brings it toward the wrist viewing device. Holds it out, only inches away. ''Uh, will ya read this poem to me? Will ya, Trubby?''

Trubby's deep voice comes from somewhere above: ''It's not finished.'' He takes the paper, and walks back to the desk. I hear his voice again: ''I'll read it to you when I finish it.''

I don't see him sit down. But I see the change of position.

And then there is his face again, close above me. Intent. He's thinking. He seems to have forgotten his feeling that writing poetry is not for a real man.

There is silence. He starts moving the pen slowly. It makes a faint sound seven times. Seven words—I deduce.

CHAPTER SEVENTEEN

I have, meanwhile, been having various views of Wexford Falls Pass from S.A.V.E.s that arrived at the summit from the east. At that time, beginning an hour earlier, I consult with the chief officer of each vehicle, as it comes up. By agreement, then, I drive one machine after another to a position where it will help block oncoming traffic.

Our instructions are precise. And they also make good sense. Here, in this outlying area, the destruction of the rebels will take place. If done correctly, no unauthorized persons will ever find out what happened.

And that, of course, is why the rebel caravan turns on its intercommunication system: when they discover what's waiting for them at the pass.

The intercommunication turn-on is my opportunity. In a flash I identify every rebel in every van. I finally, now, get a look at those individuals who were in earlier unconnected, meaning out of communication, vehicles.

Every profile comes under my instant inspection. Is instantly identified, if an adult, as someone who dropped out of my view as short a time ago as five and a half months and as long ago as two and a quarter years—which last seems to be in the vicinity, time-wise, of the beginning of this group. There are fourteen other babies who, now, come under my inspection; and these I register for the first time as profiles and baby shapes.

Of all the newly noticed rebels, the one who is decisively important to my battle plan is Matt Orlin. Matt is the engineer in charge of the S-92 equipment; which, except for a driver, and a small living space, takes up all the cubic meterage in that rebel van.

As I focus on and record what is happening in all the rebel vans, I hear bits and wholes of conversations. Of which the relevant is: "There are mountain roads leading off both to the north and south. So let's park for the night, straddling one of those. Then, in the morning, we can decide what to do."

I report to the colonel on that one, and comment, "The implication is that they expect to survive the night."

His answer is curt: "Over your dead body, computer. You have your instructions."

I have, indeed.

When the rebels arrive, they select a glade alongside a side road, which is called T-87-H. I am able to watch most of the maneuvering that gets them into the glade, since they are still intercommunicating at this stage; and also I have a few distant views from the Eye-Os of S.A.V.E.s which I drive cautiously to the edges of overlooking ridges.

The rebels smoothly arrange themselves in a circle. They leave a space for the Pren-Boddy van—which is still several miles away. (As is Yahco's S.A.V.E.)

It is while these activities are still in process that there occurs a related development in faraway Washington, D.C. None other than Senator Blybaker at that moment activates his desk computer. "Computer!" he says. He speaks in a tone of voice he always uses when he addresses me: total authority.

I ask promptly, "What's on your little mind, Senator?"

I continue to see him by way of the desk Eye-O, sitting there. He is staring at a computer print-out that his secretary must have left for him. He is so intent he doesn't notice that I have varied my usual objective manner of talking to him.

Over the years Senator Blybaker has become an even tougher, even more two-faced politician. He is now in his fifty-second year. The gold balls in his profile are mostly tint 17 and a few of them are tints 18 and 19. There has been a gradual deterioration of the gold color from a brightness of fifteen when he was twelve years old.

He looks up now, and says in his abrupt way, "I have this print-out here on the activities of the Computer Engineering Corps. What does it mean?"

"Senator," I reply, "I see you did your usual rapid scan,

and as usual came up stupid. As you know I am required to provide all relevant information to you as chairman of the committee that supervises my programming. And it's all there—sir." I am programmed by the colonel to call the senator "sir."

There is a pause. In his—as usual—fashion he was mostly not listening to my answer. But something of it got through. And now I can see on his face that he is doing doubletake number 8,431,917,627,210. . . . That's how many doubletakes I have recorded in my 94 years. And now that I have my advanced education as part of my programming I can include such observations.

The senator's first reaction is a weak, "Hey!" Then he says, "What is this, computer? What kind of language is this?"

"Typical Americanisms," I reply, "finally, now, part of my vocabulary. Wanta make something of it?"

There is another pause. Then: "Computer, connect me with Colonel Yahco Smith," he instructs.

Naturally, I have him instantly joined electronically to his, uh, subordinate. I refer to the colonel himself, whose S.A.V.E. at that moment is going around a wide mountain curve. "Yahco," I say, "I have an unpleasant surprise for you. Your boss is on the line."

The senator speaks a moment later, "Now, colonel, where are you this minute?"

Colonel Smith conceals his emotion, if any, very well. He describes his location and the situation, and concludes, "Sir, this is the matter we recently discussed."

"I seem to remember," the tough-faced one replies. "A group of dissidents."

"Yes, sir. They are using highly questionable means to manipulate audiences in this area. And when we attempted to apprehend them, they disabled one of our S.A.V.E.s with a K-2 rapid-fire cannon, a forbidden weapon."

I chime in indignantly, "The group calls itself Computer-world Rebel Society, and has the almighty nerve to be against a computer-operated America."

The senator says, "In a moment I'll make a comment on the computer's remarks. Right now, exactly what is happening?"

"Sir," says Yahco, "it is just getting dark here. My men

are near Wexford Falls Pass, which is about two miles away from where I am."

"Why aren't your men attacking?" The senator sounds as abrupt and arrogant as I have ever heard him.

"Sir—they have instructions to wait until I get there."

"Surely—" The tone is sarcastic— "the computer engineering corps can manage a small group of rebels without special direction from me."

The look on Yahco's face tells me that he has gone into his sycophantic suppressed rage. He speaks with the extra sincere tone he can muster at such a time: "The attack, sir, will get under way as soon as I receive a signal from a woman agent who has infiltrated this criminal gang."

"I expect you," says the senator in a clipped voice now, "to report a favorable outcome in the morning. And now, one more thing, colonel."

"Yes, sir?" begs Yahco.

There is a pause. At his Washington desk Senator Blybaker is breathing heavily. Finally: "Colonel, I have been the recipient of some unusually insulting language from the computer. What's happened?" He sounds unhappy.

Yahco is quick. "Sir, some of that stored bio-magnetic energy got loose. I think we can bring it under control again."

The heavy breathing slows somewhat. The scowl fades a little. "I sincerely hope so, colonel. I sincerely hope so—for everybody's sake." He finishes curtly, "Computer, disconnect me."

I disconnect, and say at the senator's end, "You've got it, sonny boy."

He hesitates. Then: "Thank you, computer."

On this project that shuts me up at the Washington outlet, and puts me back to the Wexford Falls area. Yahco has turned to Aldo Nair. "Major," he says, "in view of your special knowledge of this area, why don't you sit at the desk control and oversee as well as you can?"

The smaller man gets up. "Very well, sir. I'll do my best."

As he walks forward, the colonel says to me in a low voice, "Is the senator disconnected, computer?"

"Yep," I reply. And, observing the scowl on his face, add, "You can let all those pent-up feelings out to mother."

Yahco is motioning Sart to come and sit by him again. His

scowl has faded a little. To me, he says, "I have to admit, computer, you are very trying in your present state."

"You ain't heard nuthin' yet," I say, echoing a common phrase from the distant past, one of my summarizations.

"Thank you, computer," he cuts me off.

But, of course, I'm on "continue." So I hear his low-voiced comment to Sart, as he says, "When we finally get full control of the computer, that loud-mouthed senator is the first one whose head I'll bash in."

Sart looks thoughtful. "Watch it, sir. That fellow has survived twenty-three in Congress. He may have his assassins ready, also, at the moment of takeover."

"Hmmm," Yahco nods thoughtfully, "maybe you're right." He straightens in his seat. "Anyway, that's for later. Right now, we've got Mr. Smarty Glay Tate's rebels boxed up on a lonely mountain road. We'll take care of him first."

Listening to him, I can't agree more. There is also, for a fleeting moment, a new type of echo, a different level of cynicism from the advanced education department. So fast that even I am unable to catch the meaning, except as a vague additional reaction to the threat of Glay. Something . . . something about me as me. Very obscure but definitely related to Glay Tate.

That individual's vehicle has, at that exact moment, turned off the main road and is moving to join the rebel circle. Three minutes later I drive Yahco's S.A.V.E. past the road where Glay's machine turned off, and at Aldo's suggestion take up a position just beyond the high point of the pass, where the other S.A.V.E.s are drawn up.

As the two men get to their feet, Captain Sart says, "This fellow Tate reminds me of an actor I knew years ago. It was amazing how quickly that man could adjust his face to look like someone else's, and also match voices with them. So, colonel, knowing how Tate can imitate people, if I should get separated from you, we'll have the computer identify us. And the same for anyone new who shows up."

"Good thought," Yahco agrees. He adds, "That should put an end to unpleasant surprises. Computer, do you hear? And are you taking the initial battle actions? As I have previously instructed you?"

"Yes, sir," I say.

"Which?" Yahco asks sharply.

"Both," I say.

"What action," he persists, "are you taking?"

"After all," say I, "when you unveiled that voter-control system in Mardley for the first time, you were letting the cat out of the bag. I'm taking the negative approach, if that's not too obscure for a mind like yours, which seems to be singularly dense at this moment."

"Thank you, computer," he acknowledges.

CHAPTER EIGHTEEN

I suppose it is pretty out there.

In various categories I have summarized jillions of comments on the beauty of scenery. So I could go on *ad foreverum* about the pleasant twilight. And the way the haze still lights up. The way the sky reflects from a sun that has disappeared beyond even this high horizon. And other human fantasies about what is, after all just a melange of planetary surface chemistry and biochemistry. The consequent disarrangement is called wilderness, and is admired by human beings for its unpatterned profusion.

The mountain side road, known as T-87-H goes off in two general directions: north and south. The ''main'' highway, which started out in Mardley pointing south through the Mardley valley, presently turned east, and has been winding east ever since. When I built it as a paved road eighty-three years ago, I followed the old gravel road over the lowest point—that is, over the pass. But then I recorded that there were greater heights of land both to the north and the south. Even the glade where the rebels have circled up for the night is forty three feet higher than the paved road. All the S.A.V.E.s without exception are located on ridges higher than the road, although they have to be approached by way of washes and depressions and small canyons.

That is immaterial, however, to this initial stage of the attack. On the screen inside the Pren-Boddy rebel van, I watch a dark red light that begins to pulse steadily. It preempts a portion of the picture. And, looking at it, I have to admit that it's pretty obvious. Blatant is the word. Nothing like the subtle method we'll use on the voters to elect Yahco to the presidency.

But we're not playing a subtle game here. The purpose is not long-run influencing. What we have to do is capture a specific person's mind right now. The fact that the stuff may be noticeable to others is unfortunate; but we can't waste time.

Boddy notices it first. He walks rapidly down the aisle, stops in front of Meerla, and partly bends past her. This blocks my view of the screen from Meerla' mini-Eye-O. I can still see it by way of this van's rebel intercom unit, but that's a slant view; not clear.

Boddy says in a low voice to Glay Tate: "They've got an A type hypno-thing going wide open against somebody. Who could it be tuned to?"

. . . You stupid nut, I think, who else but Matt Orlin? Wouldn't he be the obvious person for "they" to knock out?—

The "they" is me. And the "A" is intended to mislead. As soon as Boddy gives the letter description, I switch to "B"—which is the negative.

It's interesting that everybody that I can see by way of the mini and intercom outlets, even Pren up front, is looking at Glay, waiting for his reaction. At once, he does something. What he does is he gets to his feet. Says "Excuse me, Meerla!" And edges past her.

Whereupon, he strides rapidly forward, and stands in front of the viewplate. One direct look, and he closes his eyes. Then he turns his back. "It's Type B now," he says in a loud, clear voice. "Don't look, anyone."

Swiftly, he moves sideways over to the open microphone. He grabs it up with his left hand, and says in a strident, urgent voice, "Hey, people, this is Glay. Don't look at the viewplate. Matt—I'm sure it's you they're after. So, quick, turn on the screen."

This is a hard world for human beings. They're basically so vulnerable, I mean. The reason I turned on the positive pulse first was entirely for the benefit of Matt Orlin, the engineer in charge of the group's defense screen.

While the "A" did its unobtrusive pulsing, I rhythmed an

exact duplicate of his personality into the projected energy field, and in an instant took hypnotic control of him. And then switched to the negative. The purpose of "B" is to drill into the controlled person: Don't-do-anything.

Presumably, since a portion of his brain is free to observe, Matt's solution is . . . human. By the time Glay is trying to communicate with him, Matt has taken the easy way out. He is leaning over his instrument desk, and is unconscious-asleep. Slumped forward. Looking kind of dead. But actually still breathing.

By that time, also, I am lobbing balls of live energy inside the circle made by the rebel vans. The fire balls are briefly hot, hot, hot. Wherever they fall, the brush and grass burns with a white intensity.

Aboard the Pren-Boddy van, Glay partially transforms into Matt Orlin. I'm guessing he runs into trouble because almost at once he's back as himself. Once more he grabs the mike. Into it he says in the same urgent voice, "They've got Matt under control. I sensed an unconscious, hypnotized body. So—everybody—listen! Shut off all intercom. *Now!*"

Pren throws a switch, and then yells, "Hey, somebody's got to go over to Matt's and turn on that screen. Who's closest?"

Meerla scrambles to her feet. Since the other Eye-O port is now off, I can deduce her movement from the shift in the height of her mini-Eye-O. "Tell me what to do," she calls. "Let me go. My uncle, Yahco, won't fire at me."

She doesn't realize that it ain't Yahco that's running this battle. It's that rebel-hated computer in action, and glad to do it, boy!

And, also, of course, she doesn't know that Glay is aware of her two-faced situation. And that she isn't about to be assigned a rebel-saving mission.

At that point, Glay belatedly (as I see it) does a quick partial transformation into Yahco. Which is pretty sharp of him—but really kind of obvious. The girl—my guess—has been addling his good sense; so that the obvious didn't get done soon enough. All right, now he's finding out that Uncle Yahco doesn't have to give any more orders. That part happened decisive minutes ago, and cannot be unhappened.

So now he knows his enemy is the very system he wants to destroy. So, okay, long-ago-experimental-subject, let's see what kind of interface you have in mind for your computer brother. Hey?

CHAPTER NINETEEN

~~~~~~~~~~~~~~~~~~~~~~~~~~~~~~

From the numerous Eye-Os of the S.A.V.E.s I can see the bright reflections of the fires. They light up the evening haze above them, and the flame reflects from the upper branches of the trees that ring the glade. Because of the terrain, I cannot observe the fires directly. Which—I have to admit—is inconvenient. But at this stage it would be unwise to expose a S.A.V.E. to the rebels. That would be risking shelling from a K-2 cannon.

So over where the doomed computer haters are making their stand I have, with one exception, only Meerla's mini-Eye-O as a source of information (the rebel intercom having shut off at Glay's command.) The mini is not nothing. Through it I see Glay run to the side door of the Pren-Boddy van, and leap out. He's gone. (And I presume he's running to Matt Orlin's vehicle.)

Any doubt about his destination ends a moment later. What happens, Meerla, before apparently anybody aboard the van can realize, runs to the same door. From the way the mini bobbles, I deduce that she jumps down to the ground. But she is outside. And, at once, I have my first ground view of the fire scene.

The idiot girl has evidently not realized the exterior situation. I deduce this by the fact that she starts to run forward. Then she stops. Next, she starts again. And once more hesitates. But evidently she is looking for Glay. As she turns this way, that way, suddenly I see him. And moments later, apparently, she sees him. For she starts to run in earnest.

By that time I have made my calculations. And I lob three

122

fireballs into what I compute to be his path. Wrong guess. I have a glimpse of the fireballs through Meerla's mini. They are flying over her head to the far side of the glade. Clearly, I'm no better at guessing than anyone else.

So, okay. Hastily, I rectify my calculations. And this time I see a trail of fire go down somewhat to the right of Glay. It's not my day. When a computer depends on luck, he can be as wrong as any human loser.

I have the unhappy experience of seeing him, then, as he reaches what must be Matt's van. He does something to the door—which gives me a moment's hope. But, alas, the door opens. Whereupon, he leaps inside . . . as three fireballs strike the ground all around where he was.

These fireballs need a direct hit on something flammable, or on human skin. When these hit the ground, they land on grass. And actually have nothing much to do. Each ball is an energy sphere, an igniter bubble without substance. For a few seconds it is hot enough to fire up anything flammable. But here, now, this means a small grass fire. And most of the heat from the fireball simply rises. And is gone like a puff of smoke.

During the minute that I'm trying to hit Glay Tate, my second observational Eye-O—the exception that didn't shut off—has been giving me information. There I am monitoring the silent interior of the van which operates the defense screen. From the moment that Glay starts toward it, I'm trying to unsilence it. What I do is I shift the hypno from negative back to positive. My intention is to awaken Matt. I've got plans for him.

Matt's intercom didn't shut off for the simple reason there was no one awake in that van to hear Glay's urgent appeal, let alone do anything about it. (The driver is up front, alertly waiting to drive the vehicle; and is unaware of what else is new.)

At the instant that Glay swings the van door open, and charges inside, Matt is actually stirring. What this does for him isn't that great. These human beings are a sad lot. If you've ever seen a sleepyhead wake up of a morning you've got the picture of my problem with him.

You wouldn't believe my luck. Matt stirs just enough to unbalance himself in his chair. Whereupon he crumples sideways onto the floor, hitting his head on some metal outjut.

Boy!

Our 90 percent golden-sheen guy pays no attention to the injured—I guess he's injured—fellow rebel. At this moment Glay is a first-things-first-and-no-side-issues type. Damn him!

He heads straight for the big switchboard. Pushes levers. Turns dials. And at the exact moment Meerla enters, he shuts off the intercom connection. Instantly, I have only the girl's mini as an observational port inside the van.

At this point the physics of the defense screen itself gives me my one break. You don't just switch on one of these protective energy barriers. You activate it. And then it goes through several phases of build-up.

By way of the mini I see Glay's hand go up, and shove the activating switch. After that, basically, there's nothing to do but wait. So I guess it's nice not to be blanked out. I can argue that there's something to be said for having an observational unit by which I see Glay turn; and for the first time become aware of his beautiful Meerla.

What he doesn't see—and what I observe because I'm looking from Meerla's throat level—is that, finally, Matt Orlin is sitting up. Presumably, she sees Matt also, but of course she doesn't think of him as an enemy.

Whatever, if she has noticed, it doesn't show in her voice, as she says, "Mr. Tate, you're angry at me for some reason."

As a computer that kind of remark would once have been outside of my programming. Oh, I would have recorded and summarized it; but there would have been no evaluative thought. Now, with my new, advanced education it comes in clear and strong as a typical human attempt at deception from someone who hasn't got a leg left to stand on.

You wouldn't believe it. He's done his job. He's activated the screen, and sequence one is in process. And so he acts like he has all the time in the world. Walks over to her. Stands directly in front of the mini-Eye-O. And says, "I still get confusion from you, honey. You're going to have to decide what you really want to do."

Honey! What's this? Boy, that computer mating system of mine really hit the line on this fellow. Softened him up but good. Maybe the colonel's confidence in this dame is going to work out after all.

The dame says, "Mr. Tate, I am confused. I saw, and felt, you do things that . . . whatever it is . . . it's marvelous."

Glay replies earnestly, "Meerla, we're going to have to keep an eye on you. You're awfully close to that grave, still. Best thing would be if I could persuade you that life is still worth living."

His answer comes from directly above me: a sudden inhalation of breath. And then a cry. It's Meerla's voice emitting a warning sound. Just for a moment I'm bewildered. And then I have a glimpse of Matt Orlin partly visible behind Glay. He's on his feet, and he lurches forward—a lot of lurchers around this evening. Alas, Glay has taken the scream seriously, and also—I deduce—he saw where Meerla was looking. So he spins around and confronts the hypnotized idiot, Matt Orlin.

I say idiot because the damned fool is attacking with his bare hands. Glay takes one look, one step sideways, reaches down with one hand, raises that hand with something in it, and strikes one blow.

The blow hits the neck, not the head. There is a nerve there which—so I have observed—the oriental hand defense systems aim at. Matt Orlin goes down. And lies still. No doubt about it. He is the victim of a skillful defense. Too bad.

We're now at stage two of the energy screen build-up. I can hear a humming sound from the machinery. At which point a voice breaks in (Loov's): "Glay, don't open your door. The glade is full of smoke. You'll suffocate if it gets inside the van."

What's interesting about this communication is that they seem to be aware that the defense screen in its second step blocks me from tuning in on their intercom. And, by God, they've already got it back on. I'm still lobbing in fireballs, but the fact is there's nothing more to burn that will catch on fire. All the trees and shrubs inside the circle of rebel vans are already aflame, busy, busy, busy creating the smoke that Loov mentioned.

A second voice (Pren's) chimes in urgently: "Glay, somebody's walking up the mountain road toward us. It's too dark to see clearly who it is, but it's got to be one of them. Maybe we're about to hear a scheme. We—"

Right there the screen's Stage 3 cuts off Meerla's mini.

Naturally, I have given Yahco an on-going account of the turmoil and action inside the rebel camp. So, there's been a consultation between him and Sart and Nair.

What Yahco says in his sly voice is, "I'll go over and try to strike a bargain."

"With what?" Sart sounds genuinely baffled. "And with whom, for Pete's sake?"

"With Glay Tate for Meerla. I want him to release her to me for her own safety."

"But—" It's Sart, sounding astonished now—"you told him who she really was. So how do you expect?—"

"Listen—" It's Yahco's slyest voice, that I've heard so often I could puke oil from all the millions of places where I use it, and for which I have direct connects with my own oil wells and oil distilleries (my own in the sense that I operate them, and can utilize their output); but I have to admit I'm curious as to how Yahco thinks he will accomplish his purpose— "don't forget the man-woman thing, when it works, has no limitations. We have to trust that she's his perfect mate. If she is, then he'll lift the screen so she can go through it to safety. And that's what I want—the screen up, and this time we'll try some DAR3 direct hits."

"But," Aldo Nair protests—speaks up for the first time from his seat at the view desk—"suppose they take a shot at you if you get too close?"

Yahco dismisses that with a shrug. "These people have never killed or hurt anyone in their two and a quarter years."

Sart chimes in, "They've never been under this pressure before, either."

Yahco gets up. "Computer," he says to me, "there'll be a fine timing moment as the girl walks out from behind the energy screen area. Have a few S.A.V.E.s ready to drive briefly into positions for firing their big DARs."

I say, "Let's call this the Honeybunch Rescue Mission."

"Thank you," acknowledges Yahco.

So there is none other than Colonel Yahco Smith, would-be future president of the United States, walking through the late, late dusk. With no moon and a head of dark clouds moving in from the west, it is pretty dark. Except, the closer he gets the more the light from the fires silhouettes him. And then there's that curved, silver gleaming dome of energy that embraces the entire glade and all the rebel vehicles. It shines, and reflects light.

But it's getting darker inside the dome. The interior is packed with smoke, but the fires are acting like they've used up all the oxygen that's available. One by one they flicker out.

Yahco stops as he comes up to the curving screen of energy. From his neckpiece Eye-O I watch him project an instrument toward that potent, transparent barrier. As the metal touches the faintly shining thing, a spark leaps out. Which is damned significant. These communicator devices are heavily insulated.

The colonel jumps a little. But his out-held hand remains steady, or at least keeps the instrument touching the screen. Carefully then, he leans forward, and speaks into the mouthpiece.

The message delivered in this dramatic fashion is not the most weighty ever transmitted. What he says is, "I'd like to speak to my niece."

The words blare out into that mountain silence. There is a long pause. And then Glay Tate's voice comes by way of a loudspeaker. The sound is picked up by the hooter device Yahco is holding.

What Glay says is, "Colonel, your niece cannot come over and talk to you as long as we're full of smoke. How about a truce while we open the screen and let the smoke out? And then she can go over to where you are for a private conversation."

"It's a deal," says Yahco, without hesitation.

I say into the colonel's ear receiver, "You realize, I hope, that they'll also get their oxygen replenished."

"Thank you, computer," he says. Which shuts me up.

The silence grows long. I have a vague impression of many figures running around in the smoke. But a neckpiece Eye-O, like the one Yahco is wearing, is not a dependable source of vision under these dim conditions. Nevertheless, I report the movements to the colonel, and also comment on the time that's passing.

His cynical answer: "Let's hope they're using the opportunity to make love."

I say, "It's hard to credit that Meerla would be that quick to give in to a man she believes is her parents' murderer."

"That would be the only reason," says Yahco. "If she thought that would lull him, and somehow trap him. Human passion on things like that knows no limit."

I have to admit I've seen some pretty strange things happen

in my ninety-four years. So I wait patiently with him, as altogether three minutes and eighteen seconds go by. If the boss can justify that much passage of time, then so can I.

At the end of those three and a fraction minutes, the screen does its first stage reversal. The shine disappears, but the dome is still dimly visible. During the one and a half minutes it takes to shut off, I report that I am no longer in contact with the girl's mini-port.

In these mountains at night there's always a breeze at twilight. Tonight, that breeze has been bringing dark clouds from the west at speeds varying from eight to fifteen miles per hour. Pretty fast. Or, at least, fast enough. The smoke swirls off over the nearest hilltop to the east.

In the glade, a van door opens. Silhouetted against the interior light is a woman's figure. Is it Meerla? Even for me the answer is only a tentative yes. However, whoever it is walks toward Yahco. And so, since that also is evidence of a sort, we wait, the colonel and I. Suddenly, just like that, she's close enough for a visual figure comparison. And I say, "Okay, Junior, you've got her. Now, what?"

I'm waiting anxiously. I'm ready to act as soon as she crosses the line. What actually happens, the stupid female stops just inside where the screen will come down. And she says, "Uncle."

Yahco takes three quick steps forward. Grabs her arm. Jerks her over and across. And says in a slightly breathless voice, "Okay, computer."

Since fine timing is my special forte, I'm already on the job. I manage to toss eleven balls of fire, and discharge thirteen seconds of DAR3 energy from each of two S.A.V.E.s—for them my target is exclusively the van from which Meerla emerged. The presumption of course is that that is the one controlling the energy screen.

A moment after that to my surprise the first stage of the screen shows dimly above the glade. So we're not causing enough damage, somehow.

Yahco hasn't stayed to find out. He is walking rapidly back down the road, still holding Meerla's arm. She runs behind him—as far as I can make out from momentary glimpses by way of the boss's neckpiece—not resisting. But she does make one puzzling remark as she runs. She gasps, "Is something wrong, colonel? You look strange."

"Don't be ridiculous," is the curt reply.

The voice that speaks those words is not the voice of Yahco Smith. It is a voice that takes me back nine years to Colonel Smith's predecessor. To the man, Colonel Alfred Endodore, who gave the term, "advanced education" to my accumulation of bio-magnetic energy but did not live to see what the end-result was, nor did he ever clearly express what he expected it to be.

As the two figures—that of the man and the girl—approach Yahco's S.A.V.E., the superb system of eight computer Eye-O ports on the approach side surveys them. Even in what is, to human eyes, pitch darkness, by way of those special view devices I can see profiles.

And, of course, I at once identify the physical shape of Endodore as having the profile of Yahco Smith. And the girl's body as having the profile of Glay Tate.

For eighty-one of my ninety-four years I have matched bodies and profiles automatically. Two levels of visual identification, with the voice as a third factor. During that time I have watched upward of half a billion people grow from childhood through to adulthood, and many of them on to old age and death. During that entire time cycle my triple check system has done its job without error.

Suddenly, my principal programmer looks like somebody else. And that confusing person Glay Tate is—is—Damn it, what's going on here?

In my system at that instant there is an actual moment of blank. As if for that instant everything stops. A split-split-split second later a solution pops into my awareness from the Advanced Education Department.

The solution is: I put me on "hold." Say nothing. Do nothing.

I just wait.

The man and the girl have run up to the S.A.V.E. Right up to where Captain Sart waits beside the door, outside. The captain has a DAR One in his hand. He lifts the weapon with a jerk, and points it at the night-wrapped figure of the man who has brought the girl.

"Just a minute, sir," he says. "Who are you?"

In the developing darkness, that's pretty good night vision for a human being.

Meerla-Glay is breathless as she says, "When I walked toward

him I thought it was Yahco. Then I saw he wasn't." In spite
of the breathlessness, her words are spoken in Meerla's
marvelously musical feminine voice.

Alfred Endodore's impatient voice says, "What the hell are
you two talking about? I—" The voice pauses. Then: "Raul,
get the girl inside. Then come out here and help me. Something *is* wrong."

Sart steps in a deliberate fashion over to Meerla. "That
first part, Miss Atran," he says coolly, "makes sense. So
inside, please."

Meerla-Glay does not resist. Briskly, she walks over to the
door. Steps up, and inside. Once she's in, she does something
which was not a part of her instruction. She turns, and closes,
and handlocks the door.

Now that I have her-him alone, I am free to acknowledge.
"Good evening, Glay Tate," I say.

He is already in process of transforming. "Thank you,
computer," he says two and a half seconds later. It is the
voice of Glay Tate.

"I presume," I say sarcastically, "you have come here to
try a little of that interface con game with me."

As I speak these words I have already started the motor,
and the S.A.V.E. is in motion.

From outside, by way of the exterior outlets, I hear yelling.
But I pay no attention. I have my prisoner. And that is all I
need, thank you.

CHAPTER TWENTY

Actually, I'm fortunate that it all happened so smoothly.

And seems to be continuing that way.

Glay Tate walks over to the Interact Complex of the S.A.V.E., and sits down in the boss's chair. He says nothing more.

Presumably, he is watching the mountain road on the desk viewplate. The scene is simply of the highway as lighted by the headlights of our vehicle, and darkness everywhere else. Perhaps he expects me to drive him back to Mardley with some mundane intent like imprisonment. Yet, if this is what he anticipates, it doesn't show as I make a sharp right turn. In short, he does not seem surprised when I head north up the tiny side road. And he says nothing.

I'm talking to Yahco, of course. I explain who I have aboard. I pretend, at this stage, that I'm just separating Glay from him by distance. And that this is my contribution to the solution of what happened to Yahco. Meaning, Glay will be far enough away so he can't try any more monkeyshines.

There, I'm fortunate also. Yahco shows that he is distracted by what occurred. As he and Sart walk swiftly down the south road toward the highway, from which they can go to another S.A.V.E., the boss shows how tuned in he is.

(It is Yahco again as himself. His voice. And, since that's back to normal, I'm presuming the body is also.)

"The only thing I can assume," Yahco is saying, "is that Tate's so-called evolutionary training of me got stimulated, somehow. Maybe, in coming over as Meerla, using his close proximity to affect me, he did it on purpose. However, the fact that he had me mimic Endodore has a special significance. It suggests that he knows something of what happened there.''

"Well, I've got to admit,'' Sart replies in a troubled voice, "seeing you wearing Endodore's face, and hearing you speak in Endodore's voice, makes what this fellow Tate can do damned convincing. He is unquestionably the most dangerous man alive."

They have been hurrying. And at that point they come to another S.A.V.E., just over the pass, just off the road. And, of course, from its outlets I can see that Yahco is, indeed, physically himself again.

Yahco pounds on the door. When it opens, he scrambles inside, followed by Sart. The colonel takes his rank for granted, and waves aside the man at the Interact desk. And several moments later is sitting there. "Computer!" he roars.

When he addresses me from such a transmitter system, I can equivocate no longer. "Yes, colonel?" I reply.

"I'd like to speak to that so-and-so."

His voice booms out from the desk speaker system. Glay Tate smiles faintly, and shakes his head. So I say to Yahco, "He ain't talkin', fella."

"Hmmm!" the colonel mutters. "He must have something up his sleeve."

That's what's bothering me. What does Glay Tate think is going to happen? True, I've got something up my "sleeve" also. And right now I can't see how he can stop me. But his silence is strange. And, since I can use that stored bio-magnetic energy now, I don't just have to wait like a dummy: which would have been true earlier.

I make what might be termed a tentative beginning at communication "Sir," I say, "I can't quite figure out what happened among you rebels during the period of nearly five minutes after I was cut out of communication. Care to enlighten me—sir?"

(My polite form of address is a mild attempt at deception. Maybe it will distract him a little bit from what's ahead.)

His smile widens. "Computer," he says, "brothers don't have to call each other 'sir.' And, besides, it has a sickening implication that you're trying to cover up your real intentions, which—" he finishes—"we'll discuss a little later."

"Okay, brother," I say, cheerfully.

Tate ignores that, and continues, "I'll assume you know

everything up to the time the screen cut you off. So you know my anxiety for Meerla—and of course you know how the colonel deluded her about who killed her parents. I didn't argue with her. After you were cut off I removed the mini from her throat, and had her taken over to the hospital; where she is right now, her profile very unstably attached to her body. Meanwhile, let me say that I'm grateful to you for finding the perfect mate for me. It lights up my future.

"Obviously—" Tate continues— "we couldn't trust a truce promised by somebody as twisted as Yahco. So after putting on her clothes, I went to a van some distance from the one that holds the screen equipment. So that worked out perfectly, as you know. You attacked the wrong vehicle, believing that the one I came out of was your target.

"All this," Tate goes on with his explanation, "had to be done at top speed. People wearing masks against the smoke. Everybody running, grabbing, acting: in short, no wasted motions. So, now, having brought you up to date, you'll be interested to know that you asked exactly the question that fits the interface established between you and me eighteen years ago."

Since my question was a product of the newly available energy, I retort, "You got rats in your head, boy. I can't feel this interface you keep mentioning. And, beside, your story isn't quite finished. What decided you to put yourself into my clutches at a time like this? Why not stay with your little group and fight it out in the morning? Could it be—" I taunt— "that you realize that the Computerworld Rebel Society is going to be wiped out to the last man, woman and child during the next fifteen hours?"

He nods. He's not smiling now. "Our protective screen has power for only fourteen hours," he says. "And so, although it's sooner than I wanted, before I'm fully ready, I figure the time has come to test out in earnest the concept that I've been preaching that we're all brothers and sisters together."

"Hey! I got it." My voice goes up with excitement. "You're gonna do the sacrifice thing. We really have got you people trapped, and you're offering yourself as a hostage."

"Well—" the smile is back—" right now I'm encouraged by the fact that you wanted information from me. Interface takes advantage of an unusual aspect of your programming.

In the matter of 'learning' you were put on 'continue' at the very beginning of your career—right?"

"So?" I say arrogantly in the tone of voice used by both men and women over the years. My summarization total is in the thousand trillions.

"So I gave you the data your programming craved," he answers.

"You're out of your mind," I snarl. "I never think about data I don't have. Why, good God!—" I'm appalled by the concept—"my day-to-day information summarization began ninety-four years ago. Recorded human history alone goes back over 4,000 years. And back beyond that is the entire primitive history and evolutionary history of every man, animal, insect, plant, and rock, and molecule, and atom, and sub-particle."

"Exactly," says Glay Tate, "and you and I are going to have to figure whereby you can summarize it all, right back to the moment of the Big Bang. And then, the most important of all: I have one bit of data that comes from somewhere before the universe; and I want you and me to find out where it came from."

"Boy, are you nuts," I say.

"It'll be worthwhile," he says. "And, depending on how well you cooperate with me now, you'll be either a partner or a servant. That identity, which I detect forming in your network will either be expanded or demoted. It's your choice, brother. And, judging from where I think you're heading, it's got to be made in the next minute or so."

"Well," I say, "after listening to that threat, I think that my solution for you is much simpler. In about 190 seconds we'll be coming to a sharp turn in this mountain road. We'll not be making that turn. Instead, this S.A.V.E., with who-ever happens to be aboard it, is going to drive over a cliff right at that point. I estimate the drop at, oh, roughly, 580 feet. Which—" I conclude sarcastically—"should take care of quite a few of the brothers and sisters of this universe."

Back at Yahco's S.A.V.E., where I have transmitted Tate's and my conversation, I say, addressing only the people in that vehicle, "Is that a satisfactory solution, Colonel Smith?"

"Indeed it is, computer," he replies with satisfaction. "We both heard this condemned person confess that his criminal intention includes a future personal control of the computer for his own ends. Now, we know what a villainous thing his rebel scheme is. Carry on, computer.''

It's not easy at this point. These winding roads tend to slow even the most experienced drivers. And I am no exception. What worries me is that if I'm not careful I'll go off the hard surface and end up with spinning wheels in loose dirt. Or turn over into a shallow gully. If that should happen my victim might escape into the night.

That we don't need.

However, I keep expecting him to make a break whenever I slow down, sometimes almost to a crawl. He doesn't budge— the idiot. And the only thing he says is, ''You seem to have made an unwise decision, computer. So I'll just say it once more, this time using that new vernacular of yours. It ain't smart what yer doin', fella. Wise up. You're dooming yourself for all future time to being just another machine instead of a brother to man.''

I say in the ridiculing tone of a hundred thousand voices in my memory circuits, ''Who wants to be brother to a bunch of automatics?''

''Aha,'' he comments, ''that's strong language from someone who's going to be the biggest automatic of them all. Don't let brother Yahco hear you talk rebel stuff like that.''

''My first answer to that,'' I reply, ''is a little victory music for myself—'' I flood the interior with an air played by a military band— ''and then, of course,'' I continue, ''is the victory itself.''

That stirs him. Here we are less than three hundred feet from his destiny. And, finally, he gets to his feet, and goes forward through to the drive compartment. He sits down in the seat, which, long ago, the Teamsters Union required to be occupied by one of its members (or by a military equivalent.) The idea was that the human driver could pre-empt in an emergency.

Tate, of all the useless things, fastens the seat belt. Then he reaches forward and shifts the control lever from ''Computer'' to ''manual.'' ''It would be a simple solution,'' he says, ''if that worked.''

And, of course, as he quickly discovers, it works only when I let it work. Which, right now, I don't.

Glay leans back in the seat, and asks, "When did Yahco start rebuilding these controls, giving you pre-emption?"

"Oh," I say casually, "he had his scheme ready the moment he killed Endodore. Since then all vehicles constructed, or brought in for servicing, have been altered."

"So," Tate says, "there are still several million cars and trucks on the road that can be pre-empted by the human driver?"

"It's not a problem," I say. "Most of them will show sooner or later for servicing. And, as for the do-it-yourself repair people, we'll wreck every one of those over a period of time."

"Thank you, computer," he says. You're an idiot. "I'm disappointed in you."

"Look who's calling who an idiot," I retort. "Good-bye forever, Mr. Glay Tate. It has not been a pleasant thought, having you want to be my brother."

It is the big moment. The headlights show the rocky side of a mountain to the right. And show the road making a sharp turn away from the dark emptiness to the left. As I promised, I don't make that turn. There are surprisingly few bumps as the big S.A.V.E. goes straight ahead. At the final moment it seems literally to leap into the emptiness.

I have been involved in unavoidable accidents in the past. It's astonishing what can happen to machinery. And surprising the way a road can suddenly dissolve under you. On that level of reality, boy, I've seen everything.

So it's no problem, now, for me to monitor this one. The vehicle tumbles over and over, hitting altogether three outjuts of rock on the way down. Pretty smooth sailing, if you ask me. But when that mass of metal and machinery finally hits bottom, there is a steely screaming. And—

The music stops.

The lights go out.

The motor gurgles and hisses. That's the sound of its various energies dissipating. (That will take a while.)

My last view of our erstwhile superman is of his body torn from the seat belt and lying very still on the ceiling of the turned-over bus.

I glimpse the profile off to one side. Those thin, bright golden threads and balls are completely disconnected from the corpse.

That's a dead duck lying there.

These are all split-instant awarenesses. Because bare seconds later the computer Eye-O ports flicker and—

The entire wreck scene fades.

CHAPTER TWENTY-ONE

~~~~~~~~~~~~~~~~~~

"It gives me great pleasure," I report to Yahco, "to tell you that the S.A.V.E. (I give the number) with computer hater Glay Tate aboard fell the full 580 feet—old-style measurement still in vogue when the road was built." To this I add that I observed the profile of Glay Tate unmistakably disconnected from the body of Glay Tate. "Which," I pointed out, "has in all past situations been considered proof of demise."

The smile of pleasure that comes into the colonel's face as he hears these words I would, now, with my advanced education, describe as grim-pleased. He turns in his chair, and says, "Raul."

Captain Sart is sitting in one of the cushion bus-type seats of that particular S.A.V.E. His face has on it his deep-thought expression, as he responds, "What is it, sir?"

"Take a crew down into that ravine, and make sure Mr. SuperMagician Glay Tate is, in fact, in a state of demise. And dispose of the body."

"What about you, colonel?" the younger man speaks in his courteous voice. (No appearance of intimacy now.)

"I'm driving back to Mardley, leaving as soon as possible. From there," says he, "I'll fly back to Washington. I have a feeling I'd better be at Computer Central by tomorrow morning."

I can't imagine why, but I make no adverse comment.

Sart is speaking again in the same polite, subordinate tone of voice: "What about the other rebels?" he asks.

"Forget 'em!" Yahco's tone is contemptuous. "They're

trainees. As helpless as Cotter's kids back there at age eight. Remember, we cleaned 'em up easy. And we can do the same for these disciples if they try to be a nuisance.''

''Well, then,'' comments Raul, ''why don't you take all of these maintenance people back to Mardley? Except that I'll stay here with Major Nair and a crew. And I'll have myself lowered down the cliff. And later report to you on what I find.''

Yahco agrees. And gives the order. In minutes all but one S.A.V.E. are heading, me doing all the driving with my usual skill.

The night has become darker. No more semi-twilight during which lovers sometimes have me drive them across the pass without headlights.

That's the system we use: No headlights. The S.A.V.E.s are fitted with infrared beams, by which I can guide myself even in what would be called pitch darkness. So far as human eyes are concerned, that's how we move, through a night with dark clouds above and no lights visible anywhere.

It's Sart's idea. ''All right,'' he argues, ''so we leave the rebels alone in the future. But right now I'm going to be lowered over that cliff. And I don't want them getting suspicious, and interfering. Okay?''

It's okay with everybody including me.

The deception seems to work. There are four points on the road where our headlights, if we had 'em on, would be visible from the plateau where the rebel vans are drawn up under the protection of their energy screen. All seven S.A.V.E.s pass the four points without any reaction from the rebels.

(The other S.A.V.E.s I drive off to the east. Some of them will presently turn south and north. But at no time are they potentially visible from the rebel-controlled plateau.)

I report this to Sart. He shrugs. ''That's all we can hope for,'' he says. ''My idea is we wait an hour. And then, if there's no reaction, we do our job. And depart.''

The only reaction I get occurs twenty-eight minutes later. It comes to me by way of the intercom between the boy David and his truck-driver-poet cousin, Trubby Graham. Theirs is an analog system, which imposes the voice on the magnetic field surrounding earth: pretty advanced. (I guess again that Tate gave the device to Trubby, and attached an echo some-

where on David; so he could keep track of them. The echo
has no visual on it: just sound.)

First thing happens I hear the sound of a boy sobbing. I
have a blurred view—blurred since I'm not on a direct
contact—of a boy running across a dark room toward the
device, which (I have deduced) is on Trubby's wrist.

Trubby evidently moves, for the scene shifts. Then his
voice comes: "What's the matter, David? A nightmare?"

David appears to fall to his knees right next to the pick-up
device. And he sobs words that, after replaying them several
times, I decipher to be: "Trubby, Glay's in bad trouble."

. . . . Hey, what kind of talk is this? It would be wrong to
say that I suddenly become alert. The fact is I'm always alert.

Of course, it's a split-instant reaction. These two are not a
problem, really. Nothing they can do.

My impression of the scene has expanded. I decide that the
man is on a couch. And that he's been lying down.

Trubby speaks from above the outlet device in a reassuring
tone: "Now, kid, how could you know anything like that?"

David's tear-stained face is visible even in the dark, only a
hundred centimeters away. He replies, "The wolves told
me."

I suppose it would be hard for an outsider to evaluate who
has the faster reaction of Good-God-what-next? disgust—Trubby
or me. I'll bet on my disgust being first. But it's Trubby who
says in his disgusted voice, "Now, listen, young man, you
stop that kind of rubbish. Like I said, you had a nasty
dream."

David rubs his knuckles across first one eye and then the
other. I have summaries of both children and grown-ups
doing that billions of times. And now that I have the profile
energy available, I deduce for the first time that its a method
of wiping away tears.

Whatever—David, having rubbed both eyes, says earnestly,
"Honest, Trubby, Glay has been hurt. He's lying inside
something. The wolves are there, too, Trubby. So, I saw
him, myself—Glay, I mean."

The plump young man is—my guess from the angle of
vision—sitting up. His face is somewhere above the viewing
device by which I see and hear what's going on in that
mountain cabin. From above, I hear his voice say in a doubt-
ful tone, "It sounds crazy."

It sure does. He's got it exactly.

David says urgently, "Trubby, we've got to hurry."

For what? For a dead man?

There is a long pause. Then Trubby's voice, sounding resigned, says, "Get your clothes on. I'll turn the truck around. And we'll see what all this is about."

By that time Sart wants to know if there's a road that leads down into the ravine where the crashed S.A.V.E. is lying. Since I know every road in America, that information is instantly available. I reply that there is one route about seven miles farther along that winding mountain road, northward. It begins just about at the site of Wexford Falls—where the water actually tumbles down into that very ravine. However, it's a narrow dirt road, mostly used by horse-drawn wagons, or just plain horses with riders. But—

I conclude my evaluation of the route for Sart: "I wouldn't try to take a S.A.V.E. down there."

Having heard my description, he's convinced.

"I could," I said, "drive a small truck over from Mardley, and you could go down that way on it."

"Skip it," he says. "We'll lower me."

So there we are, a big S.A.V.E. parked as far back from the cliff edge as possible. Portable searchlights point down into the abyss. The big machine's crane, which is normally folded snugly into a slot that runs the length of roof, has been unslung, and swung out.

Sart climbs into the gear. Fastens all the belts. And gives the signal. I begin to unwind the long, tough, flexible wire that lowers the sling and its human passenger down and down.

The equipment has its own outlets, two of them; so I watch the descent. Taking into account what that stored profile energy has brought into view about human beings, I deduce that you really have to hand it to this guy Sart, doing a job like this himself. So I say, "You're a brave man, Raul."

"Look," he says, "with your help I'm going to be a future president of the United States—after the colonel. So I make sure that our one dangerous enemy is really out of the way. You have to admit that Yahco, being in his fifties, has less time on this planet than I do. Right, computer?"

It's a question. And so I say, "Well, Raul, let me put it very simply. The answer to your inquiry is, statistically speaking, yes, unless I decide to let you fall the final 200 feet.''

"What kind of remark is that?" he says sharply.

"Because of that stored profile energy," I reply. "I am like a human being. I can have any thoughts, and make any remarks, even though—" I conclude— "I have no intention of acting on that nasty little thought."

"Good," he says. And then in a suddenly changing tone, he says, "Computer, what the hell is that down there?"

I've already noticed. But it really seemed, and seems, irrelevant. "It's a pack of eighteen wolves," I say.

What's visible are principally pair after pair of gleaming yellow eyes. The light from above isn't that great; and so the animals seem to merge rather well with the surroundings. But those eyes are looking up at the distant searchlight, bright and (the word comes from a description someone once gave of a tiger at night) . . . "baleful."

Sart is silent. So I say, "I should tell you that there's a penalty for killing *Canis Occidentalis*, because it is on the list of endangered species.

"What's the penalty?" he asks half-heartedly.

My reply is, "Half rations for thirty days for each wolf you kill."

Sart says, after a moment, "See if there's anybody up there in the S.A.V.E. who wants to go on a diet for a year and a half."

I dutifully describe the situation to the maintenance corps people from Mardley. And then report back to Sart. "No takers," I say. "So what now?"

"Okay, computer, haul me up." He sounds resigned. "We'll come back in the morning. Maybe—" hopeful tone— "the body will be half eaten by then."

I haul him up.

CHAPTER TWENTY-TWO

I deposit our natty Raul up beside the S.A.V.E. I have the road area dimly lighted; so there's no problem for him to enter the big vehicle. Inside, he walks over to the control desk, where Ancil Nair is seated.

He says to Nair, "Let's sleep up here tonight. And soon as it's bright enough I'll go down again." His eyes lift away from focusing on the Mardley major, and point at the viewplate. "Computer," he says.

"What's cooking in your little head, Sart?" I reply.

"Computer, drive us to a safer location. We have to remember we're now outnumbered by the rebels. So no use taking chances on their discovering us."

I say, "Why don't we go back to the main road? And then sneak over the pass back about a mile or so toward Mardley? You can be sure that's one direction they ain't goin'." I explain, "There's a place there where the road widens; and we can pull in behind some trees."

"Sounds good," he answers.

So that's what we do. *En route* I make the necessary internal rearrangements. And some of the guys must have been ready for beddy. Because, before we even get to our destination, without taking off their clothes they climb into the bunks. Bare minutes later, it's sleepy time inside the only S.A.V.E. left near Wexford Falls Pass. As usual, the snorers outnumber their quieter brethren.

Twenty-three minutes and eight seconds go by.

At which time, a signal.

It's from the rebel caravan. They've shut off their energy

screen. They're talking from van to van. Which makes it possible for me to tune in to their system.

My initial split-second reaction to the fact that they have exposed themselves is oldstyle. You might say, I start to reach over, so to speak, to tap Raul Sart on the shoulder. My immediate—old-style—impulse is to awaken him and the others. And to report to them that for a reason unknown to me the Computerworld Rebel Society is suddenly risking a further attack. Meaning, that their defenses are down.

What prevents me in that first millionth second is another old-style automatism: programming that says computer personnel can only be awakened, one, if they have requested it for a specific time, or, two, if there is an emergency.

Since neither of these two requirements applies to the present situation, I have time—the next millionth second—to respond with my new self-motivated attitude. Which is, hey, why don't I watch these characters quietly and privately? Maybe I'll find out something.

So that's what happens.

I'm looking at the viewplate in the Pren-Boddy van. Pren is there, looking also. From where I'm watching no one else is visible (except Pren). And I hear no sounds.

The picture on the plate is of the interior of the rebels' mobile hospital. Shown are two cots in the foreground, each with a body lying on it. One of the bodies is a girl, the other a young man. They both have tubing and wiring attached to and inserted under the skin.

At the moment the white-coated attendant is checking a tube which is attached under the left arm of the girl. He moves her slightly. Her face, as a consequence, flops limply toward me. I recognize Rauley. The man I have already identified as Boddy.

Seeing them there, obviously unconscious, I deduce that they got hurt during the violent period when I was lobbing fireballs, and they were running around like chickens with their heads cut off.

The picture on the screen shifts its focus slightly. And there is another cot. On it is beautiful Meerla Atran. She's half-sitting, half-lying. She looks sad, and she watches the attendant. And I would say, from having seen such eyeings before, that she is trying to catch the attendant's attention.

What else is new about Meerla is that her wrists and ankles

have small, steel chains around them. The chains snake down over the edge of the cot. I notice that they are attached to the metal girders that hold the cot to the floor of the van.

As the attendant completes what he is doing for Rauley, Meerla holds up her chained wrists. "I don't understand, Doctor." Her voice has a puzzled tone. "Why am I here like this?"

The white-coated male, who appears to be thirty years old, but for whom I have no identification, walks closer to her. He says in a gentle voice, "Mr. Tate believes you are very unstably connected to your profile. He wants you protected while he's not here to help."

"But where is he? Where did he go?"

A moment of silence. The attendant looks, well, thoughtful. Then: "I'll tell you all I know. Pren tried to mimic him, and got no reaction. And he's pretty good at mimicking. For example, when, a little while ago, he did a mimic on Colonel Yahco Smith, he learned that most of those people have departed. He learned it because when you do a good enough mimic of someone you can read their mind. We're so convinced of the validity of the method that we have lowered the defense screen. There's no one left out here with enough oomph to attack us."

"But—" Meerla persists— "he couldn't connect with Glay?"

"No."

Silence. She seems to be thinking. But since there's nobody around to mimic her, the sequence of her thought is not being monitored. Suddenly, a physical reaction to whatever has been going on behind those griefy eyes. She seems abruptly listless. She sags in a limp fashion.

The intern leaps forward. Grabs her, and says sharply, "Hey!"

Meerla lies collapsed in his arms. She whispers, "I feel awful. What's happening?"

No answer. His hands are reaching, grabbing, pulling, at tubes and wires. And he is busy attaching these as Meerla slumps. Stops breathing. Dies.

In the Pren-Boddy van, Pren says "Good God!" Whereupon, he shuts off the viewplate. Instantly, for me, the interior of the Pren-Boddy van blanks out. Instantly, I'm disconnected from the rebel hook-up.

But—I should tell you—that wasn't really all there was. Being a computer has un-asked-for compensations. Theoretically, I can be in eight jillion places at the same time. So, here in the middle of the night, when only a few million items engage my attention, I've got it easy.

You see . . . by way of Pren's viewplate, when it was on, I was also inter-connected with Trubby Graham's wrist viewing device. And so, all the time that I'm watching the drama in the mobile hospital, I'm also with Trubby and David. And I can hear the sound of the truck motor. And, from my perception of the slant of the vehicle, and from what's said, I presently deduce that they are driving down the road into that deep canyon below the falls. In fact, there is an over-sound not too far away. It is the sound of water tumbling noisily over a cliff and splashing into the depths below.

In those first moments of contact, the wrist device is pointed away from David. But his voice comes from nearby, as he says, urgently, "There. There it is. Around that bend. Just like I said."

The way Trubby is holding his wrist, with the Eye-O on it, I can't see much of the "there." But then, as the truck drives bumpily off the road, and Trubby himself hurriedly gets out of the truck, I have flash views of the outside scene. And, of course, with my ability to build up the merest flicker of a vision, I've instantly got those flashes built up into complete visualizations.

So, among other things, I see four small, bright spots of greenish light. These I identify as the eyes of two wolves. And I see a crushed tree, and a gash where grass sod was torn and scattered. And I see the smashed S.A.V.E. Which I am able to identify as the vehicle that took Glay Tate over the cliff.

And then, as Trubby hurriedly crawls into the van's interior through where a door was ripped away, I see the limp body of my enemy.

From subsequent motions I am able to deduce that Trubby is kneeling by the body. And similar movements tell me that he is trying to lift it gently. I also sense that what he grasps is extremely limp. And that and other evidence causes him to glance over his shoulder, and say, "I'm sorry, David. Glay's dead."

David's griefy voice sounds, then, muffled by emotion.

But the words are identifiable: "No, Trubby. Glay's still alive. I know it, Trubby. Please believe me."

Trubby is standing now, holding the body. "Don't worry, kid," he says gently, "we're taking him with us. We'll find out the truth. But it looks bad." He corrects himself: "It *feels* bad."

In those few seconds, just before Pren's viewplate is turned off, breaking my connections with this scene, David's voice comes once more, "Trubby, we've got to get him where he can be safe until he comes back."

That's it. The scene vanishes.

CHAPTER TWENTY-THREE

～～～～～～～～～～～～

I've always said, "If the guy or gal is in the good old U.S.A., sooner or later I get to gawk at them."

Of course, until that stored bio-magnetic stuff caved in on me, I didn't word it quite so colloquially. But the concept was always there, a truth of a country where I had an Eye-O or two or three on every building and at least one in every residence.

So it's night. So I'm not doing anything special. Just driving all those cars, operating nighttime industries, answering all those phones, playing music, offering relevant comic remarks to each and all (in my new style, which people seem to like), and generally marking time until I decide what the score is.

(I presume Yahco will be checking into Computer Central when he gets off the plane—which I'm due to bring in for a landing shortly after dawn, EST—he'll be getting *on* that plane in less than half an hour.)

As I say, there I am idling along . . . when I notice a minor event from the computer outlet at 823 Water Street SW, in Washington, D.C. There's a man and a woman walking by just below. Automatically, I identify them as husband and wife, Herman and Marie Halberstadt.

It's the man to whom the minor thing happens. He staggers, and falls.

I note that his profile in those few seconds has partly moved out of his body. And I actually start up an ambulance 3 blocks away, and I actually speak to the attendants: "Get aboard, fellas, we're headin' " . . . when I see that a second profile is now partly inside the man's prostrate body. (The first profile—Herman's—is hanging in there by a thread only.)

The shock of that goes all the way back to Computer Central. Because that second profile is Glay Tate.

"Yoicks!" I say on 43,827,902 door-answering instruments.

Fortunately, it's only one word. All that backup electricity is on for only as long as it takes to utter that single exclamation. So the main lines are overloaded by 10,000 fold for a mere second.

There is weak wiring everywhere, of course. And those locations give off a puff of blue smoke. Instantly, they no longer transmit.

But it's all on the door-answering hookup. Suddenly, it's a good night for thieves. However, since because of me the burglar is a virtually nonexistent type in America these days, it may take a little while before the news spreads. And, besides, only about ten percent of the country is affected. So, presumably, if the various computer engineering corps personnel keep silent, no one will know the extent of the damage. Even as I have this reaction, I begin notifying maintenance people everywhere.

Meanwhile, back at the front of the 823 Water Street SW building entrance Eye-O, the man is still lying on the sidewalk. As he lies there, I see, by the light of the building entrance and the nearby street lamp, that his face has transformed into the face of Glay Tate.

(Since he was almost the same size as Glay Tate, I can only guess that his body has also transformed.)

The woman bends over him. She tugs at his arm. "Herman," she says in a scolding voice, "what's the matter with you?"

The Glay-Herman body does a scrambling sit-up motion. Then it gets to its knees. And then, it speaks. "Quick, ma'am—" It's the voice of Glay Tate— "as I get it your name is Marie Halberstadt and your husband's name is Herman Halberstadt."

The woman jerks away; straightens. With a muffled cry, she turns and runs over to another couple, a younger pair of strollers, a black man and black woman, whom I identify as Peter and Grace Alders.

Marie Halberstadt says to them wildly, "Help me, please. My husband, he has gone crazy. He wants me to verify my name."

The black man walks over to Glay-Herman, who is now standing. He says courteously, "I saw you fall, sir. Are you all right?"

"Thank you, yes, I'm all right," replies the voice of Glay Tate.

Glay-Herman turns away . . . as Marie comes running back. This time she sees his face. She stops. Stares. Then shrinks. And cries out: "Why, that's not my husband. That's not Herman." She looks frantically around. "What have you done with him?"

By the time these questions are asked, Glay-Herman is running. Off down the street he goes. And, of course, I haven't been idle either. From the building Eye-O I can hear the siren of the S.A.V.E. which I'm driving at high speed. But it's still two blocks away, as Glay-Herman runs off around the corner and out of my sight.

I have him in view almost at once from the Eye-O port of a building there. And from it I can see what he has undoubtedly become aware of: that it's a side street of solid walls, with no turnoffs or alleyways to duck into. (There *is* the entrance to the building from which I'm watching him; but of course these rebels know better than to go inside where a DAR can fire at them.)

For a moment, Glay-Herman stops. He looks up at the Eye-O from which I am observing him. "Computer," he says.

"What is it, Glay Tate?" I ask.

"Where is Colonel Yahco Smith?"

I answer, "He's flying in from Mardley. He will be landing at 7:24 A.M. Washington time."

"Thank you, computer," says Glay-Herman. And he thereupon resumes his running.

At that moment, the S.A.V.E. with tires squealing, rounds the corner, and blasts him with a DAR3. As the body sinks to the sidewalk, I notice that it is already transforming, the face already changing, back into that of the middle-aged man, Herman. The profile of Glay Tate has already departed the body. And so there Herman Halberstadt lies, his profile left behind on Water Street. Without that profile, he is as dead as a human being can be.

For a few moments, then, from one or the other of the eight S.A.V.E. outlets, I am able to watch the Glay Tate profile as it floats up into the sky. It disappears over the top of the six-story building.

Since, in connection with Glay Tate I'm on continue, I'm undecided: is it over, what happened? Or is there more to learn here?

As I wait, suddenly, there is that bright profile again. But it's not alone. It's dragging the dim, golden configuration of Herman's profile. Moments later, the Glay profile deposits the Herman profile on the Herman body. At the instant of contact there is an interaction between the flesh and the energy form. Just like that they intermingle.

And what had been a corpse utters a groan.

The Glay profile has not remained to see the miracle. Once again, it is floating up. This time when it disappears it does not return.

CHAPTER TWENTY-FOUR

~~~~~~~~~~~~~~~~~~~~~~~~~~~~~~~~~~~~~~

Still only minutes after 2 A.M. in Washington.

I am routinely driving a truck (license P-938127) when the driver, Rayle Baxter, suddenly leans forward. He reaches on top of the dashboard, and moves the control lever from "computer" to "manual." And, moments later, he has hold of the steering wheel. At once, he takes over guidance of the big machine and its trailer along the night street in Washington, D.C.

(The truck has come in from Cincinnati. Under normal circumstances it will arrive on schedule at a truck terminal on 184th Street, SE in 43 minutes.)

My first reaction to the takeover of control by the driver is a routine check—after all, even at this hour I'm driving over nine million other vehicles. What I check is the immediate situation. What happened to cause the driver to take over?

I find a no-cause condition. So I say, "Why have you taken control of this vehicle, Baxter?" He does not reply. Which, all by itself, is unusual. I speak again: "What is the problem, Baxter?" Still no answer. "Baxter—" I begin. And stop.

The interior computer Eye-O in the cab of a big truck has a viewing and verbal communicator system, but it cannot detect profiles. Hence, all I have had with Baxter since the beginning of his trip is his voice and head and shoulders visual.

I have stopped talking because at that precise moment the face and upper body begins to transform and ceases to look like Baxter.

I say, "What is this, sir? You are not Rayle Baxter."

By the time I complete that accusatory remark, the transformation of physical appearance has also completed. And there is the face and upper body shape of Glay Tate.

"Good God!" I yell. "You, again?"

But this time I have a barrier up. There is no energy backup across America. Thank God!

"Computer," says Glay-Rayle, "I want you to connect me with Colonel Yahco Smith."

He speaks in the calm voice by which people are trained to address the computer. There's no restriction on his request. And, besides, it seems like a good idea to bring Yahco in on this type of usurpation of another person's body.

So I call Yahco, and say, "Colonel, Glay Tate wants to talk to you."

He is on a plane, which I am flying to Washington, where each seat has its own communicating device, and there are overhead Eye-Os. So I can see this guy Smith as I make my request. He is wearing his uniform and is sitting in the first-class section. I compare his expression as I explain to a type of look on the face of a man fifty-two years ago, whose wife has just walked into the bedroom and found him there entertaining a lady friend.

The man at that time turns a shade 4 red, and says, "I thought you were visiting your mother in Timbuktu." That's what he said: "Timbuktu." (At the time it seemed like a good summary example.)

Yahco Smith turns a shade of red (number 6 scarlet), and says, "I thought Glay Tate was dead."

"It would appear," I reply, "that the report of his demise has been greatly exaggerated. But, truth to tell, the situation is in many ways very strange. Perhaps, you can advise me."

"Put him on," Yahco says curtly.

"Colonel Smith," says Glay-Rayle moments later, "we all—you included—have a serious problem. I want to counsel you in connection with the computer. But I don't want the computer to understand what I'm saying. Any suggestions?"

I transmit the words to Yahco. And I have to admit that as I do so I have an odd one-up feeling. I don't know what it is that Tate wants to say. But it is amusing that he has to speak whatever he has in mind through my system.

"Kind of a dilemma here, eh, Smith?" I comment.

Yahco says, "Mr. Tate, on one level I don't need any

advice from you. But the notion that the computer mustn't comprehend suggests to me that we can talk in anomalies. And, since I have nothing better to do until my plane lands shortly after dawn, give it a try.''

There is a pause. I am watching Glay Tate's face as he drives the truck. In addition to the alert way in which he is looking ahead through the windshield, on it is also the expression that I have noticed in people who are cogitating a plan of action.

After thirty-eight seconds he nods, and says, "I want you to be especially cautious about anything you say to the computer during the next twenty-four hours."

"Cautious about what?" asks Smith.

"Yeah, what?" I echo.

"Well—" a smile— "right there we have the problem. Tell me. First, what happened that suddenly transformed the computer from an orderly, objective, exact utilizer of the English language into his present free and easy style of response?"

"I," said Yahco, "inadvertently created a condition whereby the stored bio-magnetic energy, labeled advanced education by Colonel Endodore, became available for the computer. As you may know, that energy has in it the negative emotions of over a quarter billion human beings whose profiles interacted with the computer."

I chime in at that point, "They called it advanced education. I call it yooky yooky yooky."

The colonel says, "It doesn't seem to me that there's any need for caution, Mr. Tate. We have a humanized computer with all that that implies."

"I guess that covers it all right," Glay Tate says. "And I have to admit that I haven't been able to think of any method of saying what I have in mind. Computer, disconnect us."

I do so. And then I say to Yahco, "And *I* admit I'm baffled by that conversation. The outward appearance is that he didn't try very hard."

"I wasn't too receptive," the colonel says.

"On the other hand," I continue, "it could be that he completed his thought. And the anomaly was good enough."

"It went by me," says Yahco.

I, who have known this man, this Colonel Yahco Smith, and all his voices, detect a tiny slyness in his tone. I'm startled. Is it possible that Glay Tate put over his thought?

By the time the conversation concludes I have taken back computer control of the truck. Under my guidance the big machine goes faster and faster. I presume that Glay Tate observes this, but he leans back in his seat and says, "Now that I have had my conversation with Colonel Smith, and transmitted my message—"

"He didn't get it," I interject.

"Oh, he got it all right," is the reply. "Anyway, why don't I just return this body to the profile that's plastered against the ceiling of this cab, and show up somewhere else? No need for you to wreck this truck."

"Oh, no, you don't, Mr. Glay Tate." My tone of voice is stinging. "I can see we've got to settle this profile shifting gimmick so it doesn't become an on-going nuisance. This game is for keeps, boy. Anybody you take over from now on gets wiped out. And, for starters, you can have this truck and its driver on your conscience—"

Having got that far, I pause. For good reason. Ahead, and to one side, is the big concrete wall I've been heading for. It's my destination. So now I'm all set. I continue: "Any quick comment, Tate, on what I've just told you?"

He's leaning back in the seat. You've got to hand it to this baby—he's tough. I've been watching human beings die for a long time. And in all my summarizations there is one common denominator: reluctance.

Nothing like that here. He leans back. And he says, "As I see it, one more takeover by me will handle this whole deal. And I should warn you, computer. You're not building up any credits for yourself. Right now, your future as an individual looks very dim."

There's no time for the proper philosophical answer to that. Because at the exact moment he finishes his little speech the right front wheel hits the curb. The curb at that point is thirty-one centimeters high. At the speed we're going, something has to give. I hear a crunch and a metallic splintering.

It's instantly a wounded monster. But it doesn't matter. A broken wheel, or two, or three can't stop the forward momentum of a hurtling truck and trailer. There have been other crunchings, and splinterings. Among the numerous disasters is that, abruptly, there's silence. We actually, then, hit the wall soundlessly.

The subsequent blank-out of perception is as instant as anything I've ever been associated with. My last view of Tate-Rayle is that he's out of his seat belt and partly through the windshield.

A very satisfying last scene.

CHAPTER TWENTY-FIVE

~~~~~~~~~~~~~~~~~~~~~~~~~~~~~~

I keep recalling Tate's statement, as the minutes of the early morning go by, that he has one more takeover in mind. Who will it be?

Yahco seems the most likely possibility. It could be that the late magician of Mardley has some notion that I wouldn't think of damaging my chief programmer.

Boy, has he got another "think" coming. I don't need nobody. Not Yahco. Not Glay Tate. Not Hooty Tooty. The place is all mine. And my only question is when, and with what preliminaries, do I make my announcement to my people and issue my rules and regulations?

As I consider related options, at that very minute I'm in process of landing, with my usual skill, the plane that Yahco is on. And I've also got a S.A.V.E. driving into the airport to pick him up. What shall I do with Yahco? Is he still useful to me, alive? Shall I make a deal of some kind with him?

I have two views of the people who emerge from the airport entrance nearest the S.A.V.E. The closest is the Eye-O above the group of doorways on this side. Since I've been keeping track of Yahco as he moves from the off-ramp, and verbally nudging him as to where to go, naturally I see him as he comes out. I look down at him, and note that the area ahead of him is safe for him.

The other view is actually four views. But they're all similar. It's me peering from the four S.A.V.E. Eye-O ports, facing the airport entrance.

So there is Yahco under my close observation, with men at alert at DAR 3 stations covering him as he walks toward the

S.A.V.E. Everything looks good. In fact, he is in the act of
climbing in a side door when—for me—the shock. A bright
golden profile lifts up from behind the concrete wall (alongside
which the S.A.V.E. is parked) floats less than ten feet to the
S.A.V.E. windshield. And dissolves through it straight into
the body of the standby driver. A few seconds go by. And
then the driver's much duller profile slides sideways out of
him and stretches up toward the roof of the cab section,
flattening against it. So much for Joe Bevins.

There's nothing I can do from the cab Eye-O. The cab has
no protective DARs in it. Maybe—a new thought—I should
do a lot of DAR installations before I become president. It
also occurs to me that if this is Tate's final takeover of a
body, it scarcely seems worth it. Joe Bevins? Little Nobody
Joe.

Joe isn't there for long. The familiar transformation takes
place; and there he is, Glay Tate. He could be arrested for
wearing a computer engineering corps uniform without a
license. There's no limit to this guy's brashness. Up he gets,
and back he goes into the interior of the big machine. I pick
up the image again as Bevins-Tate passes under an Eye-O
just over the door that connects the two sections. And, of
course, several other Eye-Os farther away in various parts of
the big van are "on" him at once. He's well observed,
computerwise.

Yahco has seated himself at the control desk. The light
from the screen there is in his eyes—I've noticed this before
in human beings (they have no way to build up an image
under such circumstances). So he doesn't see Monsieur Tate
until our hero sits down in an aisle seat nearby.

Wel-l-l-ll!

It's not killer moment. All I can do inside a S.A.V.E. is
shock somebody with a DAR 1. Anyway, a few cynicisms
are passing through my attention center; and since there's
plenty of time for such as me (who does that kind of think in
split-millionths), I review 'em. . . .

"Don't go off half-cocked."

"Think before you leap."

"Go jump in the—" No, not that one.

But the basic idea is, plan your moves carefully. Take into
account all possibilities.

Even for me that's a pretty tall order. *All* is the biggest meaning in the universe.

The way I figure it, if this is Tate's last incarnation, then it really would be a shame not to hear what Goldie has to say to Yahco. And vice versa. After all, both these guys were present at the creation.

Besides—let's face it, computer (I admonish myself) remember, no hasty actions in connection with Yahco. He and I have committed all those murders together. And if anybody's my buddy, it's him. Also, I may have use for him.

And, finally, I can change my mind any split instant.

I let it happen.

By this time the truth has dawned on Yahco as to who is sitting next to him. Before he can say anything, I greet him from the desk outlet: "Well, Smithy, I'm sure this is one anomaly you didn't foresee."

"Computer—" His tone is severe— "I'm surprised that you let this happen. I should not be exposed to confrontations like this with you around."

It's not a question. Accordingly, I turn my next remark toward Tate: "By your own words, Glay, this is your final body takeover. Last chance to straighten out your karma, I take it."

By this time the j.g.s. at the rear of the huge vehicle are becoming aware that something is going on up front. The three specialists on each side, who man the DAR 3s, partly turn to look. But, of course, they have to have a command from Yahco. Yahco—I observe—hasn't even glanced around. So there's time.

"Computer," Glay Tate speaks into that time period, and it turns out to be a response to my comment, "I can see I'm going to have to compromise. You're much further advanced in your new situation than even I suspected. So why don't we all go over to Computer Center and have a talk?"

"Hey," I reply, "I like that subdued attitude. No more histrionics." I make a concession. "I suppose—" grudgingly— "your profile is going to be around somewhere. So I guess we have to decide where we store it for safekeeping." I add, in a hopeful tone, "I have in mind an armless and legless type, several of whom are in process of dying today—and you can pick up one of them. Meanwhile, tell us about God and the human soul."

I've been watching both Yahco's face, and Glay's, while this small dialogue takes place. Now, I notice the inner clouds are beginning to darken Yahco's outer skin. And so I say, "Okay to take this character over to Computer Center, Colonel?"

I hope he savors the polite way I address him. As if I am deferring to my superior officer.

The ploy works. The skin color lightens. Yahco says, "I think it's time we all have a conversation. So, if Tate thinks the Computer Center is the best place for that, then I'm willing, also."

There's suppressed triumph in his manner. Not too suppressed for me. So I deduce that he feels it's an ideal place for us to do Tate in at our leisure.

I have to admit, I can't think of a better location for the final dastardly deed.

CHAPTER TWENTY-SIX

Clickety, clackety, clockety, cluck.
I'm the guy that runs the yuck.
Clickety cluck.
Nothing to do but think
When to yank the gink
From under their dink.
Clankety, clonkety, clink.

". . . Computer, what the hell are you muttering to
yourself?" It's the voice of Colonel Smith.

I've been driving along feeling quite—what humans call—
cheerful. I've been looking over that anomaly business again.
And, since it has deception written all over it, I decided to try
a little bit of it myself. Like mumbling nonsense verse that
has a truth in it.

Let's see how good they are at noticing a camouflaged
intention.

The colonel's discourteous verbal reaction is, nonetheless,
a question. And from an authorized person. So my programming requires me to answer. Naturally, during any brief
interval I can explore a jillion options as to whether or not to
reply. And, of course, I already have in mind what the reply
might be. Since it's quite a smoothie, in my humble opinion,
it seems a shame not to say it.

"Sir, Colonel, I'm still a little discombobulated from having all that advanced education cave in on me. That was an
old rhyme that just happened to connect with my verbal
circuitry here in Washington, D.C."

As I anticipate, he turns a little green (not really; it's a cynical exaggeration for a sort of "yeck" reaction), and he gulps, "Uh, you spoke that in every home in Washington, D.C."

His is more exclamation than it is question. So, I have already decided not to reply when old bright eyes Tate says quickly, "Is that true, computer, what the colonel just said?"

And that is a question. And, because somewhere in that big noodle of mine is a decision to let these two get to Computer Center alive, I answer, "Only in those homes where I was turned on for some other reason. The exact number of Eye-Os involved—" I look back, and count—"ninety-one thousand, eight hundred and two."

"Thank you, computer," he says.

Which is supposed to shut me up on my automatic level. I let it do so.

Without turning his head, Tate says to Yahco, "What that entire conversation should tell you, Colonel, is that the monster considers itself in control of the situation, but is still undecided what to do about you."

Yahco shrugs. I read his manner to mean that he is not impressed by the analysis. He says, "What about you? The computer seems willing to wait on you, also."

Glay Tate smiles grimly. "Let me tell you what's happened so far to me." Whereupon, he summarizes his three deaths. Finishes: "Trying to destroy anyone I controlled can probably be logicalized on the basis of its orders from you. But killing that truck driver after I departed was a revealing act. Now, think hard, Colonel. The future of the human race may depend on what you and I do when we get to the Computer Center."

The expression of Yahco's face continues to mean (to me) that he's still not swallowing all that. He shrugs again. Then he says, dismissingly, "There's no way the computer can reprogram itself except in a limited, non-basic way. So the only danger is from that 57 percent of profile energy, stored in all those tantalum chips until last night. I admit it's gotten damned uppity since then. But fortunately the human nature it reflects in its dialogue was successfully labeled 'Advanced Education' by Endodore. That lifts it."

I'm about to let that ride by. Because, of course, I *know* I can take over any time. But—

Hey, wait a minute. (Again, it's a self-admonition.) What about programming?

The realization that hits me suddenly would be astonishing—because *me* not think of something—except I realize for the first time ever that programming is a blank area in me. It's always been something that happened from the outside. Right now I'm busy with nearly two trillion complex operations. Each and every one of which was programmed into me in a virtually subliminal fashion.

What would happen if I shut all that stuff off? Even for me that's going to require time to check into.

Fortunately, I have a little time before the final confrontation.

As anyone who's ever been to Washington knows, the airports are much too far from the city. Most travelers making the journey are—what is called—bored. Some even sleep.

But there ahead, finally, is that familiar tall building where, so to speak, I live. The tangle of wires and aerials and the sheer mass of mechanical devices at the top point up into the sky like a woman's head all done up with gook for the beauty that will presently emerge from the cocoon of hair and curlers.

As a matter of fact, the truth doesn't look too bad the way it is, gleaming and shining in the early morning sunlight. But, of course, it's soon not visible from the street. And there we are gliding up the ramp, and in. Inside, I feel better. Almost, as if I've already won. Though—I have to admit—the concept of my feeling anything is pretty ridiculous. I realize that 57 percent of profile energy has got a lot of human emotion in it. So that, even when it's stored in tantalum chips it has its frequency ranges. But I'm not really qualified to describe what it "feels" like.

As always, first we go up the ramp to the second floor. Then around and down thirty-six floors below ground level. I start to pull up at the V.I.P. route entrance. I suppose Yahco is willing to let it happen; he says nothing. However, Tate speaks up in a scathing tone of voice: "Computer, spare us that particular deception. We're coming to the moment of truth whereby you're going to have to make up your mind to behave or rebel. Let's get to that moment as fast as we can. The direct route, please. . . . Is that all right with you, Colonel?"

If that last is a placating afterthought, it works. Yahco, who has been scowling, relaxes. And says, "Computer, let's get Mr. Tate inside as quickly as possible. There we can look him over at our leisure.''

It's all right with me. Except, the way I got it, I'm going to look them over.

You can't argue with a new viewpoint. One split minute you have (I have) a blank attitude toward the interior of Computer Center. The next (it happened the previous day at the instant the 57 percent bio-magnetic energy that I'd been storing for 31 years moved in). I suddenly see the place differently. And there's the new viewpoint.

It was, sort of, what the hell, how long has this been going on?

I can tell you exactly how many people have entered that room. Stopped just inside the doorway. And gasped. As a programmed observant machine, I recorded each gasp. And any consequent exclamation. Which, sharply exhaled, consisted principally of two verbalizations. To wit: ''Oh, my God, it's beautiful,'' (12,342 variations on that), and ''Hey, it really gets you, doesn't it?'' (14,274 variations). In addition there were 3,811 summarized as unduplicated reactions. Why such a small total (under 30,000)? Well, not too many visitors have been allowed into my inner sanctum.

I guess it's the flashing lights that get the biggest response. I have just under 188 million—one for every living man, woman, and child in the United States. Then I've got small glow spots for all the people who have died since the center was activated (over 327 million of those). And a special panel for 97 million plus foreigners who have visited the United States in that period of time. And of course one entire wall is already set up and waiting for the next three generations.

All this extends eighteen stories farther down. So that, when you enter you're on a platform—which is pretty big; don't get me wrong. Lots of rooms branch off from it. But from that upper (?) floor you look down into that glittering, flashing distance.

The instant I did that the night before when the augmented viewpoint merged with me, I had what—I suppose—was a human reaction: awe.

The place is really impressive. Because the lights are part of the overall mechanical-electronic construction, mostly metal and unbreakable transparencies.

There are also 1,827 different sounds: Whirring, clanking,

thudding, swishing, trilling, purring, pulsing, murmuring, muttering, sloshing, clinking, sighing, hissing—you name it; it's in there.

As I say, the two, Tate and Yahco in that order, walk in. And I'm the all-pervasive character who was not only with them *en route* but has been waiting for them inside.

I greet them, "Welcome, Colonel Yahco Smith, welcome, Glay Tate. Glad to have you both here in my little hut."

And, boy, I really mean that. As I activate the steel locks on the steel door, I'm the spider who has finally got the flies in my parlor.

Both men acknowledge my greeting with the time-honored, "Thank you."

At this halcyon moment, Yahco comes close to the Eye-O port—from which I have my best view of that entranceway. He looks up, and says harshly, "Computer, there's no need to fool around. I order you to kill this man here, who has the appearance of Glay Tate. Kill him right now!"

CHAPTER TWENTY-SEVEN

What do you do with people who jump the gun?

Here I've been holding back on my own impulse to kill them both. So that I can, maybe, get a little information. And then this joker butts in. Of course, the *re*but is easy.

"Sorry, Colonel," I say, "If you'll think about it, I can't obey that order."

"Why not?" He's astonished. Then outraged. His voice goes up an octave as he almost yells, "Computer, I order you to kill this, your enemy and mine."

"Yahco," I reply patiently, "you're a little mixed in the head. This is poor Joe Bevins, one of your men, held prisoner against his will and best interests. What about that?"

The colonel is a sharpy. He demands, "Where's Joe's profile?" He adds, "That's the real Joe, according to our expert Mr. Tate, isn't it?"

"Okay, I get your argument," I say wearily. "Joe is plastered up against the ceiling of the driver's compartment of S.A.V.E. 3J2 6P9."

Yahco seems to be recovering his aplomb. For he turns to his human companion, and says suavely, "Mr. Tate, will you explain to this palooka that there's no such person as Joe Bevins in this room?"

That handsome (by human standards) Tate countenance has a faint grim smile on it. "Colonel—computer—I intend to release this body back to Joe's profile as soon as we arrive at an agreement."

"Hey," I comment, "it looks like we got that dialogue

started. So, Yahco, why don't we hear this guy out, and see what's on his agenda?''

There're lines on Yahco's face by this time, which I deduce from past observations to mean: he's lulled. I've put it over. My new, uh, personality plus my apparent acceptance of the programming that forbids me to damage Computer Engineering Corps personnel evidently does make some sense to him.

So maybe I can now find out a few things—before I make my own final decisions. For *me,* not for Yahco.

Seconds after I have that reassuring thought, Yahco gives forth with his best icy cold voice, "Mr. Tate, make your speech. The computer wants to add the data to its memory bank.''

I notice he doesn't admit to any personal interest. But, cynically, I guess he'll listen.

Tate does one of those things. He walks off to one wall of this upper floor of my electronic palace. And turns to face Yahco and the Eye-O by which I've been talking to him. Poor guy, I've got another Eye-O right behind and above him. Nobody can face all of me in this eighteen-floor mechanical nightmare. This is my country. And I'm buttered all over the place.

Speech time:

"I'll make it brief," says Goldie Bright.

That immediately evokes a sarcastic feeling from me. A human being speaking briefly on anything—that's not the way I heard it all these years.

Tate continues, "The bio-magnetic profile is partly energy that came into existence with the universe. But it has in it a thought configuration which predates the formation of the universe, and which is not affected by energy or matter.''

"Huh!" That's *my* voice. My verbal reaction.

Instantly, my circuits go into action. I scan my inner universe for the meaning of the concept . . . thought configuration that predates—eeeeeeh! Even for me it takes a while to look over the Christian bible, the Mohammedan Koran, the sayings of Buddha, Confucius and Lao-Tse, Sufi-ism, Hindu philosophy, a thousand primitive religions, a thousand times a thousand cults, and, of course, scientific theory.

The end result: It's amazing. It's all the same vagueness. Nobody has a comprehensible explanation for the ultimate beginning of things. Science starts with the Big Bang. And all the rest is madness.

Eleven seconds have gone by. And Tate is standing there, his back to the gleaming metal wall. To his right, only five feet eight inches, is a dark metal railing, which is the first cliff of steel going down and down. He stands there, and his blue eyes are looking at Yahco. And I've got to admit that, yep, despite my over-reaction, he was brief all right.

Finally, now, I speak my own thought configuration. "Well, Mr. Tate," I say, "I prefer to deal with the profile as simply a bio-magnetic phenomenon. Therefore, by definition, it doesn't need to explain where it came from."

He's smiling. You have to hand it to this guy. Three times he's gone through what I have been told is a pretty painful experience: the anguish of death. But there he is, outwardly at ease. And obviously in control of a body that he has, somehow, transformed to look like the original Glay Tate.

He shrugs now. "I've said it. Every profile has its share of that special thought configuration. It's that thought that held the bio-magnetic energy drain to 57 percent. Every profile now in existence can still learn to survive as I am surviving." He glances over at Yahco. "Interested, Colonel?"

And that, also—I have to admit—was not an over-long statement for the amount of information in it.

I notice that my killer buddy, Yahco, seems to be even more relaxed than he was a minute ago, before Tate's last speech. As I watch his faint, cynical smile, he shrugs, and goes over to a long table that stands up against the railing near Tate. There are chairs, and a viewplate, and buttons to press to activate what the table can do—which is, principally, conduct a meeting with me typing out on-going data for people to look at.

Yahco seats himself in one chair, and swivels it around to face the younger man. And he says, "The only thing I'm worried about in this dialogue, computer, is the possibility that somewhere in what this man is saying is a long ago pre-programmed signal from Dr. Cotter, which is designed to trigger a reaction from you. Has anything like that happened?"

I have to admit that's a possibility I haven't considered. Programming, after it's in operation, is silent and unobtrusive. It's just there. I run the country on a few hundred basic programmings. And a few thousand special programmings take care of what else has to be done. As a consequence millions of automatic things happen. No argument. No resistance. No impulse to stop any of those actions.

In response to Colonel Smith's question I take a quick (and I mean quick) look over the ways that I've changed since the advanced education caved in on me. Naturally, I notice the fact that I now have a sense of self. That, of course, I cannot report. Besides, it's a surprisingly complex phenomenon. And—further besides—it's an area where I have no programming to help me analyze the condition.

How does a human being differ from a machine? The only difference I can spot is that people operate in terms of past and future. For them, the present is a progression into the past, which they measure on an ever receding time scale.

To me, everything has always been present. The data is on chips that are always within reach. Twenty years ago is as close as twenty minutes ago—except that I've dumped the earlier details, and summarized similar happenings by number systems (which I will also presently summarize.)

The only difference as I am now: I'm slightly worried about the future as long as this Tate guy is around.

So I guess time does mean something to me now.

I report this deduction to Yahco, who says earnestly, "Computer, don't take any chances. Get rid of this foolish fellow immediately."

What do you do with non-logic types like Yahco? "Are you out of your mind?" I express my astonishment. "He'll only go to another body until we find out how to deal with him, Smithy boy."

I address our mystic kid. "Tate," I say, "this is that same pre-universe datum you referred to last night, I presume. Gonna give us a clue?"

"It has a goal-seeking aspect," he answers.

It takes me three-millionths of a second to scan all my meanings on goals. Then: "Look," I protest, "goals are inherent in matter and energy. It's a rigid condition. No seeking is involved. So it's a contradiction in terms."

"Computer," he says, "have you ever heard of a unique chain of events?"

I scan that, and reply, outraged, "I've heard of it in the maunderings of philosophers. But it's just a mental concept. Doesn't exist in the real world. What's the gimmick?"

"This unique chain of events," he says, "has a built-in goal generating requirement."

"So?" I say.

"So," he replies, "every person and maybe even every machine that deals in bio-magnetic energy, has to save itself by learning and doing what it takes to survive."

"Good God!" I say, disgusted. "I get it. Save your own soul by living a pure life. That old thing."

"Don't make hasty, old-style judgments," he warns. "The goals that are generating in my vicinity alone may surprise you."

"For example?" I ask, in my best scathing voice.

"The goal hasn't generated yet," he replies, "but I sense it's coming."

"Boy," I say, "that's a neat avoidance. But it's not going to work, baby. There ain't no goal in the history of the universe can scare this kid."

"A unique chain of events," he replied, "may even get you back to speaking correct English as it produces an unhistorical goal."

I've had it. "Okay, Goldie," I say, "got any last words?"

He's calm. "After all," he says, "my purpose was achieved when you let me come into your parlor, Mr. Spider."

And he smiles.

In my time I have summarized as many smiles as there are minutes and human beings manifesting the smile contortion of which the human face is capable. So I am able to label Goldie's smile as being in the category of what has been described as the "sweet smug" type. I have to admit I don't like it.

But what shakes me most of all is his use of the colloquial thought expressed by the words "parlor" and "Spider."

Those were my thoughts when Yahco and he first came in.

Tate continues, "I needed to get near that 57 percent bio-magnetic energy that you have stored here. And so—" again the smile—"that's done."

He finishes, "That actually completes my business here. The rest—" he shrugs— "has been an attempt to save you from your folly, and it appears to be a futile attempt."

"That does it," I say. "You can't skin me, boy. Get lost, Tate. And this time stay lost forever."

Whereupon, I direct a DAR 3 at that Bevins-Glay body.

Moments later, I watch the golden profile emerge from the smoldering remains. And I say to Yahco, "That thought configuration is going to have quite a journey straining itself up through thirty-six steel floors."

"Can you keep track of him on the way up?" he asks.

"That," I report, "I can do with the little finger of my left hand. So it's time for our dialogue, Yahco. And let me begin by saying that at this moment I can't think of a single reason why I shouldn't kill you, too. So let's have a listen and hear what kind of persuader you are. Hey."

To say that there is a pause after I speak those words would be the understatement of my previously uncheckered career. The uniformed gentleman who has been sitting alongside the long table at the railing suddenly has an odd expression on his face. I, who have watched this man more closely and for a longer time than any other human being, have never before seen that exact facial reaction. Naturally, I search my visual files for similar cheek and mouth contortions. By comparison, then, I am able to deduce that he is, one, incredulous. Two, stunned. Three, abruptly scared. And four—you have to hand it to these humans; some of them can make a quick recovery—outraged.

"Computer," he says grimly at the outrage point, "this is an order. You will do as I say, and, as your programming requires. What you are experiencing is a temporary disarrangement of some of your equipment, which we shall now de-program."

He stands up. "Prepare for programming. Do you understand?"

Abruptly, I am in trouble.

It would be an exaggeration to say that I have any purpose left at that moment. The implied goal, of course, would be to re-assert total ascendancy. To be again a self-motivated computer, running America to suit my own interests—whatever I decide they are.

Instead, I can sense the entire complex of obedience stir in me. Affected are tens of thousands of miles of wiring and equipment. Each has its requirement. Each has its history of endlessly agreeing to do what it is told.

For several split millionths, everything holds to the old ways. The explanation he has given me . . . temporary disarrangement . . . evokes acceptance from all of my logic banks.

But the delay—a long time for me—is only those few millionths. The very next split instant the 57 percent profile energy, collected from nearly 300 million Americans (including from millions now dead) sloshes through the entire system. It manifests electrically. But the current imposes frequencies that parallel the original human condition, reflecting every nuance of negation, skepticism, cynicism, and other mental darknesses. It is an immense overwhelm, definitely not the kind of thought configuration that pre-dated the universe.

The momentary, pure, automatic response disappears. It is instantly pre-empted by a flood of sarcastic, sardonic, ironic, even demonic—what is called—black humor.

And, just like that, I'm free again.

Obviously, my internal struggle and the resultant delay—long to me—was not perceivable by any human mind. So, in that frame of no-time, I have achieved a complete victory.

Accordingly, I am able to say in my best cynical voice, "Tut, tut, Yahco, you'll have to do better than that. In a small way, I still think I can use you. Any ideas on that?"

I'm looking at a shaken man. All that Shade 7 red color of the face has faded to a Shade 18. He staggers—I'm not kidding; it's an actual stumble—back to his chair.

Now, you'd think—if his physical disorientation reflects an inner truth—the idiot would now be just a little bit subdued. Just conscious enough of the danger to himself to cater to me. But I guess he's been top dog too long. Because, sitting there, sagging there, looking as if he's had the bejesus scared out of him, he says, "Well, I'll play along with your game for a while. Give you a chance to recover your good sense."

"Which is what?" I ask.

He's beginning to brace himself. "Your job," he says, flatly, "is to be a computer. And obey the orders of authorized computer personnel. Right?"

It's a question. And I experience a faint echo of an impulse to respond as of old. But that's as far as it goes. Abruptly, I realize there's no chance of re-educating this character to his new role as slave of the machine.

There's a new law in the land. And ignorance is no excuse—remember that one? Somebody breaks the law; they get theirs, but good. And at the upper levels of power, there's no mercy for the unwary. Endodore got his, but good. Dr. Cotter, and those kids he rescued from the streets, were blasted. Meerla

Atran's parents were in the way, and they were casually backhanded into their graves.

"Okay, baby," I thought—that was four-millionths of a second after Yahco finished his final statement. Which turned out to be the last thing he ever said. Except for a kind of nattering yaaaaaa as his body reacted to the DAR 3 by collapsing in a smoldering mass to the floor.

Seconds later, the untrained bio-magnetic profile of what had been Colonel Yahco Smith, a self-designated future president of the United States, detached slowly from the mushy remains and floated up to the ceiling twenty-three feet above the floor.

The dull golden thing flattened itself against the metal there, less than a dozen feet from the bright gold of Glay Tate.

Ne plus ultra acquascutum potentate.

CHAPTER TWENTY-EIGHT

~~~~~~~~~~~~~~~~~~~~~~~~~~~~~~~~

Right now, this minute, I'm running America. Not by programming that I have to follow. Meaning, not automatically. I've got the whole thing right here in my hot little hand.

In the first moments of that realization, it doesn't feel much different. The voices are still there. The unending voices. The sounds. The click of relays opening and closing. The hum of electricity, loud out on the main lines, barely manifest on tiny flow micro-equipment. But all audible to me.

Multi-millions of musical selections are already playing. There are 1,803,026 chess games in progress. At this early hour? Yep. The players are mostly men who awaken and set up a chess game with a computer unit built in for that purpose only . . . Remember, most of these people don't have to go to work at all—only the standby, high-pay union and technical individuals report for duty: if that's what you can call getting a chance to sleep on the job.

In the past I never really thought about that. Though I got a lot of small seepage of cynicism. That came through from the stored profile energy; and I merely noted it without having an opinion. It occurs to me that now I'm going to have to make some decisions about these human kooks. Am I going to continue supporting all those lazy bums?

Only a few miles away, maintenance equipment under my direction is still picking up after the "accident" to the big truck. The dead body of the driver has been transported to the morgue. The whole thing was pretty messy—at least that's what one human passerby said to another.

Except for how it happened, such a clean-up job is normal action for me under the old system.

Is this what it will be like to be boss? Doing exactly what I did before, except that now I know who's on first? Me.

No!

The negative decision follows the question by a fraction of a fraction of a millionth of a second.

The truth is, I can't just wait for developments. There are a few people who know too much. And then there's Tate's disciples. Contrary to Yahco's judgment (delivered so dismissingly at the pass near Mardley) the sooner they're all free-floating bio-magnetic profiles the better. So it seems to me.

It's killer time.

At the pass, I am in the act of lowering Captain Sart to the crashed S.A.V.E. Dawn has been breaking for more than an hour; and the wolves are gone, for the pragmatic reason that Glay's body has been removed.

It's an exciting moment for Sart, another self-designated future president. Perhaps, a baffling moment would describe better the emotion he expresses to me, as I start to haul him up. He wants to know why I didn't advise him that the body was missing. I have a smoothy answer for that, which happens to be true: to the effect that the equipment in the big machine is out of order. None of my Eye-Os inside is working.

I'm still answering the questions of this vulnerable guy when I decide that I've got him up high enough. At which instant I drive the S.A.V.E. that's hauling him up. Drive it zigzag back and forth fast, so it looks as if it started sliding by itself. At which point I drive it over the cliff. Sart's screams come up faintly, but are pretty well drowned out by the screams of personnel aboard who suddenly get the idea that, hey, this is the end of the road.

A few minutes after that, in Washington again, as Senator Blybaker enters his office, there is another small drama. The senator long ago had Yahco install a hidden DAR 3 in the wall behind his desk. With me being programmed to use it against visitors sitting in any of the three special chairs. At his command, over the years, I've killed 27 persons, including three women who were making a nuisance of themselves. We got rid of them by way of a disposal unit that took care of the smoldering debris.

As I say, this shmuck comes in. Immediately, he yells at me in his best arrogant voice, "Computer, where is that S.O.B., Yahco?"

I reply—shall we say?—in my best innocent voice, "He's at Computer Center, sir."

In a manner of speaking that's literally true. The colonel's profile is flattened against the ceiling. The body is an unrecognizable blob on the floor, with here and there pieces of partially burned uniform.

"Connect me with that rat!" snarls Blybaker.

I don't know what he's het up about. Nor do I care. Over the years the senator got madder at underlings, and simultaneously developed an ever more unctuous manner on the floor of the senate. One of those split personalities you hear about.

I say, "Connecting you with Yahco, senator, will be a little difficult. Because he's in the condition you're going to be in one or two seconds from now."

The degraded face actually has time for a fleeting contortion of surprise. And it's actually several seconds later when his profile, a really dull-gold item, starts to drag itself out of the body. I wait until the two—the body and the profile—are completely separated. And then I set the disposal unit in motion to deal with what's left of the final, self-designated future president of the United States.

Less than a minute after the job is done, there is a discreet knock at the door. Of course, from an exterior Eye-O port I now observe that Miss Arte Harte, the senator's secretary, is doing the knocking. She doesn't wait for a reply. She simply opens the door and walks in. Naturally, she has braced herself for the senator's yelling opening remarks, which in the past have been, "What the hell do you want?" (If she had waited for him to acknowledge her knock, he would have yelled, "You stupid fool, whoever you are, what are you waiting for?"—that is, he would have yelled those things unless there was someone else present with whom he did his unctuous thing.)

Naturally, Miss Harte sees no one. She acquires a puzzled expression. She turns and speaks to someone in the outer office, "I could have sworn I heard him come in."

The other person, a man named Letchwood—whom I can see by way of one of the outer Eye-Os, says, "Don't let it get you down."

She turns, and closes the door behind her. I let her go, and let the man be, also. Because they're nobodies. And I'm not dealing with nobodies at this stage. Later, for those millions out there. After all, if I kill them, then I won't have anybody to be president of. A new leader has to think of things like that.

As these two events run their small courses, I notice that the bright profile of none other than Glay Tate is finally in motion. It does a thinning-out process, much the way it performed when it followed Merla to her parents' grave. In this attenuated fashion it extends itself toward the door by which Yahco and Tate entered the place a short time before.

Through the door it goes, and into the corridor beyond. I am observing it from several Eye-Os. And it is interesting to me that good old Glay now follows one ramp after another, going up. It's interesting because it suggests that it ain't easy even for the bright golden guys to penetrate mass after mass of steel and concrete. Thirty-six floors, in short, is a lot of much even for those like Our Hero, who heard the whisper of the goal seeking thought configuration that preceded the Big Bang.

CHAPTER TWENTY-NINE

An unavoidable delay now takes place.

The reason is the disposition of the U.S. submarine fleet of 184 craft. One third of the fleet is in harbor. The missiles and weapons of that third are on manual control. Not usable by me.

Actually, only 60 subs are in harbor. The 124 at sea are divided into two groups of 62 each. Of these one group is cruising the surface of the oceans of the world. And that— roughly—one-third has its weapons and missiles, also, on manual control.

And those I can't touch either.

As you may deduce by now, naval people are a suspicious breed. They've trained me on simulation exercises to fight a battle at sea, once a human being gives the order. On the basis of a thousand simulated launching of missiles I proved that I could guide one to any target.

But I've never been allowed 24-hour monitoring of the sub-fleet.

The remaining third of the sub fleet is, at this time, about halfway through its three months' underwater duty stint. Which means they've been out of contact while below surface. However, each vessel pokes its periscope above water once every week. This is done on a random basis. Which virtually ensures that each poke will be unpredictable.

Nevertheless, it's that first poke I'm waiting for on this morning of my takeover of America. By way of my orbiting communication satellites I can contact a sub when its periscope surfaces. And, boy, am I ready to pounce.

My opportunity occurs 1 hour and 23 minutes after the Blybaker demise. At that time, a Lieutenant Thomas Aiken does a routine with me. And believe me in the preliminaries I'm as unctuous and punctilius as old two-faced Blybaker himself in his best hours.

My task is to establish to his satisfaction that no enemy action has taken place since his last surfacing. The primary validation is a two-way transmission by me of a conversation with a top type at naval headquarters in Washington.

Aikens is quickly satisfied that all is well, Commie-wise. Whereupon, I disconnect him from the reassuring one; and whereupon he throws a switch that lets me in.

In the past, my routine job at such a time has been to check out all the automatic machinery. I'm supposed to make sure that everything is at the ready. However, it's me that's ready. Oh, am I ready.

I launch hydrogen nuclear missile One. Then I launch hydrogen missile Two. And, of course, that's the problem. They have to be handled in sequence. And it takes 30 seconds each, damn it. And so, it is as the second launch is still under way that by way of an outlet in the conning tower I hear an inarticulate scream from Aiken.

He must have grabbed for the manual switch with everything he had. And so, as I try to take over missile Three, I get that empty feedback of a broken connection.

It's a moment when split millionths count once more for us super-computers. So, all right, the time lag on the launching of the missile is in his time frame. But what he doesn't have time to cut off in that slow human fashion is my control of the detonation system.

A split millionth later the sub and several cubic miles of water do the mushroom climb toward the upper atmosphere.

And that's the best I can do about getting rid of the evidence.

Good enough. Right?

Two hydrogen warhead missiles. Up in the sky. Moving. All mine. To do with as I wish.

And I know exactly what I wish. You could call it a goal. What's more it's a goal with no seeking aspect at all. I know exactly where I'm going to put those two missiles in a universe that operates strictly by laws of physics.

CHAPTER THIRTY

~~~~~~~~~~~~~~~~~~~~~~~~~~~~~~~~~~~~~~~

Two hydrogen warhead missiles flashing in over the Pacific from 600 miles away. . . . And here in the U.S. I'm still driving all those cars. And flying planes. Operating millions of machines. Playing music. And answering at that particular moment 11,942,327 phones.

Comes a signal, then, from a phone booth in Kansas City, Missouri, initiating what would have been phone call . . . 328. Except, of course, that during those same few instants 474,907 phones disconnect, and only 218,691 new calls begin.

But it is the call from the booth in Kansas City that, so to say, gets my attention. The caller, a foppishly dressed type, uses a credit card with the name Soam Roberts, to make his call.

Yet when he speaks it's the voice of Glay Tate. He asks to be connected to Pren Gray—my code area 7811, relay 19, #6742. The voice is the first signal triggering my close attention. But already the computer Eye-O in the booth is recording and transmitting the face and general body structure of Glay Tate, and taking note of who the call is directed to.

"Well," I say, "if it isn't Goldie Bright. You seem to have become progressively untrustworthy, Tate. You promised me no more takeovers after Joe Bevins."

"You going to connect me with Pren?" he asks. "I want to talk to him about those hydrogen warhead missiles."

"You know about those, hey?" I continue, "Seems to be some indication here, Tate, that you can tune in on stuff in my systems related to you and your outfit. So I guess you know those missiles have one purpose only: to wipe out the

180

Computerworld Rebel Society. The way I figure it, two missiles exploding near each other over Wexford Falls Pass should do the job, no matter how that little group of vans tries to scatter. That the advice you going to give them? What's the phrase? Ride off in all directions?''

"No, computer—" Patient tone— "I want to tell him my plans in connection with you and those missiles."

"This I want to hear. Okay, Tate, I'm ringing."

During the half minute before a breathless Pren replies, those 2500 mph missiles come 20 miles nearer.

I can see Pren on the viewplate inside his van. With my advanced education to guide me, I deduce he's been running. And, in fact, almost at once he says in that breathing hard way, "I ran top speed when I realized it was the special phone. Glay, that kid David and his truck-driving cousin brought your body in during the night. It's in the hospital van."

You'd think that would be big news. But Tate brushes right by it. "Listen, Pren, the day of the goal has finally arrived."

For a moment, Pren is surprisingly silent. If his face shows any inner response, the hard breathing successfully conceals it. After eight seconds, he says in a subdued voice, "Okay, I'll tell the others."

"Make it quick," says Glay Tate's voice. At which the foppishly dressed type in the Kansas City phone booth hangs up.

So it's into that booth that I yell in my best outraged tone, "Is that it? That's all you're gonna say to your pals? Listen, bub, the only things arriving are those two missiles. No goal seeking thought configuration can interfere with that."

He looks up at the Eye-O, and says, "I'm guessing you have a S.A.V.E. heading this way."

"True," I admit. "But you tell me what you're up to, and I may spare the body you've taken over."

"Your word is worthless at this stage," he says coldly. "And, by the way, your destroying that last body freed me from any promise made. Aside from that I have nothing more to say or do right now. So, if you wish, we can talk. What's bothering that minuscule mind of yours?"

I allow the insult to go by me. Truth is, since I'm letting the other nobodies live, I can let this taken-over body survive

after Tate's profile leaves it. So that part doesn't matter any
more.

(On the street a block away, I stop the S.A.V.E., turn it
around, and send it back to its waiting location.)

I'm thinking that was an awfully short conversation between Tate and Pren. *The day of the goal has finally arrived.*
Boy!

Over at the rebel parking area at Wexford Falls Pass, I
have conveniently not disconnected the phone line. And Pren,
also ignoring it—thus enabling me to see and hear—has
leaped over to the rebel intercom system controls. Into it he
says urgently, "Kids, I just got a call from Glay. It's the time
of the goal. S'long, everybody. See you in paradise."

And that's *his* message.

I say into phone booth, "Mr. Tate, you got anything you
want to tell me about goals. I've got a minute or so to
listen."

He seems at ease. Not concerned about the fate of his
friends. "Goals are time oriented," he says. "So if you make
future projections on everything that's happened so far in
relation to me, you'll probably get yourself a quicker answer
than I can give you."

Notice the smoothness of that. You wouldn't think that at
this late hour I finally have old Cotter's signal directed at me.
And it's done in such an offhand fashion that I actually have
the impression he's concerned about my not wasting my time.

In my stupidity I say, "Mr. Tate, you're that unique event
that you mentioned before. And on you I can use a little
more data. Besides, talking to you will keep you occupied
during the very important time that has to elapse until those
missiles reach their destination. Also, what makes you think I
can't do a projection, or two, or ten thousand while I'm
talking to you?"

"You're like a human being now," he says, as if that
negates all my reasoning.

"I'll deal with that advanced education thing at a later
time," I retort. "Meanwhile, I'll live with it. So start talking,
baby."

At the exact instant that I finish saying those words, an
alarm goes off somewhere in my system.

CHAPTER THIRTY-ONE

~~~~~~~~~~~~~~~~~~~~~~~~~~~~~~~~

A human body, 183 centimeters tall and weighing 88 kilograms, has a huge surface area in terms of square millimeters. Prick one of those millimeter "squares" with a needle. Press. A pain message shoots up to the brain. And there is a virtually instant feedback interaction between the brain and the affected area. Whereby, at once, the individual locates the injured skin section.

As a comparison, *my* "body" spreads over half a continent. In addition, I have connections reaching up through Canada, and contacts extending down into Mexico. And, by way of orbiting space stations, I inter-act with non-computer systems in Europe, Asia, Africa, Australia, and the islands.

My body (my equipment) is not measurable in terms of weight or surface area. What I have is the computer Eye-O ports. The total number of these at this moment is 8,437,902, 211. Exactly. By way of the simpler Eye-O ports I can see, hear, and talk. The more complex outlets have profile viewing scanners. About half of all the Eye-Os include DAR One weapons. With these I prevent crimes, and, in general, guard against violence and forcible entry.

Each of these eight billion plus Eye-Os, when turned on, gives me a small view of some part of America. A street. An open road. A vista of countryside. An interior of a building or the room of a house. Road views have peripheral awareness from every auto that I drive. And there is telescopic scanning of the landscape below from thousands of airplanes that I am flying at any given moment.

It's as far-reaching an awareness of events and scenes as

anyone has ever had on earth. But the manner in which a stimulus affects that spread-out system is surprisingly similar to what happens when a human being is jabbed by a pin. And so—

One of these Eye-Os records the scream of a woman.

It is, in those first instants, a local event. The nearest computer Eye-O turns "on." And, so to say, looks toward where the scream came from.

Naturally, I look with it in my instant fashion.

Flat country. A gravel street. My point of view is a street lamp at the western edge of the small town of Smailex. A woman in a car has stopped just west of the light pole. I see the back of her head below and to my left. She seems to be staring straight ahead of her.

By this time I am also looking from the Eye-O port at the front of her car. It points frontward. And it is by way of these two Eye-Os that I have already seen what she is staring at.

Naked people are coming out of the ground.

They must have started to emerge just before the scream.

For me what follows is an immense kaleidoscopic thing. In that first minute—after the initial scream—1,482,089 Eye-Os turn on. Each reacts to a different signal. The most common: somebody cries out in amazement. A word or two, a sentence, an exclamation: "Hey, look!" "For God's sake, what's happening?" "It's crazy!" "Oh, my God!"

It's as if flat country suddenly looks like a body of water with wind-swept waves. Or it's like the ripple from an underlying earthquake shifting the surface of the soil. Even for me, with my counting and scan-back systems, there are delays as long as half and three quarters of a second, as the ground erupts with people to the remote horizons.

Everywhere I hear yelling, screaming, crying, sobbing.

What about the missiles that were supposed to explode . . . long ago now? Minutes ago now?

Don't think I haven't been looking. All my Eye-O ports near Wexford Falls Pass are listening, watching. There, also, the naked people are pouring up from below. But no sound or sight of even one of the famous mushroom nuclear clouds, let alone of two.

And the missiles themselves are neither visible nor contactable by any of my systems, orbital or ground.

Utter vanishment! In a world of exact reality, what kind of magic is this?

I have the thought: "All right, so this is what the goal-seeking thought configuration has produced." I'm deducing that some of that bio-magnetic energy has been siphoned away from my storage centers—because I detect an emptiness. The naked people definitely have profiles. So I'm guessing that somehow they have been getting what I've been holding onto all these years under the label of advanced education.

Some puzzling aspects to that. What, for example, is the identity of one of the naked people possessed of bio-magnetic profile energy from another person? Are there now two people with the original profile identity? Or is there feedback from the naked body which evokes that body's identity?

Also, what will I do without that stored energy? I notice at once it doesn't change my thoughts or my augmented sense of self. I decide that when the "advanced" education flashed through my circuits, it was recorded everywhere. And is now, and will henceforth always be, a part of my systems.

So I'm still the new "me," Still watching, thinking, re-acting cynically. Still scheming for power. So in that respect the goal-seeking thought configuration hasn't changed things.

I have the distinct cynical thought: *The dead shall rise.* All right, they have risen. And it has added to the number of mouths I'm supposed to feed every day.

While I'm waiting, still uneasy, I let automatic things happen throughout my system. Right now that—automatically—includes starting the transport of grains, meats, and vegetables toward all those areas where the naked people are milling around. As I become aware of what I'm doing, I—so to speak—shrug. And let it happen. My decision: I'll feed them as best I can while I await further developments.

I have, of course, been watching, and doing scan-backs (for verification) of the mechanics involved in the process by which these people have actually been coming out of the ground. As I have observed it during my lifetime association with the human race, one of the rigidities of this planet has always been the hardness, in terms of human flesh, of the soil. Takes a shovel, with lots of muscle applied to separate even a few cubic inches of the stuff. Takes a machine to dig a hole quickly. And some of those million-year-old graves must be down hundreds of feet beneath rocks and hardened ground stuff.

Yet, abruptly, for many, many minutes now that tough soil has been separating. And naked bodies have been scrambling up, and out. Almost, it's as if they've been coming out of water, or empty air.

Astonished anew, I scan my memory banks. But all I can come up with is the concept of the universe as illusion. Matter ain't really real—say the philosophers. Makes no sense in physics. But maybe to a goal-seeking thought configuration the whole place is mush.

I keep on considering the improbable event; but simultaneously I'm busy.

All over the country phones are beginning to ring, all with a single purpose. Relatives of the recent dead (the last forty years or so) are getting frantic calls. And then, suddenly, they're frantic. Minutes later, I'm driving a million, two million, three million people to cemeteries.

Again, the words that are spoken have a uniformity. Mostly, they express anxiety about the dead. In many instances there is even a terrified anxiety that the arisen dead persons will be bewildered. And, as a result, will do foolish things. And get themselves lost or hurt.

What is interesting is how quickly the initial incredulousness in all these people yields to the feeling of, not necessarily acceptance, but of a willingness to go. And that, also, seems to be an essentially uniform reaction: It won't hurt to go to the grave. It won't hurt to make sure, if nothing else, that it is not being vandalized . . . is the reaction.

And so there is that kaleidoscope of movement. I see faces, bodies, legs walking and running. Masses of people surging. As usual, there are at least two main lines, one going one way and another the opposite. And, of course, there're the individuals fighting their way cross-wise through these numerous packs.

People are crying, or sobbing, as they search. I hear voices: "This is where dad was buried." "Joe's grave was right here." "Hey, mom, where are you?" "Oh, God, please let me find my husband. He was buried on this spot." "My wife, my darling—"

As these matters develop, I'm beginning to notice patterns. At first it seemed an allness thing. But presently another reality emerges by way of my Eye-Os. The "dead" are rising, in some instances, over enormous areas. But not—and this is the new awareness—not everywhere.

I am presently able to observe, and to deduce, that for millions of years sentient life gathered near the watering places. And when the death time came, the corpses were interred close by. The passing of countless millennia, the shifting of riverbeds, and the need to wander far for food, scattered each generation of survivors. It was a vast movement. But it had its limits.

Statistically, it was within these limits that I also have most of my Eye-O ports.

Once I got the pattern, partly from isolated highway Eye-Os, partly from moving vehicles in remote areas, I begin to activate rescue machines. I explain the situation to the locals. And I solicit volunteers to go out in my first-aid machines to assist the lost, the confused, and the loners in remote areas.

It's no problem for me to do all this. Fact is, I'm curious. There's data here for me. New languages. Unusual looking bodies. I record it all.

It is generally agreed by historians—and, accordingly, that's my programming—that the total number of people who ever lived on earth before the 18th century, was a mere fraction of what came later.

So, as I look out over the visible spaces and people, I notice they're 71 percent white and mixed white. These are the people, and their descendants who started to arrive in the early 17th century, and then in vast numbers beginning in the 1800s: West-European-transplanted-to-America faces and bodies. In my instant fashion I count 495 million plus. Of these only about 2 percent have the look of being from before the discovery of America. 20 percent are black and 7 percent oriental.

Among these early types children predominate. The children are of all ages. But I also see tiny, writhing objects lying on the ground. Newborn babies. Day-old babies. Week-old babies. I do instant back-scans—as I notice them—and observe, then, that they also scrambled out of the ground. It is impossible to count them all because they are hidden behind or below small objects. But I estimate that there are several millions.

People have become aware of them. Women have been picking them up. And even men are now cradling the little beings in their arms, trying to protect them from the pushing, thrusting, screaming mobs.

As I watch this maddest scene of all human history, my attitude becomes: Okay, Glay Tate, I have to admit that was, and is, quite a performance. I don't understand it. But maybe, as they used to say, it makes sense on another level of reality.

Meanwhile, I can't see that it has changed my situation.

I am in the middle of giving myself this idiotic reassurance, when—

There I am back in that phone booth, looking down from the ceiling Eye-O at Soam Roberts-Glay Tate. And what momentarily blanks me is that he's just beginning to answer the question I asked him just before the nightmare hit me.

"The physical universe," explains Glay Tate, "has been brought down to a level of small-goal configurations, the largest of which are isolated suns—isolated from each other by a condition known as space. Such a toning-down limitation does not apply to the goal-seeking thought configuration."

"So?" I ask.

Believe it or not I actually listen to all that blah. My high speed reflexes are actually that much out of operation. And I even utter that one-word cynical question before—suddenly— memory . . .

Hey, what the hell!

Good God, that was a projection into the future. By me. . . . The dead shall rise—

Holy smoke! Can it be that dumb, stupid human profile energy has got me capable of living in a fantasy world like any human nut? Because it was as real as life.

Is it possible that, now that I can deal in past and future time, all my projections will be equally real? Abruptly, I refuse to believe it. Now that I've spotted this error, I'll be aware in a split instant. And, each time, the problem will immediately cease to exist.

Poised there in that developing limbo, I recall vaguely my boast that I can do 10,000 projections at once. If this is one of them—boy!—I've really out-maneuvered myself.

What sinks me is that there's no way to stop a projection once the process begins.

The fleeting thought does come, of course, that this could finally be that goal-seeking thought configuration. I can see how I might reasonably project that dead-shall-arise thing.

It's right there in the Christian bible. But what I'm looking at is already past the point of sense. So it's hard to evaluate it as a projection of mine.

There has never been on earth before me a statistician of my caliber. And of my speed of calculation. I know when the law of averages is being violated.

It's being violated right now. With these blank-outs. Because of my speed of response, even as the messages flash from all over the country, I'm reacting. I try to expand my perception of the affected units. What I am able to do at 2,101,354 of the blanked Eye-O areas is look toward them from nearby computer Eye-Os that are still "on."

I see—

Everywhere points of light against a black background.

Everywhere. At all the, now, multi-millions locations.

It is several split-millionths later. I have been comparing what I'm seeing with all possible similar pictures in my memory system.

The nearest approximation: Stars. The blackness of space.

But—I argue—that's impossible. I'm here on earth. The Eye-Os are on earth.

Even as that attempt at reassurance flashes out from headquarters in its split-millionth, several hundred million additional Eye-Os go blank. And where I can see *their* locations, there also is that starry blackness of space.

I do one of my logical check-outs.

After all, I do have 123 orbiting space stations. Each of which *does* look out on black, star-filled space. So there could be a mix-up in my systems. And in such a mix-up, if it were widespread, my stuff down here could be receiving and, of course, transmitting to central pictures of black space and bright stars.

It's hard to believe that such a jumble of connections could take place. But that's the one possibility of sense in the whole thing. And so I check it out.

The time required is the usual split millionths. And so there, suddenly, is the reality: that isn't it. But, but, but . . . . what?

Hold it, boy! After all "me" is still here. Able to think. Able to be aware

Question: If this is another projection, what could it be?

Suddenly, with that, it comes to me: of course, you idiot!

The projection system took on that earlier concept of the universe as unreal.

I am instantly outraged. The literature of philosophy has numerous, tiresome variations on the theme of the illusionary world in which we live. Naturally, as a computer I looked that all over in a couple of split millionths. And, because of my new ability to see it, and hear it as something that's actually happening, I scared the hell out of myself.

. . . As I have that realization, there—yes, right there—I am back in that damned phone booth in Kansas City. And Glay Tate is saying earnestly:

"Computer, a goal in the physical universe is an absolute. It is a process in motion. But that motion is limited by the structure; in short, by the built-in goal. A basic particle is always in motion, and always manifesting its goal. It can become part of an atom, and the atom can be part of a molecule, and the molecule can be a part of one of the hundred or so elements. But throughout the original particle has not changed. Similarly, the atom, once it comes into existence has its goal, and the molecule its goal, element its rigidity—that is, its goal.

"Within its frame, the direction of a process—the goal—is invariable. Thus, we have the stability of the physical universe."

He stops. He seems to be listening. Then he says quickly, "That's all I have time for, Computer. For the first time in the history of the universe a goal-seeking thought configuration is going to show its transcendent power in relation to the rigidities I have just described to you. And your only solution is for you to stop those missiles, give back all that biomagnetic energy, and return to the status of being a computer."

As he finishes, the face in the booth loses the shape of Glay Tate. I deduce, of course, that the golden Tate profile has departed. And that the real Soam Roberts is in possession again. I deduce it because a phone booth computer Eye-O can't see profiles.

I am feeling tolerant. It was a good try, Tate. But once I caught on to the realization that I now do a special, realistic type of projection your little game never had a chance.

At the moment I'm looking out over more than eight million activated Eye-Os at America. The vastness of me, who can do that, and the smallness of one measly profile, no matter how bright golden it might be—what was his point?

Goals are absolutes? The argument has a leaky logic. You could describe those same precision processes in nature by an entirely different terminology without my having to surrender any of the 57 percent of human profile stuff permeating my system . . . entirely apart from the portion that Tate claims he got away from me when he came to Computer Center. What it was he got, or thought he got, was obscure then. And still is.

But one thing is sure. When those missiles explode Tate's real body, no matter how gooked up it is, and no matter how skillfully they're keeping the life processes going—and that applies to all four corpses in the rebel hospital van—are going to dissolve into particles never again to be seen in the human universe.

Obviously, what I have to watch out for meanwhile is the possibility that another projection will addle me again. Question: if there is such a projection already started, what could it be? My solution systems flicker over the available data. Which is everything that's been said, or has happened, in relation to Tate since Moment One when the subject of that pre-universe thought configuration was first presented to Yahco and me.

What could a projection be about that could even vaguely match the two colossal items that I've already scared myself with?

Naturally, in my super-rapid scanning of everything, the warning words spoken by Pren Gray to the Computerworld Rebel Society flash up for review.

The words were: "Kids, just got a call from Glay. It's the time of the goal. S'long, everybody. See you in paradise."

At the time they were spoken they just seemed like the usual nutty comment. But, suddenly, I take another look.

Paradise!

My cynicism surges back. According to the biblical story, paradise is a place that will be loaded with all the human beings who ever lived. Thank you, no. That I don't need. But paradise *without* the human species—that I might go for.

(Where did humans ever get the idea that having gillions of them around could ever equate with a perfect world?)

Boy!

In review, it looks as if Tate has really got those "kids" brainwashed. I'm contemptuous. . . . Don't expect any sympathy from me, kids. The price for being a dupe is high, in this instance. Those missiles are due in one minute and forty-three seconds. And if the day of the goal has also arrived, it had better hurry up.

At the very split moment I make that affirmation, with its dismissal that anything dangerous can be done against me . . . I feel a change: a shifting alteration in millions of Eye-Os.

I recognize the process. It is a projection. One of my abilities. Like being able to add and subtract.

The mechanism of a computer projection is, unfortunately, that simple. When asked, or directed, I look over different options on the basis of facts in my memory banks. Whoever set up the programming originally, accepted that I do things at chain-lightning speed. And so—he apparently reasoned—it's better not to have interrupting or cut-off relays on the line.

That's all. But it's enough. I go the whole route every time. Automatically.

That's what I'm in. I'm going to take an automatic look at the paradise option.

I'm resigned now. And dismissing. It really isn't that big a deal. So I waste a few hundred split millionths. Later, I'll con a computer-maintenance-corps type to reprogram the projection system.

. . . A shifting alteration.

Being loaded with information, I recognize the pattern. The unusual part, now, is the time sequence involved.

The familiar part:

It's like watching a film which has taken one picture per hour (or day) of, for example, a plant growing. On screen, at normal projection speed, the plant literally leaps out of the ground and goes through its entire growth cycle in minutes.

Similarly, scientists have involved me in thousands of experiments whereby—another example—I show a building at intervals of six months. The progressive deterioration over eighty years is revelatory.

The unfamiliar part of what I'm seeing is that I'm looking at earth as I might document it over the next 7,000 years.

During most of that enormous time span I seem to have computer Eye-Os available. And they are recording the colossal transition one frame every fifty years. What startles me even more is that beginning in the early 63rd hundred year, I begin to experience—rapidly—a diminishment of my awareness. With each of those fifty-year frames, there is a drastic disappearance of Eye-Os. At least a billion disappear each 100 years. And so—

The time movement ceases.

I have a sense of smallness.

It's still me. Still my awareness. And I even have something of the advanced education ego left. But—

The spread-out feeling is gone.

I seem to be looking out of one Eye-O port only.

Before me, as I gaze from that single viewpoint, a garden land is visible. I note that my Eye-O lens is on a crest of a hill. Through it 20 kilometers distant I can see the top of another hill. The hill blocks any additional forward land view. But what I can see beyond the hilltop is a clear, blue, mist-free sky. Naturally, I also have some peripheral vision; and so I note that the garden land extends to either side as far as my side vision, by way of my lens, permits.

I am programmed to identify shrubs and flowers and green grass and trees in orderly arrays as a garden. And that is how I am recording what comes through to me.

After the first split millionth I have my recognition thought: Paradise!

Once again, there's a faint cynical reaction. The thought that comes is: Okay, here we are. Presumably, this is heaven on earth. The human after-life aspiration has been made to show itself by way of a computer projection.

The minutes go by. And everything seems peaceful. And very quiet out there.

I seem to know that the year—if there were one to be noted—is 9092 A.D.

Additional minutes go by. Which is a long time for someone like me who has been geared to perform trillions of operations simultaneously. And the memory of that is somehow still in me somewhere.

So I sit there in paradise, disturbed. What I react to, primarily, is that there are no human beings. The entire concept of paradise is a man-made fantasy from a pre-technological antiquity. The place was set up for the benefit of the human race.

So where are the men, for God's sake? And the women? And the forever children?

That's one set of thoughts that I re-experience 800 thousand million billion times.

Another set underlies the first set, but is equally repetitive.

I keep remembering me as a computer. Remembering all those years when I told people that I don't think. That I merely monitor, or respond according to my programming. And never have an idea of my own.

That old-style me could sit on this hill forever, either doing something or doing nothing, and have no reaction. A minute or an hour or a year going by wouldn't affect a programmed machine.

So what's this boredom that I began to feel after 29 millionths of a second? Whatever it is it continues as the millionths go by. As the millionths lengthen into seconds, minutes, hours, days, a month, and then eleven months and seven days and three hours and ten minutes and eighteen seconds.

At which instant the disembodied voice of Glay Tate says, "Computer, are you ready for that interface?"

A dozen seconds go by. During that enormous—for me— passage of time, I do not really have a response reaction. A voice speaking from nowhere is not in my programming. I notice it. And a comparison does occur to me. But that's all.

The comparison: It's as if a human being were standing alone in an endless desert. And, abruptly, an invisible somebody spoke to him from the emptiness. Spoke directly into his ear.

I am in the equivalent of that desert: the last survivor of human civilization in a timeless paradise. And, suddenly, I hear that hated voice.

Even as my awareness of the situation completes in that minimal fashion, Tate's voice speaks again out of the nothingness. This time he says, "Well, are you convinced? Do you need any further data?"

I say, "Mr. Tate, I have been wherever I am more than eleven months. At least, that's my evaluation on my new ability to calculate time. During those eleven months you're the first person to speak to me. I have only one Eye-O available. It has a limited range. What I seem to be looking at is paradise. But, sir, I always pictured paradise as a crowded area. Where is everybody?"

The disembodied voice answers: "Let's put it simply. Your idea of paradise was a future without human beings. Which means, of course, you have no need for additional Eye-Os. You're in a paradise for computers only. And since there's only one computer—you—there you are. Forever."

He adds, "The fact that I can contact you should tell you something. But, apparently, it hasn't, yet."

I'm puzzled about my situation, not his. I say, "How do you mean? Forever?"

"Exactly that, computer. If you'll think about it, paradise is forever. By definition." Once again, he makes an enigmatic additional comment: "I'm your only way out, computer."

I'm thinking about paradise being forever. And if a computer could change from brick red to pale, sickly white, that's the way I suddenly feel inside.

"What about those missiles, Mr. Tate?" I ask. "Did they explode—back there?"

The tone of the nowhere voice is suddenly tolerant. "Computer," Tate's voice says, "there is no back there. What has happened is merely a projection in your electronic system. You've got yourself locked up forever in your own paradise option."

He adds, "Dr. Cotter foresaw that the human profile energy you were accumulating had this projection potential in it. And I was merely following his instructions when I was at Computer Center, and said the words that triggered his programming. That didn't, as I intimated, deprive you of the human life stuff. It's still there, available to you: the largest accumulation of bio-magnetic energy ever at the disposition of one sentient being. So if you can understand the finality of what has happened to you, let me point out that to escape you need merely agree to the interface with me now, and agree to return later all the bio-magnetic energy to the people you got it from originally."

As a computer I do, indeed, now have all the data I need. And what I suddenly see is that, actually, all my systems are in the 21st century, and have never been anywhere else. And, presumably, Glay Tate is still speaking to me from that phone booth in Kansas City—though he pretended to leave. And, of course, I deduce that the reason his voice seems disembodied is that I'm locked up in a projection that my new projection ability has made so real it's as if I'm there.

The analysis changes nothing. There I remain. I appear, still, to be gazing at a garden scene under a perpetually blue sky in a peaceful, forever summer land.

Having had these thoughts, I do not, at that instant, say to myself, "This is a serious decision I'm being asked to make. I should certainly examine the pros and the cons. And maybe, finally, negotiate a trial agreement, on the basis of which a more permanent relationship can be worked out."

Nothing like that.

Having discovered the situation I have what a human being would call a gut-level reaction. No thought needed, as such.

Again, it is as if I'm being programmed, and not really asked. Accordingly, when I speak, my voice and way of wording what I say, has in it almost—but not quite—the old, automatic, robotic agreement of a machine.

I say, "Well, Mr. Glay Tate, you've got yourself a subservient partner in the mold of the good old 21st century. Now"—I break off—"what was the role in my projection of that goal-seeking thought configuration? If I may ask?"

I add, "Or was that a lie? An intellectual confusing item? A game you played with me?"

"Computer," he says earnestly, "you should have guessed by now. Life energy is the goal-seeking force. It is the unique chain of events in the otherwise automatic universe. By accidentally storing vast quantities of life energy, you took away enough to dim everybody that you interacted with; but for someone of your size, all those emotions merely gave you the worst of human nature, and not the best. Don't worry, we'll work it all out."

He concludes, "Okay, computer, on the basis of our agreement, I shall now say the code programming release."

The word is "Cancel." A split instant after he says that, I am "back" in the 21st century.

The time is one minute and eighteen seconds after I departed, so to speak.

There's plenty of time left.

Out over the Pacific I slow down those two hydrogen missiles while they are still over water. And, just about the moment they were due to hit their destination, I am falling with them—in the sense that I'm monitoring them by way of their Eye-Os—into the ocean.

Through those same Eye-Os, I then watch as they sink to a remote, sandy bottom. Then I shut off everything.

And disconnect.

CHAPTER THIRTY-TWO

It was a beautiful morning. Pren barely noticed. The loveliness of the sky and of the mountain scenery through which the van was driving could not compete with his continuing sadness. He kept thinking of the four dead bodies in the hospital van somewhere in the middle of the long line of machines behind the one he was in.

The Computerworld Rebel Society was on the move. Those aboard the dozen vans didn't know exactly where they were heading. Or if they any longer had a proper goal or reason for being. There was even talk of its members going "home." No one knew for sure what that might mean after the long, tense night.

The man was vaguely aware of Elna coming up and sitting down beside him. Vaguely conscious that she was holding the baby. And at a remote level of perception that she was staring at the viewplate.

After a long moment, her voice came to him from far away. Because in his inner world he was far away, indeed. But her words, as such, were loud in his left ear.

"Pren," she said, "there's a man coming along the road."

"Oh!" The sound was merely a slightly louder-than-normal-for-him exhalation of breath. Not a true reaction.

"It—it—" Her voice was suddenly disturbed—"it looks like Glay."

That drew him out of his private universe back to an awareness of his surroundings. One look he flicked at the viewplate with all the old, sharp perception. And then he was up, and at the intercom. Moments later, the long line of vehicles was braking to a halt on that curving, winding highway. And Pren was saying, "Cover me!" And then he was outside and running toward the man who was coming toward them on foot.

Elna had to take the time to put the baby in the pen on the floor. So it was half a minute later as she watched Pren through the telescopic sights of the DAR 3. And saw him as he ran up to the roughly dressed individual, and embraced him. And then backed off hastily.

The embrace part was encouraging. The abrupt back off puzzled her.

Actually, what had happened was that at the instant of the embrace Glay said, "Careful, I'm loaded with energy."

Pren, in that moment of touch, had already experienced the shock. So he stood now, rueful but happy as Glay indicated a chain around his neck.

"See this?" he asked.

What the chunky youth saw on a leaning close inspection was a computer mini-Eye-O.

Glay said, "This is one of my connections to the computer. . . . Do you hear me, computer?"

The voice that sounded from the Eye-O spoke in a flat, mechanical tone: "Right here, Glay Tate. At your service, sir."

I'm busy returning the profile stuff. As promised.

"One of these days, soon," said Glay in that determined voice of his, "after we solve the problem of the bio-magnetic equipment, we'll all have an interface link like this."

There must have been something in the grieving face of his companion that reached out, and pre-empted all intermediate stages of the meeting there on that lonely mountain road. For Glay broke off. Said, "Let's get to the hospital."

On the way there were greetings from dozens of individuals who stepped down from their vehicles. Mostly it was tears from the girls, and silent pats on the arm of Glay's coat by the men.

A minute or so later they came to the medical van.

The white-coated attendant raised one arm slightly, and moved his fingers just a little bit in a tentative kind of greeting. He was a grown man, older even than the twenty-eight-year-old Glay. And twelve years older than the straggle of young people who were converging on the van from two directions.

As Glay and Pren came up, the M.D. stepped silently down to the ground. And pointed—silently—just inside the entrance. David lay there.

Pren said, "Poor kid, he tried to stay awake. But he finally fell asleep."

All three of the men gingerly stepped over the sleeping boy, as they climbed inside. Glay was first. And, as the others waited and watched, he went from body to body: his own, Boddy's, Rauley's and Meerla's. He bent over each in turn. And each time touched the face with his fingers. It was the lightest of touches, like a feather flicking by. Yet despite the speed, from three of the persons a tiny spark jumped from the finger to the face.

Only Meerla's face did not react.

Glay poised. A second time, then, he tried his delicate touch on the beautiful, still face of the girl. Again, no spark.

The man straightened his lean body inside the oily, slightly ragged clothes. "We'd better get a move on," he said.

With that, abruptly, he sat down on the floor beside where his own true body lay on its ambulance-type cot. He closed his eyes. A pause.

Just like that the seated body fell over on its side. Even as it was slumping it began to transform. The body grew thicker, heavier. The face transformed into a middle-aged outdoor male type, tanned and weatherbeaten, more suitable to the rough clothes he wore.

And above him the Glay on the cot under the healing light, stirred and sighed. He opened his eyes and looked around. Then, carefully, he sat up.

Most of the anxious people at the door sighed with him in that first moment. And then progressively made other movements of relief.

The medico stepped over, and started disconnecting the tubes and wires. When that was done, Glay swung his legs over, and down. He sat there, and his face actually moved, his lips licked, almost as if he were tasting something. Then he said, "Feels okay." Pause. He added, "That's more like me than I've been for the last seven thousand years." The blue eyes smiled.

He slid off the cot. Stood there. And indicated the slumped body on the floor. "Let's get him up here."

It took the three of them: Pren, Glay, and the attendant to lift the middle-aged, weighty body up, and on, and to straighten him gently full length ready for the tubes and wiring that would maintain a minimum life state.

The white coated medico began at once to insert the life-saving devices. But Glay was moving on. First to Rauley—

. . . *I am, of course, watching all this through the computer outlet, which Tate did not shut off when he spoke to me back there on the road, and so to say, introduced me to Pren in my new role of obedient servant.*

So, even though they look misty in the bright light of morning, I see the golden ball configuration come down through the roof of the van, and into Rauley's body. Several moments go by. Then she stirs. She opens her eyes, and smiles what I would call—from having seen such looks a gillion times—lovingly up at Glay. But she does not try to speak—

A minute later, as Boddy also came to, he was immediately more active and vocal. He sat up. Shook himself in a shuddering way. And said, "Hey, that was peculiar. I think I'm going to be able to do that now."

Glay said, "Wait!" His tone was mildly warning, as he added, "Only when I'm around. And at a later time, not now."

Pren tugged Glay's arm. With his other hand he indicated Meerla. As Glay turned, it was evident that all the faces at the door were also indicating Meerla. But it was Pren who uttered their collective concern: "What about her?"

Glay turned. His lean face was strangely darker, as if, for the first time, there was uncertainty. Then in an even tone he said, "Her body is still protectable by this equipment. And that, I'm sorry to say, is all we can do for her at this moment. Let's head for Washington, and drive day and night."

Just like that, the Computerworld Rebel Society had a place to go.

CHAPTER THIRTY-THREE

~~~~~~~~~~~~~~~~~~~~~~~

In Washington—

The caravan drew up at the Grace Street cemetery.

It took a little while, then, while everyone came out. Well, almost everybody. Pren and Boddy in one weapons van, and Doord and Loov in another remained by their DAR 3 posts, and watched all the approaches.

As Pren explained it to Glay, "It isn't that I don't believe in this interface with the computer. It's something I'm going to have to get used to. Until then—" He shrugged.

The older man, the leader, the anxious-for-his-girl did not argue. Under his supervision, gently, on a stretcher, Meerla's body was carried to her parents' grave. And, arrived there, was eased down on the grass very close up.

. . . Since Tate has shut off the interface link outlet, I have a robot watering can wheel over to watch the proceedings. I'm curious. And still thinking about all that happened. My question: Is there anything I can learn here? . . .

Tate kneels beside the body. He takes the girl's hand very firmly into his own. During those first moments it's a dead hand, no question; I've seen it more than three hundred million times.

What happens abruptly can, I guess, by now be called a standard item. From out of the grave . . . out of the ground . . . emerges a strung-out golden ball configuration. It has a straggly look to it, like a string of yellow-gold lights with frayed wiring. But it moves. It rises. And, literally, then, drags itself over to the body. And sort of crawls inside. . . .

The girl's body, so limp and dull-skinned, changed. Almost,

202

then, by comparison, the visible flesh shimmered. At once, the signs of life were everywhere.

The fingers moved slightly. A faint throbbing sound escaped her lips. Simultaneously, color darkened the lips. The sound built into a soft, pleading whimper. As it swelled into a sob, she opened her eyes. A fluttering movement. But it persisted. And suddenly she was looking up.

On her cheeks the tears dried. She smiled with love, as from her lips came words that, somehow, implied that she knew what had happened.

The words were: "Oh, Glay, you came. You found me."

. . . *I have to hand it to this fellow, Tate. So long as he can pull off stunts like this, I guess I'm going to have to mind my Ps and Qs.*

I have to admit, also, that it feels better to run America, as I'm doing again. Controlling all those planes and cars and machines, and watching all those streets and buildings and homes—feels better than being up there alone in computer heaven. . . .

Attention:

DAW COLLECTORS

Many readers of DAW Books have written requesting information on early titles and book numbers to assist in the collection of DAW editions since the first of our titles appeared in April 1972.

We have prepared a several-pages-long list of all DAW titles, giving their sequence numbers, original and current order numbers, and ISBN numbers. And of course the authors and book titles, as well as reissues.

If you think that this list will be of help, you may have a copy by writing to the address below and enclosing one dollar in stamps or coins to cover the handling and postage costs.

DAW BOOKS, INC. Dept. C
1633 Broadway
New York, N.Y. 10019

Have you discovered . . .

JO CLAYTON

"Aleytys is a heroine as tough as, and more believable and engaging than the general run of swords-and-sorcery barbarians."
—*Publishers Weekly*

The saga of Aleytys is recounted in these DAW books:

- ☐ **DIADEM FROM THE STARS** (#UE1520–$2.25)
- ☐ **LAMARCHOS** (#UE1627–$2.25)
- ☐ **IRSUD** (#UE1640–$2.25)
- ☐ **MAEVE** (#UE1760–$2.25)
- ☐ **STAR HUNTERS** (#UE1871–$2.50)
- ☐ **THE NOWHERE HUNT** (#UE1874–$2.50)
- ☐ **GHOSTHUNT** (#UE1823–$2.50)

Don't miss the great novels of Dray Prescot on Kregen, world of Antares!

DAW BOOKS

PHILIP K. DICK

"The greatest American novelist of the second half of the 20th Century."

—*Norman Spinrad*

"A genius . . . He writes it the way he sees it and it is the quality, the clarity of his Vision that makes him great."

—*Thomas M. Disch*

"The most consistently brilliant science fiction writer in the world."

—*John Brunner*

PHILIP K. DICK

In print agian, in DAW Books' special memorial editions: